Scandal at the Midsummer Ball

Suitable matches or salacious seductions?

The Duke and Duchess of Brockmore
are hosting *the* event of the Season—
and arranging the most powerful marriages
in England. But when two of their promising
protégés decide to take fate into their
own hands, scandal abounds!

Don't miss this sizzling duet from

Marguerite Kaye and Bronwyn Scott

Read Fergus and Katerina's story in
The Officer's Temptation
by Marguerite Kaye

and

Zara and Kael's story in
The Debutante's Awakening
by Bronwyn Scott

Marguerite Kaye writes hot historical romances from her home in cold and usually rainy Scotland, featuring Regency rakes, Highlanders and sheikhs. She has published almost thirty books and novellas. When she's not writing she enjoys walking, cycling—but only on the level—gardening—but only what she can eat—and cooking. She also likes to knit and occasionally drink martinis—though not at the same time. Find out more on her website: margueritekaye.com.

Bronwyn Scott is a communications instructor at Pierce College in the United States, and is the proud mother of three wonderful children—one boy and two girls. When she's not teaching or writing she enjoys playing the piano, travelling—especially to Florence, Italy—and studying history and foreign languages. Readers can stay in touch on Bronwyn's website, bronwynnscott.com, or at her blog, bronwynswriting.blogspot.com. She loves to hear from readers.

SCANDAL AT THE MIDSUMMER BALL

Marguerite Kaye
and
Bronwyn Scott

First published in Great Britain 2016
by Mills & Boon, an imprint of HarperCollins*Publishers*
1 London Bridge Street, London, SE1 9GF

© 2016 Harlequin Books S.A.

ISBN: 978-0-263-26318-3

The publisher acknowledges the copyright holders of the individual works as follows:

THE OFFICER'S TEMPTATION © 2016 Marguerite Kaye
THE DEBUTANTE'S AWAKENING © 2016 Nikki Poppen

Our policy is to use papers that are natural, renewable and recyclable products and made from wood grown in sustainable forests. The logging and manufacturing processes conform to the legal environmental regulations of the country of origin.

Printed and bound in Great Britain
by CPI Antony Rowe, Chippenham, Wiltshire

CONTENTS

THE OFFICER'S TEMPTATION

Marguerite Kaye

Chapter One

Saturday June 14th, 1817
Brockmore Manor House Party

Programme of Events
Welcoming Party in the Drawing Room
Exhibition by the World-Famous
Russian Acrobat Troupe
The Flying Vengarovs in the Ballroom

The drawing room of Brockmore Manor faced due west, looking out over the extensive formal gardens of the Duke and Duchess of Brockmore's country estate. The heady scent emanating from the nearby rose arbour wafted in through the open windows on the faintest of breezes. A veritable cornucopia of English roses both inside and without, Colonel Fergus Kennedy of the Ninety-Second Regiment of Foot thought wryly, eyeing the fluttering groups of ladies, their pale after-noon gowns in stark contrast to the vibrant co-balt blue of the heavy painted silk wall hangings that gave the room the appearance of an under-water cave. The marine theme was continued on the blue damask sofas which lined the draw-ing room walls, where naked mermaids and gro-tesque sea creatures were carved into the gilded arms and legs. Similar creatures were carved into the white Italian marble fireplace, and the works of art which adorned the walls had a maritime theme.

Fergus tugged at his starched neckcloth and edged closer to the open window. A trickle of sweat ran down his back. It was unseasonably hot. It seemed his host, who had a formidable reputation for scheming and machinations, had also organised the weather. He envied the ladies their light muslin gowns, so much more suited to the heat than his silk waistcoat and heavy dark-blue coat, but a quick glance around the room confirmed that he had correctly interpreted the 'informal' dress code stipulated for this welcom-ing party as being 'London-smart.'

Fergus was not particularly in the frame of mind to be welcomed. In fact, the prospect was distinctly unwelcome. The truth was, Fergus was beginning to have some reservations as to the wisdom of accepting this invitation and the potential consequences.

'I have made a small wager with myself that you are Colonel Kennedy. May I pat myself on the back and preen indulgently?'

The man who stood before him was of indeterminate age. Clad in what looked to Fergus like an emerald-green silk dressing gown emblazoned with gold-and-scarlet dragons, he carried a similarly painted fan. His skin was powdered, but he had a disconcertingly determined chin, and the pale-blue eyes which shone beneath the perfectly plucked arched brows were piercing.

'You may do both if you so wish, though attempting them simultaneously may prove problematic. Fergus Kennedy, at your service. I am afraid you have the advantage of me, sir.'

The thin mouth formed into a delighted smile. 'I knew it! One look at those shoulders and that ramrod straight back, and I knew you must be a military man. What a shame you decided against wearing your regimentals, Colonel, the ladies do love a Red Coat. I'm rather partial myself. But where are my manners! Allow me to introduce

myself. Sir Timothy Farthingale, and it is a pleasure to make your acquaintance.'

'How do you do.' Farthingale's exotic appearance was decidedly at odds with his firm
handshake, Fergus noted. 'May I ask if you are
acquainted with our hosts? I have not yet introduced myself to them.'

'Never fear, they will make an appearance directly,' Sir Timothy responded with an airy wave.
'Marcus and Alicia always choreograph their
grand entrances carefully, and I believe we are
still several guests short of a party. You have
been based in London since Waterloo, I believe?'

'I am, at the War Office, on Horse Guards.' Fergus winced inwardly. How he hated that blasted
desk in that poky office. Tedious did not begin to
describe his administrative duties. Someone had
to keep track of supplies and equipment but why
did it have to be him? It had been bad enough
when he was recuperating from the injury he'd
sustained at Waterloo, but he'd been fighting fit
for at least eighteen months now.

'I am surprised our paths have not crossed before now, Colonel,' Sir Timothy said, 'I know
everyone who is anyone. It cannot be a lack of
invitations which keeps you squirrelled away,

for I understood you to be one of Wellington's brightest protégés.'

As had Fergus, though his belief had waned, as request after request for a transfer to active duties had been refused, and Wellington's vague promises of saving him for the right appointment had remained unfulfilled. Until now. 'You seem uncommonly well informed about a man you have never met,' Fergus said.

Sir Timothy's smile was knowing. 'Oh, I make it my business to be well informed, Colonel. One never knows when the information may prove useful. That man over there, for example, the one who is dressed like a vicar with the face of a cadaver, is Desmond Falkner. A very rich fish indeed, though he reeks of the city. I might— or I might not—choose to dangle a little business proposition in front of him. The three young bucks standing beside him are Douglas Brigstock, the Earl of Jessop, Jessamy Addington and Jeremy Giltner. Now, they are the duke's ideal pawns—personable, popular, not too bright, not too dim, well connected and, I am sorry to say, utterly interchangeable.' Sir Timothy smiled archly. 'No doubt Brockmore has plans to match each of them up with one of the gaggle of young ladies over by the fireplace. They make a pretty picture, do they not? And don't they know it!'

Fergus, who himself was required to have a particular interest in one as yet unidentified young lady, eyed the group with a mixture of dread and anticipation, though he made sure to keep a neutral expression, having quickly deduced that the apparently eccentric Sir Timothy was as sharp as the proverbial tack. 'Your knowledge of our fellow guests is positively encyclopaedic,' he said, knowing full well that the man would be unable to resist rising to the bait, thus providing him with much-needed intelligence.

He was rewarded with an indulgent smile. 'But I have barely scratched the surface. The buxom blondes are, needless to say, the Kilmun twins, Cecily and Cynthia. Anything you wish to know about anyone—provided you cannot locate me— you will glean from them. The demure-looking lady in white over by the windows is Florence Canby. Don't be fooled by those innocent doe eyes of hers, Colonel Kennedy. A kissing miss, who never misses a kiss, if you take my meaning?'

Fergus shifted uncomfortably. Sir Timothy tittered. 'I see you do. I see also that one of the most lovely of the ladies has not yet arrived. Miss Zara Titus, are you acquainted? No? She is indeed a true beauty but, I regret to say, a jilt. Quite a scandal, our Miss Titus caused less than a month ago. I will wager you any amount that her mother will bag a husband for her before the week is out. There are a few candidates, though she would do well to ignore that tall, rather intimidating gentleman who has just joined the young bucks. That is Mr Kael Gage. I am not at all sure why he is here, but it is certainly not to make a match. I wonder, Colonel, if you could possibly be a candidate for Miss Titus's hand?'

'You have, then, eliminated yourself from the list of runners and riders?' Fergus quipped.

'Most people of my acquaintance would assume that I would ride a horse of a very different colour.'

'I'm sure that's exactly what you'd like most people of your acquaintance to think, Sir Timothy, but over the years, I have commanded men from all walks of life, and all persuasions. Your secret is safe with me.'

'Bravo,' Sir Timothy responded with a silent clap of his hands. 'A man who has a sharper eye even than I. I congratulate you, Colonel Kennedy.

I find that my little charade encourages people to underestimate me, which from a business perspective suits my purposes very well. You are no doubt wondering where Lady Verity is. If you will cast your eyes to the doorway, you will be rewarded. A lovely piece, the duke's niece. You see, I do know why you are here, but *your* secret is safe with me. You will excuse me now. I do believe I must delve a little further into Mr Gage's motives for turning up uninvited.'

Alone again, Fergus watched the Brockmore party make their stately progress around the room. The Duke of Brockmore, known as the Silver Fox, was a handsome man, with a broad intelligent brow under a thick coiffure of silver hair that was more leonine than fox-like. His wife, her gown of watered silk the exact same shade as her husband's waistcoat, Fergus noted with amusement, had the kind of elegance and grace that gave the impression of timeless beauty.

And then there was the duke's niece. Feeling slightly sick, Fergus turned his attention to Lady Verity Fairholme. Lustrous golden locks, china-blue eyes, a swan-like neck, a retroussé nose and a rosebud mouth, she was, in her blue-and-cream gown, perfection itself. Wellington had not, for once, exaggerated in order to get his way. Fergus, ridiculously, wished he had. He ought to be relieved, and extremely grateful. He ought to remember why he had agreed to be here.

He did not need much reminding. Wellington's summons a week ago had been an enormous relief. Finally, his days languishing behind a desk were over. 'Egypt,' Wellington had told him with one of his rare smiles. 'Henry Salt is the Consul-General in Cairo. A good man, though his penchant for collecting antiquities could prove a problem. Locals don't like it. Italians and French want to beat him to it. Tricky situation, potentially. We need a practical, trusted man on the ground, and that's where you come in.'

Relief had given way to excitement. Until Wellington explained the price. The diplomatic posting required a suitable wife to host social events and entertain guests. Apparently his friend, the Duke of Brockmore, required a husband for his niece. An excellent piece of serendipity, Wellington called it. Unfortunately, Fergus could not have one without the other—and on this, his commander-in-chief was implacable. 'Such prestigious postings as this come up very rarely, Colonel. You may have to wait two, three, perhaps even four or five years before another becomes available. Do you really enjoy counting muskets that much?'

The Duke of Wellington's smile this time had been thin. The threat was barely veiled. Sixteen years, Fergus had served obediently in the army. Now he must march to a different drum, or he might never march again. It stuck in his craw to be manoeuvred in this way, but if he was to be stuck behind a desk for the rest of his service, he'd likely die of boredom. A wife, an apparently beautiful, accomplished and well-born wife, was a small price to pay for such an exciting posting. Egypt—that was the thing he had to keep in mind. Egypt and escape from drudgery. Though now he was here…

Now he was here, he'd better stop wasting his time wishing that he were not. Whatever doubts he might harbour about this arranged marriage, he had no doubts at all about Wellington's judgement. If he said that his friend's niece would suit Fergus 'admirably' then it was up to Fergus to make sure that she did, because the consequences, if he failed to make a match of it, were unthinkable.

The Duke and Duchess of Brockmore were

now only a few feet away. Fergus braced himself. Looking across the room, he saw Sir Timothy Farthingale deep in conversation with a statuesque flame-haired woman of about thirty, clad in a scarlet dress which clung in all the right places to her voluptuous figure. Sir Timothy, he noticed with an inward smile, was having to work very hard to keep his eyes from that magnificent bosom. Maintaining an act was hard work, it seemed.

'Colonel Kennedy, I presume? A pleasure to make your acquaintance at last. I have heard a great deal about you from my friend, Wellington. May I present my wife, the Duchess of Brockmore, and my niece, Lady Verity Fairholme?'

Fergus bowed first to the duke, then to the duchess, and then to the niece. Lady Verity's hand was limp in his. While they made the usual introductory small talk her eyes glazed over and her gaze drifted to the painting behind his head. Suppressing his irritation, he nodded and smiled, responding automatically to the duchess's remarks about the weather, the duke's enquiries as to Wellington's health. Lady Verity's eyes continued to drift around the room. She fluttered her fan in the direction of the Kilmun twins. 'Excuse me,' she said, to no one in particular, then turned her back, making for a large footstool in the middle of the room, where she ensconced herself, and was immediately joined by the twins.

'It may be that my niece finds the heat trying,' the duke said stiffly, for the affront was clearly deliberate. 'I am sure she did not intend to be rude.'

'Indeed not,' Fergus said tightly. 'I am sure that if Lady Verity intended to be rude she would make a better fist of it than a mere flounce.'

'*Touché*, Colonel Kennedy,' the duchess said with a forced smile. 'Now, who else would you like to be introduced to?'

He had already met the one person he'd come here to meet, and it had been a far from auspicious beginning. His nerves had given way to a horrible flat feeling, as if he'd been waiting all day to confront an enemy who did not show up. Not that Lady Verity was the enemy—though dammit, she had appeared more enemy than ally.

One of the many lessons Wellington had taught him was that on occasion it was prudent to beat a strategic retreat and regroup. 'Thank you,' Fergus replied, making his bow, 'but I'm finding the unseasonable heat a little oppressive myself. If you will excuse me, I think I will retire outside momentarily for some fresh air.'

The sun blazed down from a cloudless, azure sky. Fergus glanced at the handy little map he'd found in his bedchamber—another example of the Duke of Brockmore's legendary attention to detail—and reckoned he was at the top of the steps leading down to the South Lawn. Sure enough, the waters of the ornamental lake glinted in the distance. It would be much cooler there. He'd be tempted to wander down, were it not for the fact that he'd be spotted from the drawing-room windows.

He descended from the terrace to a lawn so perfect he reckoned the Duke of Brockmore's gardeners must have trimmed it with grape scissors. Behind him, the house itself seemed to glitter in the sunshine, looking as if it was constructed from spun sugar. The beauty of the country mansion could not be denied, with its pleasing symmetry, its surprising lack of ostentation. It reminded him of an Italian palazzo he'd been billeted in once. He couldn't remember where, but he did remember it was summer, like this, and the marble floors had been blissfully cool on his feet, which were aching and blistered from long days of marching. There had been a lake there too, where he'd swum.

And there had been a woman. Fergus smiled. There had been a good many women back in those days, and a good many wild parties too, when they were not fighting wild battles. Though he did not forget the tedium of endless drills and weeks of tense waiting, though he did not wish to relive the horrors of the aftermath of battle, he missed—oh, how he missed—the excitement, and the danger, and the thrill, the desire to make the most of every single day, knowing it might well be his last. His smile faded. Those days were most definitely long gone. He tried to conjure the elation he'd felt when he'd first heard about the Egypt posting, but that awkward moment with the woman he would have to share his future with made his doubts surface once more. He couldn't afford to have doubts.

The formal gardens were laid out on the right-hand side of the house. There was a maze there. He'd be sure of some privacy in the maze, but his thoughts already contained enough dead ends and wrong turnings to be going on with. Instead he took the left-hand path, which his plan informed him led to the kitchen gardens.

Deciding that he could risk some concession to the heat, Fergus shrugged himself out of his dark-blue coat with some relief. Why was it that fashion went hand in hand with discomfort? He tugged longingly at his starched neckcloth, but knowing he'd only have to re-tie the blasted thing before returning to the drawing room, contented himself with rolling up his shirtsleeves.

Peering curiously into the Duchess of Brockmore's famous Orchid House was like opening an oven. Hastily closing the door, Fergus decided against an investigation of the pinery and the huge succession house where reputedly grew the largest vine in England.

The stone archway in front of him must lead to the walled garden. Sure enough, neat vegetable plots vibrant with greenery took up most of the available space. Precisely pruned peach and apricot trees fanned against the walls, and regimented ranks of raspberry and gooseberry canes filled one sunny corner. In the centre of the garden, on the large rectangle of lawn, stood two tall poles with a thick rope strung between them. And on the rope, improbably, dressed in a tiny tunic, balanced a woman.

Fergus drew back against the archway out of the line of her sight. She was slim, slight in stature, but the flimsy fabric she wore revealed a lithe and extremely supple body, with shapely legs and slender, elegant feet clinging to the rope. Her hair was auburn. Her skin, in contrast, was creamy white. She moved expertly and fluidly along the rope, her arms spread wide, as if she were about to fly.

He watched, fascinated, as she balanced, first on one leg and then on the other, traversing the length of the rope before, to his astonishment, she leapt high into the air, executed a perfect, graceful somersault in impossibly slow motion, and landed soft as a cat on the grass. Bouncing back to her feet, she tumbled over and over in a series of one-handed cartwheels so fast that her body was a blur of cream and auburn, until she came to an abrupt halt and finished with a theatrically flourishing bow. Fergus could not resist giving her a round of applause.

Startled, she glared fiercely at him. Her eyes were emerald green, her heart-shaped face flushed. 'This is a private area,' she said in heavily accented English. 'The Duke of Brockmore assured us that we would not be disturbed. Mr Keaton, the head gardener, has instructed his men to work elsewhere. Though you,' she said, raising one brow and giving him the faintest of smiles, 'I do not think that you are an under-gardener?'

He made an elaborate bow. 'Colonel Fergus Kennedy at your service. And you can only be Madame Vengarov. I am sorry to intrude, but in truth, I couldn't take my eyes off you. You looked as if that rope was glued to your feet.'

'*Spasibo.* Thank you, but I am a novice compared to Alexandr.'

'Your husband, and the other half of the famed Flying Vengarovs, I presume?'

'Yes, but you presume too much. I am not married. Alexandr is my brother.'

'Then I am even more delighted to make your acquaintance, Miss Vengarov.'

She smiled. Her teeth were very white. Her lips were very pink. There was a smattering of freckles across her little nose and a teasing light in her almond-shaped eyes. 'I don't know why my lack of a husband should cause you delight.'

'You are quite correct,' Fergus said, with a

guilty pang. 'It should not, especially under the circumstances.'

'Which are?'

'I am here at the behest of one duke to make a match with the niece of another.' His words, spoken without thinking, wiped the delightful smile from Miss Vengarov's face. Put like that, she would think him the worst sort of social climber, and worse, a compliant pawn in someone else's game. Fergus could feel himself flushing. What he ought to do was beat a retreat. Though he told himself the exotic Miss Vengarov's thoughts were irrelevant, he felt compelled to explain himself. 'It's not how it sounds,' he said. 'The first duke in question is Wellington, my commander-in-chief. The second, my host the Duke of Brockmore.'

'Wellington ordered you to marry Brockmore's niece?'

Her tone was starkly disbelieving, and no wonder. 'Not ordered, precisely. I am to take up a diplomatic posting to Egypt. A wife is apparently standard issue in such situations,' Fergus said, more flippantly than he intended.

Katerina eyed the soldier in some surprise. He looked decidedly uncomfortable, clearly regretting blurting out such private matters to a complete stranger. She ought to allow him to drop the awkward subject, but she was intrigued. He must want this posting very much if he was prepared to marry a stranger in order to secure it. 'What is so appealing about Egypt?' she asked.

'It is not Whitehall, for a start,' he said with a wry smile. 'I won't have to sit behind a desk and compile endless lists that no one will read. I won't have to drag myself out of bed knowing that today will be the exact same as yesterday and the day before. In Egypt, every day will present a new challenge.' His smile lightened. 'I'm a soldier. Peacetime can be a bit of a double-edged sword. Inactivity doesn't suit me at all.'

'That, I can understand. When I am not performing, I am not living. Inactivity does not suit me one little bit either,' Katerina said with a smile. 'We have that in common, Colonel.'

'It's Fergus. Call me Fergus.'

She ought not to call him anything. She ought to ask him to leave. This was precisely the kind of situation and he was precisely the kind of man that experience had taught her to avoid, but against her will, she was interested in him. And yes, also against her will, she had to admit she was attracted.

His eyes were the most startling shade of blue—or was it green? Turquoise? Colonel Fergus Kennedy was tall, several inches taller even than Alexei, and every bit as muscular, though the colonel's physique was broader, more solid than her brother's, the result of a lifetime of marching and fighting presumably, rather than endless hours of acrobatic training. War had etched the tiny fan of lines around his eyes, though the grooves at his mouth, the natural curve of his lips, made her wonder if laughter had also been a significant contributor. His fair hair was cropped close to his head, though there was a rebellious wave, a little kink on his brow that mitigated the severity of it. Attractive, he was most certainly, in a rugged way, but first and foremost, the impression she had was of a man of authority, a man accustomed to giving rather than receiving orders. Slightly intimidating, he was the kind of man that turned heads when he walked into a room. Or a walled garden, come to that!

'Fergus,' she said. 'And I am Katerina. Forgive me, but why can't you marry someone of your own choosing if a diplomat must have a wife?'

She wrinkled her brow. 'I cannot believe that you would be lacking in eager candidates.'

'Thank you for that vote of confidence,' he said mockingly. 'If only it were true.' He ran his fingers through his hair, making the kink stand up endearingly. 'It has been decided that this will be strictly a one-horse race, if I am to claim the prize.' He sighed heavily. 'And so, Miss Vengarov, I fear that I have no choice at all, if Lady Verity—that's the Duke of Brockmore's niece—will have me.'

'Do you doubt that she will?'

'I don't know what to think. She was certainly not been effusive in her welcome.'

'So you have already met her?'

'A wee while ago.'

'And she did not warm instantly to you?'

He laughed shortly. 'Is that so difficult to believe?'

His smile was charming. Not that there was any possibility of it charming *her*. 'Come now, you do not need me to tell you that you are an attractive man, Colonel—Fergus,' Katerina said. 'Most likely, under the circumstances, the lady was simply nervous, embarrassed or both. Everyone knows the Duke of Brockmore's Midsummer Party is simply a notorious matchmaking fair.'

'You disapprove?'

'I am sure it is a foolproof way to find a wife. As you see, we lowly performers are kept within the boundaries of this walled garden so there can be no confusion as to whom are the suitable candidates.' *On either part.*

Fergus Kennedy was looking quite taken aback. She had not meant her own bitter experience to colour her tone quite so much. Katerina gave a careless shrug. 'It is none of my business.'

'True enough,' he replied, 'though in a sense I've made it so, by confiding in you. Perhaps I should not have. I don't know why I did, to be honest, save that perhaps I disapprove a wee bit myself.'

His admission disarmed her. For some reason, she was relieved not to have to think quite so ill of him. 'I don't know you at all,' Katerina said, 'but I confess I find it strange that a man like you, so clearly accustomed to command, is allowing someone else to make such an important decision for him.'

'The "someone else" is my commander-in-chief.'

'Yes, you said so.'

'I did.' He was silent for a moment, before sighing heavily. 'You're right. If I was happy with the situation, I'd be back there at that welcoming party making myself amenable, instead of out here, embarrassing you with my problems in the hope that you'll reassure me.'

She had no idea how to reply to this, as confused by his indecisiveness as he was. Was it simply an ingenious way of engaging her sympathy? He did not seem the ingenious type, but she had been fooled before. 'I am sorry,' Katerina said, somewhat helplessly.

'Ach no, don't be. You've not said anything I've not thought myself. That's enough about me,' he said, giving himself a little shake. 'You're much more interesting. Brockmore pulled off quite a coup bringing you and your brother here. The Vengarov name is one of the most respected in your field.'

'What do you know of my field?'

'I've seen a few acts such as yours in my travels, and I've visited that man Jahn's gymnasium in Berlin.'

Despite herself, Katerina was impressed. 'The Duke of Brockmore will spare no expense in obtaining the very best entertainment for his guests,' she said drily. 'He does not, however, share your respect for our reputation. Or our artistry. We are, in his eyes, I suspect, little more than performing monkeys.'

'Then the man is an idiot. What is it like up there on the tightrope?'

'Oh, there is nothing to compare it with.'

'Save flying? You must feel as if you're in your own wee world.'

He had one of those smiles that was impossible to ignore, and his interest really did seem genuine. 'Wee world,' Katerina repeated, surrendering to the temptation to smile back. 'Your accent is strange. You are not English?'

'Scottish. And you, I believe, are from Russia.'

'R-r-r-russia,' Katerina repeated, in a fair enough imitation of his accent to make him smile. 'Yes, I am Russian.'

'You speak excellent English.'

'And French, and German, passable Italian and a smattering of Spanish. All my life, I have been travelling, you see, and performing too. I come from a great tradition, as you said, a long line of performers. The Vengarov family, we are the aristocrats of our world.'

'I am aware of that, even if Brockmore is not. I'm looking forward very much to tonight's performance. I see from the Programme of Events that you're also holding a demonstration class for the party guests.'

'Aristocrats from one world, mingling with the aristocrats of another,' Katerina said sardonically. 'Will you be taking part, Colonel Fergus?'

'I most certainly will. Do you include the ladies in this class? I'm not sure I can picture the duchess wearing one of these wee tunic affairs. Or, indeed, care to!'

Caught up in their conversation, amazingly, astonishingly, Katerina had quite forgotten that all she was wearing was what he called her wee tunic affair, in part because Fergus too seemed to have forgotten. But now he had drawn attention to her state of dishabille and was looking at her most appreciatively, she became acutely aware of how much of her flesh was on display, and Fergus seemed to be having difficulty dragging his eyes away from her modest cleavage, and the way he was looking at her was making her flush more, with a mixture of awareness of him and anger at herself, rather than embarrassment.

'It is not possible to practise real acrobatics

in corsets and morning gowns,' Katerina said tightly. 'We will restrict ourselves to teaching more seemly and decorous moves.'

He flushed very faintly, making a point of turning his gaze away. 'Curses, then I will be denied the sight of a tumbling duchess.'

'And I will be denied the opportunity to witness a soldier falling from the tightrope.'

'You seem very certain I will fall.'

'You won't have a chance. It will not be offered as an activity in the masterclass,' Katerina told him. 'It is too dangerous.'

Fergus eyed the rope speculatively. 'It doesn't look so high.'

'Because this is merely a practice height—so I can reach it without a ladder. It makes no difference to me what height the rope is set at, but for the spectacle—oh, then the higher the better, as you will see tonight.'

'Aren't you ever afraid of falling and injuring yourself?'

'The trick is to convince yourself that you are not afraid.'

'It's the same on the battlefield.'

They were no longer looking at the tightrope. He was smiling at her again, but there was something more than laughter in his eyes. Though he was not touching her, her skin tingled. Heat, that's what it was. Katerina's stomach fluttered in response. 'There is no comparison,' she said. 'I am not brave in that way.'

'Perhaps not,' he replied softly, 'but definitely fearless.'

There was a trickle of sweat on his brow. She noticed a tiny shaving nick, right in the cleft of his chin. His fair lashes were absurdly long for a man. A sharp gust of desire took her by surprise. She saw it reflected in his eyes, and the air in the walled garden seemed to still, the sun's heat to intensify. Even the birdsong seemed momentarily muted. She curled her toes into the grass and realised she was waiting, longing for him to kiss her.

Confused and startled by her reaction, Katerina launched herself up on to the rope, taking them both aback. Safe from her own desire, she perversely fed his, wanting to show him what he could never have, what he could never attain, walking, leaping, dancing, tumbling on the rope, aware of his eyes fixed on the shapes her body was making, her naked limbs, her supple flesh. Only when she stopped, her chest heaving with the effort, and her eyes met his again, did she re-alise that desire fed desire, that her feelings were as nakedly exposed as his.

She hovered on the rope, furious at herself for surrendering to temptation, yet unwilling to put an end to it, waiting for the proof that he was, after all, exactly like the rest. When he gave a tiny shake of his head, turning deliberately away, it took her off guard. She vaulted down. Still averting his eyes, he disconcerted her further by holding out her robe, the robe she should have donned the moment he had appeared in the garden. Her fingers fumbled with the sash.

Fergus made a show of consulting his watch. 'I've deserted the reception currently underway in the drawing room for far longer than I intended. I must re-join the others lest I blot my copybook at the first opportunity. Even in a one-horse race, one can't afford to fall at the first fence.' Finally, his extraordinary eyes met hers again. 'It has been a privilege to see you prac-tise, a privilege to make your acquaintance, but you will be wishing to return to your practice. I should not have taken up so much of your time.'

She was in danger of liking this man. She was in danger of thinking him different. She'd thought that before, and look what had happened. 'I spend most of my time with my brother, Colonel Kennedy,' Katerina said dismissively. 'Any other company is a welcome distraction.'

'Well, that's a fine compliment indeed. Here was me thinking you enjoyed my company for its own sake. And it's Fergus, remember?'

His quip, his smile, made the awkward moment pass. She was forced to laugh. 'Indeed, *Fergus*,' she said, 'if the charming Mr Keaton or one of his under-gardeners should happen by, you will please send him straight in.'

'A tour of the pinery would no doubt be entertaining.'

'And there is the orchid house too. I believe the duchess has some rare specimens on display.'

'Oh, when it comes to displaying rare specimens, I believe her husband has the edge.'

'What do you mean?'

'You,' Fergus replied. 'I doubt very much there's another exotic flower in the garden quite as fragrant as you. It has been a pleasure, Katerina.' It was there again, as he covered her hands with his, the tug of desire between them. The long fingers which covered hers were calloused. His knuckles were covered in a fretwork of tiny scars. Powder burns? He lifted her hand to his lips, brushed a tantalisingly brief kiss to the tips of her fingers, then gently released her hand. 'I very much look forward to enjoying your performance tonight.'

A straightening of the shoulders, a firming of his mouth, and his purpose was set. With a sketched bow, Fergus turned away, marching briskly across the grass in the direction of the house, looking for all the world as if he were marching into battle.

The impressive ballroom of Brockmore Manor ran the full length of the house from front to back and opened out on to the large terrace, the ceiling twice the height of the other reception rooms. Painted alabaster white, with only the ornate Adam cornicing to relieve its plainness, the pilasters running down one side gave the room the look of a Roman forum. Three huge chandeliers blazed down, their flames reflected in the highly polished wooden floor. The centre of the space was taken up by the tightrope and poles, set about fifteen feet off the ground now, surrounded by thick mats. A stack of hoops and skittles were laid out neatly to one side, beside a shallow tray of chalk.

Marcus, the Duke of Brockmore, surveying the scene from his vantage point on the balcony, permitted himself a small smile of satisfaction and a flutter of anticipation. The welcoming party earlier in the day had been but a prelude to the main event. Tonight's performance would set the tone for the rest of the week. A spectacle never before seen in England. The Vengarov siblings would be a symbol for his guests, a reminder of how they too could fly—with his assistance.

Marcus leaned over the balustrade to direct a footman in the more precise arrangement of chairs for the audience. He swept his mane of grey hair back from his forehead as he took in the bustling scene below. The Silver Fox, they called him behind his back, and he rather enjoyed his reputation. It was not as if any of the guests were unaware of the subtle games they were being invited to play here. The Brockmore Midsummer Party was well established now, as the stage for all sorts of alliances to be made— and in some cases unmade. He and Alicia did not manipulate, but rather facilitated these affairs—of the heart, of politics, of business. Yes, they greased the wheels of power, but they did not force those wheels to turn in any particular direction. Though more often than not, of course, they did. In their later years, they would be able to look back with pride and satisfaction on their achievements. The children of the marriages they had brokered would be consolation for their own tragic lack of progeny.

The customary pang this engendered in his heart made Marcus's thoughts turn towards his wife, and as if on cue, she entered the room ahead of their guests, glancing up and smiling, that special smile she saved for him and him alone. She was looking splendid this evening, her pale-green evening gown carefully chosen to complement the darker-green stripe of his own waistcoat. His diamond-and-emerald cravat pin matched the magnificent set of diamonds and emeralds she wore around her swan-like neck. It was these little attentions to detail that were so important. No, he could have no regrets.

He watched his duchess making her graceful way through the throng of specially invited guests, admiring the way she gently manoeuvred each into their allotted place with the skill of an orchestra conductor. There were the obvious matches to be made—and by and large he left those in Alicia's capable hands. Viscount Monteith's daughter would be marketable enough, a shy beauty and therefore a desirable catch, but that dragon of a mother of hers was bound to interfere. The Kilmun twins—Marcus smiled to himself as he eyed those two ladies. Cecily and Cynthia, wasn't it? Damned if he could tell which was which. It would be interesting to see if their intended bridegrooms could—or cared to. Brigstock, Earl of Jessop, and Jessamy Addington were lined up for them. Cynthia and Cecily. Jessop and Jessamy. Sound fellows with excellent connections. He had plans for both, and frankly an alliance with either twin would suit his purposes just as well. Let them sort it out between them.

Verity now—where was Verity?—ah yes, there she was, seated as planned beside Wellington's protégé. Colonel Kennedy looked to possess a strong will, just the type to take his headstrong niece in hand. It was not a great match in the eyes of the world, not compared to some of the offers Verity had already rejected, but in some ways this man was likely more suitable. If Wellington was in the right of it—and his old friend invariably was—the colonel would very quickly make his mark abroad, giving the Brockmore family another string to their many bows. Mind you, that first meeting between the pair today had not been auspicious. It was to be hoped that Verity had indeed been merely out of sorts due to the heat in the crowded drawing room.

As for the rest of his guests? His Grace scanned the audience, now seated, and made a rapid inventory. Sir Timothy Farthingale would be easy enough to accommodate, all he desired was to be pointed in the direction of a generous benefactor with deep pockets, but Desmond Falkner might prove just a little tricky to bleed. A canny man, he had seemed at dinner earlier, and something of a prude, if truth be told. Farthingale's flamboyant appearance had made quite the wrong impression. What possessed the man to wear a pair of Turkish slippers and a scarlet coat to dinner, Marcus could not fathom. Alicia had seated him in the back row, but he looked more like he should be performing in tonight's entertainment. A quiet word might be in order. A task for Lillias, perhaps? By odd coincidence, the woman he and Alicia liked to think of as their eyes and ears was already seated by Sir Timothy in her customary scarlet. The duke winced at the clash of colours. Though the Titian-haired Lovely, Luscious Lillias Lamont was a stalwart of their Midsummer Party, her flamboyant taste in clothes was really almost as suspect as Farthingale's.

'Your Grace?' He turned, to find the Russian duo whose services he had secured at great expense beckoning him from the doorway. 'We are ready to begin the performance.'

Marcus fought the urge to inform the rather arrogant young Russian man that the performance would commence when he decided it could begin. He was paying a small fortune to hire the pair for the whole week, yet each time they spoke, he had the sense the man was looking down his nose at him. There were not many people who discomfited the Duke of Brockmore. Marcus couldn't understand it, but there was something about Alexandr Vengarov that made him feel as if he should be doing the kowtowing.

Though the blasted man was right, it was high time to get the evening's entertainment underway. Marcus nodded his assent and the Russian performers disappeared. Moments later, the pair of them appeared in the doorway of the ballroom.

His Grace leaned over the balcony and cleared

his throat. 'My Lords, Ladies and gentlemen, it is my great privilege to present, for your delectation, the most extraordinary, the most talented, the most graceful and indeed the most flexible acrobatic performers in the civilised world. Prepare to be both astounded and amazed. I give you the Flying Vengarovs.'

Conversation stilled. Skirts rustled, painted fans were snapped shut and quizzing glasses prised open as the audience settled into their gilt-edged chairs.

The duke gestured to the performers. They were a striking pair, he so tall, and she so tiny in comparison. Both wore long cloaks, hers dark blue and his black, studded with paste diamonds that sparkled and shimmered in the candlelight. There were paste diamonds in her burnished auburn hair too. They seemed to float across the floor together like a walking constellation of stars. A hushed silence pervaded the ballroom as they stood in front of the tightrope, facing the expectant crowd. He had to admire their professionalism, the pair possessed real stage presence. The duke felt his own heart pick up a few beats. Catching his wife's eye, they shared a smile, but his eyes were drawn, almost against his will, to the duo below. They did not look like siblings. Vengarov's square-cut jaw, brown eyes and dark-brown hair were in stark contrast to his sister's colouring and appearance, though they shared the same high Slavic cheekbones, and there was something about the mouth too.

They made their bow. Vengarov's cloak dropped to the ground and there was a sharp intake of breath. The man was half-naked, wearing only a shockingly tight pair of knitted pantaloons. His muscled torso gleamed in the candlelight. The duke smothered a chuckle. Fans were being hurriedly opened, but he had no doubt that behind them the ladies were gazing with flagrant admiration at the chap's sculpted physique. The men present, on the other hand, were bristling with purported indignation. Intimidated no doubt, rather than offended. Save Kennedy, who was smiling. And Farthingale who was looking like a dog salivating over a particularly juicy bone.

Another sharp intake of breath followed when the female acrobat dropped her cloak, and to this the duke contributed enthusiastically. She was virtually naked. A scant flesh-coloured tunic studded with more paste diamonds and little else clung to her perfectly proportioned body. It was indecent. It was also rather exciting. The rumours he'd heard regarding the exotic allure of the Vengarov siblings had not been wide of the mark. If anything, they had been understated, especially regarding the delicious Katerina. No bristling from his male guests now, that was for sure. And the smile had been wiped from Kennedy's face. Rapt, was an accurate description of his expression. Marcus congratulated himself. He had provided something for everyone, an audacious spectacle no other host would dare commission.

Then the girl put her bare foot on her brother's linked hands and he propelled her upwards on to the tightrope. He followed her, too fast for the duke to work out how he'd managed to leap so high. The show began, and Marcus, along with everyone else in the enthralled audience, forgot everything else and concentrated on the two graceful and impossibly skilled acrobats.

Chapter Two

Sunday June 15th
Brockmore Manor House Party

Programme of Events
A Tour of the Gardens for the Ladies
Al Fresco Luncheon at the Lake Summerhouse
Boating to Follow
Cards and Conversation

Katerina gazed out of the window of her bed-chamber. A ripple of wispy mare's-tail clouds streaked the hazy blue sky. It was another beautiful day, the sun already warm on her face, though it was not yet eleven in the morning. She pushed the casement as high as it would go and leaned out. A light breeze ruffled her hair, which was coming loose from its tight night-time braid. The sleeping quarters she and Alexandr had been allotted were on the top floor, one below the servants' cramped garrets which were squashed into the attics, and one floor above the luxurious guest chambers. It summed up perfectly their place in the grand scheme of things: coveted by the elite but excluded from polite society; envied by the hoi polloi but treated with a mixture of admiration and circumspection.

Her window overlooked the working gardens. From this height, she could see down into the stables, over the top of the glinting glass of the succession house, pinery and orchid house, and into the walled garden beyond. Alexandr was walking on his hands along the practice rope. She had never seen anyone more skilled than her brother, and though she had watched him perform this trick countless times from much more vertiginous heights, she still felt that familiar combination of fear and awe. She had only managed to complete just over half the rope in this manner herself, and certainly never attempted to perform it in public. Alexei was most likely going to feature it in his solo performance scheduled for later in the week.

A small group of women had entered the walled garden. They did not usually permit an audience to watch their practice sessions, but the Duchess of Brockmore was paying them well over the odds for their residency this week, so even Alexei would not be so bold as to deny her female guests this unscheduled opportunity to gawp at him as he went through his paces. He did not look at all enamoured though, his brow furrowed deeply in one of his most formidable frowns.

He was however, like her, an artiste above all, and once back on the rope lost himself in his performance. His audience watched him, rapt, their expressions as openly admiring as ever. To those rooted to the ground, there was a cachet and glamour attached to skilled exponents of the tightrope. For those at the very peak of their profession—as the Flying Vengarovs were—this manifested itself as a form of fame, and sometimes notoriety. Alexei professed to despise the slavish admiration he habitually received from women, but he was no saint—there had been countless *affaires* over the years.

She could not blame him. It was a lonely and itinerant life they led. But while her brother was happy to take what he called comfort in the arms of his admirers, Katerina had foolishly longed for something more lasting. What she had discovered was what she should have known all along. There was nothing more thrilling than the tight-rope. Not for the performer. Certainly not for the men who watched her, who had no interest in the woman who walked it. And most certain of all, not that particular man who had caused her to fall to earth, where she had landed with such force that she carried the bruises still, two years later.

In a way, she envied Alexei. He stuck to the rules. *He* never made false promises. *He* never pretended to emotions he did not feel. He loved and he left. He was no more interested in the woman behind the beguiled spectator than his lover was interested in the man behind the artiste. When the Flying Vengarovs packed up their act and headed for the next venue, the next country, he did not leave behind any broken hearts or shattered dreams. He never dallied where he could compromise. His lovers were as discreet as he. Being women, they had to be. It was different for men.

Katerina pulled a chair over to the window and sat down, resting her chin on her hands. With the possible exception of the voluptuous redhead in the clinging gown, the ladies down in the walled garden were quite safe in their summer gowns the soft shades of the English countryside—rose-pink, primrose-yellow, leaf-green. Clustered together, their parasols in matching colours raised to protect their complexions from the sun, they looked like a posy of pretty blooms. Very elegant, delicate and much-prized hothouse flowers.

Though her own petite frame suited her artistic requirements to perfection, Katerina felt a pang of envy watching the tall, willowy figures possessed by the duke's aristocratic guests. Two in particular stood out, one a disdainful blonde, the other a dusky brunette, perfect foils for each other. Perhaps one of those two was Fergus Kennedy's intended bride. Though he'd tried not to show it, he had been hurt yesterday by whatever snub she had handed him. Perhaps she was the type who took pleasure in humiliating her admirers, or perhaps she was the type who thought her value enhanced by constant refusals. After all, men desired most what they could not have, Katerina thought bitterly, until they had it, and then it became a mere trophy.

But the Duke of Brockmore's niece had no need to play games. Foolish woman, whichever of these beauties she was, if she continued to do so, for Fergus Kennedy was most certainly not the type of man who would meekly play along.

At least, she would not have thought he was. But then, she would not have thought he was the type of man who would allow himself to be ordered to marry. He was neither spineless nor passionless. Yesterday, when she had worked the rope as he looked on, desire had connected them like another, more ethereal, rope. Last night, when she was performing, she had had felt it tug powerfully at her again. He never took his eyes off her. Knowing that he was watching had given her display a new soaring quality, almost as if she had grown wings.

It was a sobering thought. Rather a frightening one. She could fly perfectly well without Fergus Kennedy. He was no different from all the other male admirers who found her skimpy costumes and flexible limbs alluring. Men who would boast to their friends of their exploits, but who would never dream of introducing her to their family. Men for whom the conquest was all, and the woman they had conquered—valueless. She knew that. She could not afford to forget that. Yesterday, Fergus might well have seemed interested in her, but yesterday, Fergus had arrived in the walled garden with a bruised ego and a wish to forget, for a moment, why he was here at Brockmore Manor in the first place. She had been a short-term distraction, no more. She'd do well to keep her distance from him.

A burst of applause startled her from her melancholy musings. Alexei stood in the centre of the circle of women, his arms crossed, his expression stormy. Finally, the duchess realised that she and her ladies were *persona non grata*, for she was leading the way out of the garden, presumably to resume their tour of the gardens and the legendary orchid house. A posy of traditional English roses to be introduced to the duchess's exotic blooms.

Fergus grasped the oars of the rowing boat and concentrated on gently pushing it away from the little jetty on the island and out on to the lake. Lady Verity had been his allotted passenger for the return trip after the picnic luncheon, but when he'd dutifully invited her to step aboard, she had demurred, thrusting the Kilmun twins at him in her stead.

He had not attempted to cajole her. In truth, he'd felt guiltily relieved. She was very beautiful, but there was something about the haughty way she surveyed the world, the cold, clipped way she conversed, that he found most off-putting. At dinner last night he'd tried to be attentive, but to little avail. He had tried to persuade himself that she was most likely nervous given the circumstances, but today during the picnic, watching her perfectly relaxed with the other guests, he had caught glimpses of the vivaciousness that had by all accounts made her the toast of the *ton*. Yet in his company, he could almost see the icicles forming. And if he was brutally honest, lovely as she was, eminently suitable as she was as a diplomat's wife, as a woman, she left him as cold as he appeared to leave her.

He wasn't the kind of conceited dolt who expected every woman he met to fall at his feet, though he'd never before failed to charm when that was his stated intention. Was she one of those women who were incapable of feelings? No, that was his male pride talking. Besides, the point of this week was not to charm or woo, but to forge an alliance. A matchmaking fair, Katerina had called this Midsummer Party, and she was right. A marriage market is what it was.

Clear of the shallows around the island, he

began to row towards the boating house with long, powerful strokes. The Kilmun twins smiled their almost-identical smiles at him.

'You handle the oars like a master mariner, Colonel Kennedy.'

'We are in safe hands, Sister.'

'I rather think you were intended to be in different hands,' Fergus said, relieved to turn his thoughts away from his own matrimonial prospects. 'Brigstock, the Earl of Jessop, and what's-his-name?—Addington?'

'Yes, they were most put out, weren't they? Brockmore has earmarked them for us, as you have correctly deduced, Colonel, but our swains cannot even tell the difference between us,' Cynthia informed him, her pretty nose in the air.

'And until they can, we shall make a point of snubbing them,' Cecily added. 'It is insulting, Colonel Kennedy, to imagine that simply because we look alike we are the same person. We are not interchangeable. I notice that you can easily distinguish me from Cecily.'

Fergus laughed. 'And I notice that you like to exploit your remarkable likeness to play games on the unsuspecting. That is Cynthia. You are Cecily.'

The twins clapped their hands together in unison. 'Oh, well done. You have no idea how refreshing it is for a man to take the time to tell us apart. If only you were one of the duke's candidates for our hands.'

'Alas,' Cynthia chimed in archly, 'I suspect Brockmore has other plans for you, does he not, Colonel?'

Hearing the truth spoken aloud deepened his unease. He did not like to think of himself as a fly caught in the duke's web. 'I have no firm plans,' Fergus said stiffly, 'save to enjoy the pleasant company.'

'Oh, come, Colonel,' Cecily exclaimed, 'there is no need to equivocate. We are all here for a purpose. Sir Timothy for example, clearly *he* is not here to secure a wife.'

Cynthia giggled. 'Like all rich men, he is married to his money. And of course some, such as the Lovely, Luscious Lillias Lamont, are here to oil the party wheels, should it flag. Have a care what you say around Lillias, Colonel, for she reports everything back to the duke.'

The dinghy bumped against the jetty. A waiting manservant caught the rope. Fergus wondered, as he helped first Cecily and then Cynthia on to the shore, whether they too would dance to the duke's tune, by the end of the week.

Would he? He'd been so carried away by the promise of a far-flung posting, a new, exciting life away from his Whitehall desk, that he'd not really weighed up the price to be extracted. A suitable wife was all very well in theory, but the reality of this bloodless and frankly calculated marriage was proving trickier to swallow. Marriage was not a commercial transaction. A wife was not a commodity, but a flesh-and-blood woman. A husband was also a man. It disturbed him deeply, that his blood heated when he looked at Katerina, and yet it seemed to freeze in his veins when he was in Lady Verity's company.

Katerina, now, she was another matter altogether. Not only had there been a spark between them, it had threatened to become incendiary. He'd been so close to kissing her, it made his blood heat just thinking about it. Last night, on the tightrope and on the mat, her supple body had formed impossible yet perfect shapes. She was so lithe and yet so elegant in that tiny tunic, like a tumbling constellation. It had been there again as he watched her performance, he was certain of it, that visceral pull of attraction between them.

'A penny for them, Colonel Kennedy. You were miles away.' Cecily slipped her arm in his, her gaze speculative, as Cynthia took his other arm.

'I was thinking how fortunate I was to be a Scots thistle between two English roses.'

'I am not at all convinced that is what you were thinking, but it is a delightful image. Though not as delightful an image as the thought of you in your regimentals, for we ladies love nothing more than a man in a Red Coat,' Cynthia teased.

'Save perhaps, a man such as the rather formidable Mr Vengarov, who wears no coat at all,' Cecily added, with a giggle. 'It has been a pleasure, Colonel. We trust we will see you at dinner.'

With a flutter of hands and parasols, the Kilmun twins headed off in the direction of the orchid house. Immediately lost in his own thoughts, Fergus took himself in the opposite direction through the heavily scented rose garden and into the maze. According to the Programme of Events, there was to be cards and conversation after dinner. He'd eschew winning at cards and instead do his best to make winning conversation with Lady Verity. Perhaps when she came to know him a little better she would thaw somewhat. And he would warm to her too.

Perhaps. The uneasiness in his gut was becoming more persistent. It was the same feeling he had when something wasn't right in the field, the same instinct that had saved his life and that of many others on numerous occasions. It was becoming a struggle not to listen to it.

A false turn took him to a dead end in the maze. Fergus stared at the dense wall of hedge. The trick was always to turn right. Or was it left? There was no performance on the tightrope to look forward to tonight. He wondered how Katerina occupied herself when she was not practising. Another turn, and then another, and soon he was in the centre of the maze, and Fergus's question was answered for there she was, in the shade of a large copper statue of Atlas.

She was asleep, her cheek resting on her clasped hands, her back against the plinth. The Greek god, crouched down carrying the world on his shoulders, cast a shadow over her, protecting her from the blazing heat of the afternoon sun. The statue was likely the duke's little conceit, a reference to his role in underpinning English society, Fergus reckoned. 'Though right now, I know how you feel,' he said under his breath, eyeing the copper god's straining muscles and pained expression with a stir of empathy.

He returned his gaze to the much more enticing sight of the sleeping Katerina. Her gown was lemon-coloured sprigged with pale green, the puffed sleeves drawing attention to her slim, toned arms, the modest neckline displaying the curve of her bosom. She had taken off her slippers, Fergus noted with amusement, and her legs were bare. Though she was wearing a great deal more than when he had previously seen her, the sight of her naked toes peeking out from the hem of her gown made his blood stir. A long tendril of hair had fallen over her face, glinting fiery red highlights in the sunshine. He fought the urge to tuck it behind her ear. He tried to force himself to turn away, to leave her undisturbed, but once again the allure of her was almost irresistible. He could not take his eyes from her.

The intensity of his gaze must have registered with her, for she woke, blinked, pushed back her hair herself, and Fergus told himself it would be rude to retreat straight away, so he remained where he was, and was rewarded with a sleepy smile.

* * *

'Fergus.' Katerina rubbed her eyes, just to be sure she was not still dreaming.

'I didn't mean to wake you.'

She got to her feet, shaking out her crushed skirts. 'I didn't intend to fall asleep. I was reading.' She handed him a rather dog-eared book. '*Les Liaisons Dangereuses.* Are you familiar with the work?'

'I'm afraid my French is not up to reading anything more substantial than captured battle orders and dinner menus,' Fergus replied.

'It's quite shocking. The Vicomte de Valmont is even more of a schemer than the Duke of Brockmore—though his purposes are a good deal less benign.'

Fergus was frowning, looking distinctly uncomfortable. He ran his hand distractedly through his hair. 'I am not sure that I'd call the Silver Fox benign. If Brockmore is anything like his good friend Wellington—and I suspect he is very similar—then he'll take as good care to avenge his failures as to reward his successes.'

'Perhaps he models himself on the Vicomte de Valmont after all,' Katerina said. 'For your sake, I hope you will be one of the duke's success stories.'

She meant it lightly, but his frown deepened. 'Which would be worse, do you think, a miserable marriage, or a miserable career?'

'Must it be one or the other?'

'The army is my life. I can't imagine another, any more than you can.'

'But you won't be a soldier in Egypt, will you? I thought that the point of diplomacy was to keep the peace, not go to war.'

'I'll be serving my country. It's the same thing.'

She couldn't see how it was the same thing at all, but she could see that it was what Fergus wanted to believe. 'I know nothing of these matters,' Katerina said. 'My only dealings with diplomats have been to secure appropriate travel papers. Which, given the itinerant nature of our performing life, has been a regular requirement.'

'We must have travelled a good few of the same countries, you and I.' Fergus lowered himself on to the grass under the statue and stretched his long legs out in front of him. 'Mind you, I doubt we saw them in the same light,' he added with a grin. 'When you visit a place, I expect you're welcomed with open arms, rather than the barrel of a gun.'

'That very much depends on the arms,' Katerina said wryly. 'There are those who find our act shocking. In the early days, before we were famous, we occasionally had to abandon a performance, flee a town, having raised the ire of the local populace.'

She sat down beside him on the grass, tucking her bare feet under her skirts. 'Our presence was not always universally welcomed. So you see, we have more in common that you thought.'

Fergus chuckled. 'Wellington's army never fled—at least, that's how Wellington would tell it.'

'I would like to hear *you* tell it.'

'Do you want the death-and-glory version, or the real one?'

'The real one, though I will be very disappointed if it contains no death or glory.'

Fergus talked reluctantly at first, but gradually, as they identified places they had both visited, as they compared and contrasted their experiences of those places, he became more at ease. He was modest when it came to himself, glowing when talking about his men. He was renowned in the Mess as the last man standing, he joked, but confessed, when she probed, that he did remain on the battlefield long after the last shot was fired, until every one of his men was accounted for. Shadows crossed his face at times, dark memories scudding past like black clouds, but they were few in number—or perhaps he was at pains to limit their appearance. By and large, those startling turquoise eyes were alight with humour, aglow with remembered excitement.

'Enough,' he said, too soon. 'That's more than enough about me. I want to hear about you.'

'Do you want the death-and-glory version, or the real one?'

Fergus smiled. 'Definitely the real one.'

His knee brushed hers as he turned towards her. It would be silly and churlish to move away, when he most likely had not even noticed. 'The real one is very tedious, I doubt you will be interested.'

'I'll be the judge of that.'

Katerina leaned back on her hands. 'The glamour of the tightrope accounts for a very small part of my life. When an audience watches me up there, they don't realise they are seeing the result of countless hours of practice. They see an exotic wingless bird flying effortlessly through the air, and know nothing of the pain of torn muscles, the tedium of packing up our equipment and our travelling tents, the boredom of long days spent travelling from town to town.'

'Then the life of a Flying Vengarov, and the life of an officer in the Ninety-Second really are pretty similar.'

She smiled, but shook her head. 'On the surface, perhaps. All the time that you are packing up, marching, drilling, writing letters for your men, talking in the Mess, you are still Colonel Kennedy in his uniform, with his stripes or flashes or whatever it is that shows your rank. When I am out of my uniform, I am a shabby thing whom no one notices.'

She had not meant it to sound so pathetic. She did not like the rather too-perceptive gaze which rested on her. 'Shabby is the very last word I'd use to describe you,' Fergus said. 'Then again, I didn't have you down as the type of woman who fishes for compliments any more than I thought you were the self-pitying type.'

'I'm neither,' Katerina said awkwardly. 'I'm simply not accustomed to talking about myself.'

'Now that I can believe, though I find it difficult to believe that it's for lack of interest.'

'Oh, there is never any lack of interest in my ability to cling to a rope, or to bend myself backwards or in half, or—or any way you choose.'

'Oh, if I could choose…' Fergus said with a wicked smile that made her blush, but then immediately shook his head. 'I'll not pretend it isn't a fascinating subject for any red-blooded male, but it's not the only thing I'm interested in. I want to hear about you.'

Once again she found herself both aroused and disconcerted by him. Katerina gazed down at her hands. 'What do you want to know?'

He raised his hands expansively. 'Everything. Where you were born. Have you any brothers or sisters? Are your parents still alive? What is your favourite colour? Your favourite country? Your favourite food? Can you ride? Shoot? Swim? What frightens you most?'

'Stop. Wait.' Laughingly, Katerina counted his questions off on her fingers. 'I was born in Kerch, in the Crimea. No sisters, only one brother. Yes, my parents are still alive. My favourite colour is the blue of the Mediterranean Sea. My favourite country—I should say Russia, but there are so many places I have not been—I would like to visit America. My favourite food is *coulibiac*, which is a pie, filled with salmon and boiled egg and rice. Yes, I can ride well enough. No, I have never fired a gun. Yes, I can swim very well, from having spent much of my childhood near the Black Sea. There, I think I have answered them all.'

'You missed the last one.'

'What frightens me the most?' At this moment, her feelings for this man, who was frighteningly good at making her feel as if he really was interested in her. But she could not have such feelings for him. 'Falling,' Katerina said ambiguously.

He pressed her hand, giving her a smile that was as ambiguous as her own words. 'I hope you don't think my curiosity satisfied. I want to know a lot more.'

She surprised herself by obliging, not because he was persistent, but because she wanted to. She forgot all about her resolution to keep her distance, surrendering to the temptation to talk and to laugh with someone new and beguiling, just for a little while.

Though it was not such a little while. The gong sounded from the house to warn guests that it was time to change for dinner. Katerina jumped to her feet. 'Goodness, I had no idea—we have been talking for hours.'

'By far and away the most pleasant hours I've spent here.' Fergus caught her hand, pressing a kiss to her palm. 'Thank you.'

His touch changed the atmosphere between them. It was there again, that tug of awareness, that tension that thickened the air, made her breath catch in her throat. The way he looked at her made her blood heat. 'You had best go, or you will be late for dinner, which would never do.'

'Watching you last night,' Fergus said. 'It was like watching stars tumbling from the sky. I was mesmerised.'

'I know. I felt it. Felt you. Watching.'

He pulled her to him, his hands resting lightly on her waist. Heat was spreading through her in all directions. Her skirts were brushing against his legs. Her bare toes were touching his boots. 'I hope it didn't distract you too much.' His hands slid from her waist to her arms. His skin on hers. 'If I thought that you might fall, especially now I know how much it frightens you…'

'Once, I fell.' Katerina surrendered to the temptation to step closer. 'That is why I will be very careful never to fall again,' she said, shivering as her body brushed his.

He shuddered in response. 'Never?'

She pulled his head towards her. 'Absolutely never,' she said, and closed her eyes as his lips met hers.

It was a kiss that felt long, long overdue. As his mouth covered hers, his hands slid around her back and moulded her to him. Too quickly, he came to his senses and with a sigh, he let her go.

She could not bring herself to be sorry. What she felt was cheated, and frustrated. If she felt regret it was only because their kiss had been all too brief. A taste, no more, of what a kiss might be.

What was Fergus thinking? He looked as confused and discomfited as she. The uncomfortable silence stretched between them. Busying herself in an effort to break the awkwardness, Katerina slipped her foot into her slipper and began to cast about for the other one.

'Is this what you're looking for?'

She held her foot out. He made to place the shoe on her foot, and then at the last moment handed it to her, leaning down instead to pick up her book.

Didn't he want to touch her, or didn't he trust himself? What did it matter! 'Thank you,' Katerina said, 'That's exactly what I'm looking for.'

Chapter Three

Monday June 16th
Brockmore Manor House Party

Programme of Events
Masterclass in the Acrobatic Arts to be
held in the Ballroom
Expedition to a Mystery Beauty Spot
Musical Evening with Recitations and
Recitals from the guests

Alicia, the Duchess of Brockmore, settled into her lone seat, strategically placed on the balcony of the ballroom, with a keen sense of anticipation. The acrobatic masterclass about to be delivered by the Vengarovs promised to be highly entertaining, though not necessarily for those guests bold or perhaps foolish enough to participate.

Engaging the services of the two Russian acrobats had been a masterstroke. They lent enormous cachet to this year's party. Alicia had no doubt they would be the talk of the *ton* for months to come. The session she was about to witness was pushing propriety to the very limits. Were it being held anywhere other than Brockmore Manor, under the auspices of anyone other than a duke and duchess, she doubted very much that any of her guests would dare turn up. As it was, she had guiltily high hopes that at least some of them would be quite literally tied in knots.

The doors to the terrace were open, the gauzy curtains tied back, filling the ballroom with sunlight, which shimmered over the huge chandeliers. The polished dance floor was piled high with thick rugs to provide a soft landing in the event of mishap. Goodness knew where Mrs Phydon had found so many. Her venerable housekeeper was a positive treasure. Several stacks of equipment had been placed in the centre of the room. Their guests were to be given the opportunity to try their hands at juggling, the art of spinning hoops or, for bolder gentlemen in rude physical health, tumbling.

Alexandr Vengarov was the first on the scene,

rather disappointingly quite respectably dressed in a shirt and a pair of leather breeches. My, but the man had a fine pair of calves. And really, those cheekbones could sharpen knives. The gentlemen arrived in dribs and drabs, all attired in breeches and shirts. Admittedly there were some shapely legs and fine shoulders on display, but there were some, Alicia noted, eyeing them critically, who must surely resort to padding when more conventionally dressed—and not just of the calf. However, their unexpected and indeed uninvited guest, Kael Gage, stripped down very well indeed, as did Colonel Kennedy, which was to be expected of a military man.

There was no sign of that desiccated twig of a man Falkner, and surprisingly Timothy Farthingale had made the rare decision to pass up an opportunity to make an exhibition of himself. Perhaps the pair of them were closeted elsewhere talking business. Marcus would be pleased about that, it was a partnership he was most eager to promote. Lillias would likely brief him on any progress there. She seemed to be spending an unfathomable amount of time with Farthingale.

The little Russian acrobat, demurely dressed, led the posse of blushing and giggling ladies in.

This event offered an excellent opportunity to take an inventory of the early progress of the various liaisons this year's party had set in train. Alicia studied them as they filed into the room, shockingly corsetless, wearing divided skirts. It would be fair to say that not everything was going exactly to plan. The Kilmun twins, for example, seemed determined to resist the ardent advances of Addington and Brigstock, the duke's personal protégés. As to the other business closest to her dear husband's heart—now that, Alicia thought with a weary sigh, was going deuced badly.

It was a relief to see that Verity had decided to honour the company with her presence. The girl had made very little attempt to endear herself to the colonel, despite the fact that her duty had been made very clear to her. Last night, in the drawing room after dinner, had been positively embarrassing. While Colonel Kennedy had made a point of seeking Verity out, the girl sat there like a wooden effigy, forcing Alicia to intervene lest further damage was done. But the conversational seeds she so carefully planted had fallen on stony ground. There was no evidence of Verity's normal sharp-mindedness, nor of her much-vaunted wit. The poor colonel! The duchess fanned her cheeks at the memory. He at least, had emerged from the encounter with distinction. The man had shown remarkable restraint, though his mouth grew tighter with each successive silence, and those remarkable blue eyes grew stormy. In the end, she had resorted to escorting him into the card room herself.

What the *devil* was wrong with the girl! Colonel Kennedy was not simply presentable, he was an extremely attractive man, and quite, quite charming. Verity could do a great deal worse. He had an air about him that made one wish to do his bidding, but also made one rather tremble at the thought of not doing so. Wellington had gone out of his way to recommend his protégé to Marcus, and though Kennedy was a second son of a mere Scottish peer, Wellington's seal of approval more than made up for a somewhat watery pedigree. Kennedy would go far under his own steam, but he would go further with the appropriate help-meet. Just as Marcus had, Alicia thought, smiling fondly. Verity was simply being stubborn. In some ways, the girl was very like her uncle. She would remind her in the sternest of terms of her obligations.

Unless the damage was already done? Rather worryingly, despite Verity's fetching appearance in the divided skirt, Kennedy was at this moment showing little interest in his prospective wife. The duchess leaned forward over the balcony, risking discovery. It was the little acrobat that he was leaning close to, bestowing a smile on her that brought a flush to Alicia's artfully powdered cheeks. The Vengarov woman was smiling back. She touched his arm, lightly enough, though she withdrew hurriedly. Had Verity noticed the little exchange between the female acrobat and her intended? A pinch of jealousy might rouse her from her torpor. No, blast it, Verity was pointedly staring in the opposite direction.

'Ladies and gentlemen, if you would be kind enough to gather around, please select your preferred activity and we will begin.' Alexandr Vengarov clapped his hands imperiously and the duchess pushed her exasperation with her niece to one side and settled back to enjoy the spectacle.

'Very good,' Katerina said to Lady Verity Fairholme, 'you have excellent co-ordination, if

I may say so. You are the only one to have mastered juggling with three balls.'

This was a fact not lost on those male guests who had taken what they no doubt considered the easier option. One of them, Brigstock, who was the Earl of Jessop, was all fingers and thumbs, and could barely throw and cleanly catch a single ball. When she had noticed that his lack of dexterity was an enormous source of amusement to some of the spectating ladies, Katerina had quickly moved him to the hoop-spinning group. Unfortunately, he proved no more adept at this simple trick. His face a grim mask of fierce concentration, he gyrated violently as if being assailed by a swarm of hornets, but despite his determined efforts, the hoop refused to remain around his waist and clattered repeatedly on to the rugs. It was all Katerina could do not to burst out laughing herself.

Her star pupil turned out to be the Duke of Brockmore's niece, the woman intended for Fergus. She was extremely beautiful, though rather haughty, her manner distant at first, but during the last hour as she immersed herself in the art of juggling, she had been quite transformed. Eyeing her flushed countenance and sparkling eyes, Katerina felt an unaccustomed twist of envy. Family, breeding, looks and charm, as well as that certain something, a supreme kind of confidence that came from the security of her position in the upper echelon of society, this woman had it all. Including Fergus, if she wished. And why would she not wish for that!

Somewhat annoyingly, Lady Verity was proving to be easy to like. Her smile was completely lacking in self-consciousness. The glee she took in mastering what none of the other guests could manage was infectious. 'You have a natural talent,' Katerina said, and meant it.

'Thank you.' Her pupil beamed. 'You are an excellent teacher. Am I ready for the skittles, do you think?'

'You wish to learn in a morning what it takes most people years to perfect! Why not, but start with just two. Here, hold them like this. Now watch me.'

Katerina demonstrated several times, then handed two skittles to Lady Verity to try for herself. Keeping one eye on her pupil, she allowed her attention to drift back to the group of intrepid gentlemen whom Alexei was coaching in the basics of tumbling. Unsurprisingly, Fergus was one of the most successful of his pupils. He had actually managed to string a handstand and a cartwheel together. Her brother, who was ridiculously competitive, was making a point of picking holes in his technique.

Instead of taking offence, Fergus listened intently, nodding, requesting a demonstration. His next attempt was a vast improvement. He had only a fraction of Alexei's flexibility, but he was extremely strong, with an excellent sense of balance. And he was determined. His shirt came untucked from his leather breeches on his next attempt, revealing a tautly muscled belly, a smooth, tanned expanse of chest. His next combination of handstand and tumble was almost perfect, with momentum enough to take him into a second handstand. Alexei had no choice but to applaud. Fergus caught her eye and grinned.

Flushing, for she suspected she had been staring rather too openly, Katerina turned her attention back to her pupil. Fergus, his shirt clinging to his heaving torso, rested against a nearby pillar to watch. Lady Verity, intent on her skittles, did not seem to notice, but Katerina found him too distracting for her own liking. Every time she looked over, his eyes were on her.

Why was he not looking at Lady Verity! The woman was perfect for him, for goodness' sake. Making eyes at the hired entertainment would not assist his matrimonial cause, and it most certainly would not get him anywhere with the hired entertainment, who had no interest in him whatsoever. None!

Torn between anger and a creeping awareness engendered by his blatant staring that would not desist, she decided to give Fergus something else to look at. When Lady Verity dropped the skittles, Katerina picked them both up, setting them off using one hand, bending down to snatch another skittle with the other. She sent them in an arc high above her head. She threw them behind her back. She launched them higher, leapt after them, and caught them before her feet touched the ground. She knew Fergus was watching her. She would not look at him. She scooped up another skittle and threw it to Lady Verity who, catching on quickly, and with impressive timing, began to send and return the skittle on Katerina's nod. She forgot about Fergus, caught up in the sheer childish pleasure of it now, until her assistant finally threw up her hands in surrender, doubling over, panting with effort and laughter, to make a bow.

Katerina, rising from her own theatrical bow, saw Fergus walking towards them. Intrigued, she glanced at Lady Verity to gauge her reaction. The smile disappeared abruptly from her face. Katerina watched in astonishment as her body seemed to freeze, her expression ice over.

'That was most impressive, Miss Vengarov. And Lady Verity.'

Her response was as frosty as her demeanour. 'It was a private performance, Colonel Kennedy, for our own amusement.'

'You really were very good, my lady,' Katerina said, now utterly bewildered. 'I am sure the colonel merely intended—'

'I find I am not particularly interested in the colonel's intentions,' Lady Verity interrupted. She gave Katerina a forced smile. 'Thank you for your patience, but I fear I am fatigued now, and I have taken up enough of your time. You have other pupils to teach.'

Fascinated and appalled in equal measures, Katerina turned to Fergus as Lady Verity stalked off. 'What on earth have you done to provoke such enmity?'

His eyes were stormy and dark, his mouth a grim line. 'As you can see, my mere presence offends her. Not interested in my intentions! That, at least, has the merit of being the truth.' He shook his head, wiping the sweat from his brow with the back of his hand.

'I don't understand.'

Fergus thumped his fist into his palm, staring off into the distance. 'No more do I, but I intend to demand some answers. You will excuse me, if you please,' he said, and with a curt nod, strode swiftly from the ballroom.

Fergus finally tracked Lady Verity down in the music room an hour later, where she was supervising the repositioning of a pianoforte from its normal place in the corner, into the centre of the room. She was wearing one of her pastel-coloured gowns. Her hair was freshly pinned. Her countenance was no longer flushed and her expression was, as ever when she deigned to meet his eye, quite blank.

'I am rather busy, Colonel Kennedy,' she said. 'I would like to complete preparations for the musical evening before setting out on today's mystery tour, so if you will excuse me…'

She turned her back on him. Fergus held the door wide open. 'Leave us, if you please,' he said firmly to the butler.

She waited until the last of the footmen had closed the door in the butler's wake, before she turned to Fergus with raised brows.

Fergus leaned back against the closed door, eyeing her appraisingly. 'I wish us to speak plainly.'

'I suspect that is more of a command than a wish,' she replied with a shadow of a smile. 'May I assume, Colonel Kennedy, that this plain speaking does not involve a proposal?'

Her expression remained aloof, but in those china-blue eyes, there was a tiny hint of fear. There could no longer be any doubt that her snubs had been deliberate. Oddly, Fergus found this reassuring. 'You may indeed,' he said, crossing the room towards her and pulling out a chair from the stack waiting to be set around the pianoforte, waiting until she sat daintily down upon it before sitting astride another, facing her. 'What I want to know, Lady Verity, is not whether or not you'll accept my hand, but why you agreed to consider a proposal from me in the first place.'

He watched her closely, the struggle between prevarication and truth well disguised but there, none the less, in the tightening of her clasped hands, the way her eyes roamed restlessly around the room. Finally, to his relief, she seemed to reach a decision, straightening her shoulders and meeting his eyes unwaveringly.

'It is not that I find you in any way objectionable, Colonel. On the contrary, you have borne my appalling behaviour with admirable restraint.'

She smiled then, a reserved smile, but a genuine one, allowing him a glimpse of the attractive woman behind the ice-maiden façade she routinely presented to him. He could, finally, understand why her admirers were legion, but knew too that he would never be one of them. There was still an element of calculation in the way she teased, something in her manner, a sense of entitlement that made his hackles rise. Lady Verity was lovely, and she was charming, and she knew it.

'It is not I, but your uncle who will mete out any punishment when he discovers we are not willing to make the match he has engineered between us.'

Lady Verity blanched. 'I fear my uncle will be furious with me.'

Fergus cursed under his breath. What a selfish oaf he had been, so caught up in his own dilemma that it hadn't occurred to him that his were not the only strings being pulled by the twin puppet masters. 'I apologise. I have been so concerned with the implications for my own fate that I had not thought of yours.'

'What implications, Colonel?'

'My posting to Egypt will be cancelled. My career as a tallyman of numbers will be extended indefinitely.'

'How ironic. It is the posting you desire so very much which is precisely the stumbling block for me, you see. I confess that I have, to my surprise, found you to be honourable, and intelligent, and—yes—extremely attractive,' Lady Verity said, blushing faintly. 'Colonel Kennedy, under different circumstances, I am sure we would suit very well, for you are clearly a man whose star is on the rise, and without false modesty, I believe I would make an excellent diplomatic helpmeet, were you to be posted somewhere civilised like Paris or Rome. But Egypt! Heaven forfend, that does not suit me at all. I simply won't be despatched to some fly-blown outpost. There, is that plain enough speaking for you?'

Completely taken aback, Fergus laughed.

'Plain, and very unexpected. It is ironic indeed, that my idea of heaven is your idea of purgatory.'

'No doubt you think me shallow. Perhaps I am. I prefer to think that I recognise that this particular English rose would not flourish in the desert, would rather wither and die. I know my limitations, Colonel.'

'One of which is an inability to speak as frankly to your uncle, or even your aunt.'

Lady Verity sighed. 'You don't understand. I owe the duke and duchess a great deal. Since my mother died, I have been treated as the child they could not have. I have already turned down several advantageous proposals. I am testing their patience to the limit.'

'And so this time, rather than incur your uncle's wrath once more, you thought to shift the blame on to me.'

'I am sorry. I had no way of knowing how much it meant to you. It is easier to think only of oneself when one is not actually acquainted with the other party.'

It was a very uncomfortable truth. 'You are quite right,' Fergus said, 'it is a chastening thought.' He got to his feet and began to pace the room. He ran his fingers across the strings of a harp, producing an appropriately discordant, jarring sound. There was no getting around the facts. He could not marry Lady Verity. The loss of his precious posting made his heart sink, but almost at once, his mood felt lighter. The uneasy feeling he'd been carrying about with him since he arrived at Brockmore Manor was quite gone. After all, a posting was hardly a lifetime's commitment, while a wife—lord, but he'd had a narrow escape.

'I do wish you would stop pacing, Colonel. I feel as if I am up on some sort of charge.'

'I fear that will be my fate, when Wellington hears—but that is none of your concern.' Fergus resumed his seat. 'I wish I had not agreed to come here, but now that I have, and the eyes of your uncle and his guests are upon us, I think the worst possible course of action would be for me to leave, and leave you exposed to the inevitable gossip and ensuing scandal.'

Lady Verity shuddered. 'No. Good grief, no.'

'Aye. Well, in that case I suggest we pay lip service to our allotted roles. We'll be polite to one another—you'll stop publicly snubbing me—but there's an end to it. And at the end of the week, I'll speak to your uncle and tell him that I don't think we'll suit. I'll make sure he understands that the failure to do his bidding lies at my door and not yours.'

Lady Verity flushed. 'That is very good of you. I wish—I do sincerely wish, Colonel, that I was brave enough to shoulder the blame myself, but...'

'There is no need for you to feel guilty.'

She smiled tightly. 'I am afraid that if I try hard enough, I won't. You make me rather ashamed of myself, Colonel.'

'It was not my intention.'

'None the less.' Lady Verity got to her feet. 'You are a good man. A most admirable one. I hope that the Duke of Wellington can for once overlook his ego, and award you the posting regardless. His loss would also be Egypt's.'

'But not yours?' Fergus said, smiling.

She laughed. 'I am a good deal less sure of that than I was this morning, but I suspect that matters not a jot. You would not have offered for me, Colonel, had I set out to charm you from the beginning, would you?'

'I honestly don't know.' He frowned, running his hand through his hair. 'I came here with every intention—at least, I thought I did, but—it's such a cold-blooded way to make a match, is it not? I think we've both had a lucky escape. Best leave it at that.'

'Unflattering as the sentiment is, I am forced to agree. I can only hope that the next suitor my uncle produces for me feels quite the opposite.'

'Perhaps you should consider finding your own suitor.'

'A novel thought.' Lady Verity extended her hand.

Fergus brushed her fingertips with his lips. 'It is indeed.'

Slipping her feet into a pair of soft leather slippers, Katerina quit her bedchamber. The house was quiet in the lull between the flurry of housework and the laborious preparations for dinner. The duke's guests were, according to the Programme of Events, off on a mystery tour. Descending the stairs to the main guest floor in the hushed silence, she felt the eyes of the ancestral portraits which lined the walls around the stairwell on her, and succumbed to curiosity. Each painting was neatly labelled and in chronological order. The illustrious history of the Brockmore family was laid bare in picture form, from the first earl, his countess and their nine children, through to the current, fourth duke and his duchess.

Bloodline and pedigree, those most valuable things to the aristocracy—of their children and their horses, Katerina thought sardonically. And after that, power and influence. Oh, and wealth, of course, though that seemed to come a poor third. Pomp and circumstance, those were the things that mattered when a match was made. There was no place for love, and as to desire— desire, as she well knew, was sated in less formal relationships, with those who could not claim blood or pedigree, or whose blood and pedigree, no matter how revered in their own world, was not revered in the *right* world.

It did not matter what one was, but how one came to be. A mere accident of birth, yet in the Duke of Brockmore's world, which was also Fergus's world, her birth excluded her for ever, no matter how much of an aristocrat she was in her own right. The guests at Brockmore Manor might look up to her on the tightrope, but they would look down their noses if they encountered her on the ground. More likely, they would not even recognise her. Should she make the unforgivable mistake of trying to enter their world however, that would be a very different thing. Not that she would try. Not that she wanted to.

The space next to the portrait of the current duke and duchess, unlike all the others, was not filled with smaller portraits of children. Instead a painting of a weak-chinned man in his forties was hung just below their images. Katerina peered at the label. "'Robert Penrith,'" she read. "'Nephew to the Fourth Duke, and Heir to the Brockmore Title.'"

Pity stirred in her breast, looking at the painting, for it starkly drew attention to the Brockmores' childless state. A very galling state for such a dynasty, she suspected. So much power and influence, so much wealth, so much pomp and circumstance the Brockmores had, yet they were forced to expend it on nephews and nieces and cousins.

Perhaps one day Fergus's children would adorn the walls here, if he married Lady Verity. It was an unpalatable thought. Turning away from the gallery, Katerina ran lightly down the central staircase, across the polished chequered tiles of the reception hall, through the ballroom and on to the terrace. The blue waters of the lake were irresistible. Crossing the velvet green of the lawn, a flutter of scarlet silk caught her eye. The statuesque beauty clad in her habitual crimson, Lillias Lamont had not joined the mystery tour and nor had her companion, also dressed in red silk. Sir Timothy Something. They made a very odd pair as they disappeared into the maze. Proof that opposites could attract.

Katerina did not need proof of that. She and Fergus were not so much opposites, as from opposite worlds. In many ways they were so similar, yet in that most important regard they were utterly different. Fergus and Lady Verity, now they ought to be a perfect match, yet that scene between them this morning—if she had not witnessed Lady Verity's transformation herself, she would not have believed it. Had they resolved their differences? Fergus had been furious when he'd gone after her, but Fergus had an enormous amount at stake. Enough to force him into obeying orders, no matter how unpalatable?

He was, as yesterday's conversation in the maze had proved, an honourable man, and at heart, above all, a soldier who loyally carried out orders. But marriage to a woman who for reasons quite unfathomable, did not understand how fortunate she was? He deserved better.

Turning the corner of the boating house, she saw the subject of her musings standing on the edge of the jetty, staring out over the water and quite lost in thought. He had changed out of the clothes he'd worn for this morning's acrobatics. His black boots were so highly polished they shone like mirrors. Since his coat lay over one of the pier's bollards, Katerina had the opportunity to admire the way his sand-coloured pantaloons clung to the taut contours of his rear, and she took unashamed advantage of it. The back of his waistcoat was fawn-coloured silk. The sleeves of his shirt were rolled up, as they had been the first time she'd met him, displaying tanned, sinewy forearms. There were golden streaks in his hair that she'd not noticed before.

As she stepped on to the jetty, Fergus turned around. He had been frowning, but the instant he saw her, his expression cleared, his mouth softened into a smile that made her stomach lurch, and he held out his hand in welcome.

'I was just thinking about you,' he said, 'and here you are.'

'I was just thinking about you,' Katerina replied, 'and here *you* are.' She took his hand. His fingers twined with hers. 'You did not go on the mystery tour?'

'I've a mystery of my own to resolve. What to do with my life,' he clarified, when she looked confused. 'I've come to a—let's say an arrangement—with Lady Verity, that we won't suit. Truth is, she could just about stomach me, but she couldn't stomach Egypt.'

'Oh, Fergus.' She stared at him wide-eyed, more horrified than relieved.

'Aye, I know, it doesn't bear thinking of, but at the end of the day, I'd rather be stuck behind a desk than stuck in a marriage of someone else's making.'

'Have you spoken to the duke?'

'Which one of the two do you mean? We've agreed that it's best to wait until the end of the week for me to inform Brockmore. Until then, I'll join in enough to keep face, and no more. And after the weekend—well, then I'll face the other duke, and—ach, but you know I will think about that later. To be honest, at the moment I'm just relieved. I should have known, when it was so bloody—blasted difficult to bring myself up to the mark, that it was wrong.'

'You are too hard on yourself. The pressures—especially from Wellington. All of your life as a soldier, you have obeyed him.'

Fergus smiled warmly at her. 'You understand. I somehow knew you would.'

She could not resist reaching up to smooth down his rebellious kink of hair. 'I think it will be very difficult for you to tell him so, to his face. I think you will need every bit of your courage.'

He caught her hand in his. 'I'll think of you, when I do. I'll think of you flying high on that tightrope, defying gravity. But right now, I'd rather not dwell on it, if you don't mind. In fact, what I was actually thinking was that I'd like to get away from the machinations of the Brockmore family tomorrow. A day out, the chance to explore a bit of the countryside. I don't suppose you'd like to accompany me?'

Katerina did not have to think twice. 'I would like that very much.'

Fergus turned her hand over to press a kiss to her palm. 'The pleasure, Miss Vengarov, will be all mine.'

Chapter Four

Tuesday June 17th
Brockmore Manor House Party

Programme of Events
Performance of Aerial Dexterity by
the Legendary Alexandr Vengarov

'This looks like a perfect picnic spot. What do you think?'

'Perfect,' Katerina agreed, though she was looking at Fergus rather than their surroundings. Dressed in a bottle-green riding coat and leather breeches with top boots, there was none the less an unmistakably military air in the way he sat imperiously astride his horse. The mount which Cade Retton, the Duke of Brockmore's discerning Master of the Horse, had selected for him was a huge, highly strung stallion, but Fergus

had brought the massive beast to heel with remarkable ease. Katerina had been relieved when
Mr Retton graciously provided her with a docile,
impeccably behaved mare.

They had set out mid-morning, riding across
country, skirting the little estate village of Brockmore, through narrow lanes redolent with the
scent of honeysuckle, past fields of wheat and
hops waving lazily in the breeze. Now, in the
shade of a little copse, where a shallow stream
burbled contentedly along its pebble-strewn bed,
they dismounted, Fergus loosely tethering the
horses while Katerina spread a blanket out on
the grassy banks that flanked the stream.

He took off his coat and sat down beside her,
stretching out his long legs in front of him. 'I
hope I've not bored you to tears with my stories
of home.'

The skirts of her blue riding habit were brushing his leg. The hairs on the back of his hand
were golden in the dappled sunlight. He was so
close, and not close enough. When he smiled at
her, as he was doing now, she found it hard to
concentrate. 'I've never been to Scotland,' Katerina said. 'You make it sound so beautiful.'

'Absence makes the heart grow fonder. It is

lovely, though it is also very wet. We have a hundred different ways of describing rain.'

He rolled on to his side, leaning his head on his hand. Automatically, Katerina did the same. 'Tell me some of them,' she said.

'Well, when the sky's gunmetal grey, and a constant drizzle of soft rain drifts down in a fine mist like this,' he said, brushing his fingers lightly along her forearm, 'we say it's *gie dreich*.'

'*Guy dreeck.*'

He laughed. 'Not bad. And when it's that heavy rain, the kind that cascades straight down like stair rods and soaks right into your bones,' he said, drumming his fingers on her arm, 'we say it's pelting. Though in France, they have a much better expression for it, involving the—er—natural functions of a cow.'

'I know that one, it is very rude indeed,' Katerina said, smiling. 'I thought you could not speak French, save for battle orders and menus.'

'Oh, I have some other handy wee phrases up my sleeve in a few different languages, should circumstances demand it.'

'Oaths and curses?'

'Aye, a few of them, right enough.'

'And compliments?'

'There's no denying they do come in handy on occasion.' Fergus's smile deepened. 'Though I'm thinking that a bonnie lass like you, and one so talented, must have received a great deal more of those than I've ever doled out.'

'When a man looks at me, he does not see what you call a bonnie lass. He sees a half-naked artiste seemingly flying free of any fetters, and assumes that means I am also free of any morals, and therefore easily persuaded to remove the other half of my clothing.'

Fergus sat up abruptly. 'You jest, surely.'

Katerina shrugged. 'You saw for yourself the reaction to our performance the other evening. It is the same wherever we go. Women are drawn to Alexei like moths to a flame, and men are likewise drawn to me. They don't know me, they don't want to know me, but they covet—I don't know what it is they covet to be honest. Alexei and I, we are like trophies to be collected, you know?'

'No, I don't,' Fergus said shortly. 'You talk as if they see you as a courtesan.'

'A very exclusive one, if that's the case.'

'That's not funny.'

'No, Fergus, but it's true,' Katerina said, with

an edge of bitterness. 'Not that I am a courtesan, but that is how your society views me. No matter how innocent I may be, I am not and never can be respectable. And I am not—I am not wholly innocent.' She could feel the heat flaring on her cheeks, but she refused to look away. She had not meant to speak so frankly, but it mattered to her, that he understand. 'I did—there was a man, once.'

'Only one.' Fergus covered her hand with his. 'There have been a great deal many more women in my life.'

'It is different for a man.'

'It is, but it shouldn't be.' He touched her cheek, brushing her hair behind her ear. 'I get the feeling that it's not a very happy story.'

'Why do you say that?'

'Because there has been only one man. Did he hurt you, Katerina?'

His unexpected tenderness brought a lump to her throat. 'I thought he was different from the others. I thought he loved me. He said he did, and I wanted to believe him.'

'Did you love him?'

She blinked furiously. 'I thought so. I thought my heart was broken when he left me.'

Fergus cursed softly under his breath. 'What happened?'

She scrubbed at her eyes. 'He wasn't different. He didn't love me. I was wrong on both counts. He wanted only to prove he could have me, and then, when I did—after I had—after he had— then he wanted to tell all his friends that he had had me, and of course his friends assumed that they could have me too and...' Katerina fumbled for her handkerchief. 'He said we would be married. No, that is not quite true. He never actually said the words but I thought—I assumed—I was such a fool. I know that now, but at the time...'

It was too much. She covered her face with her kerchief, overcome not only by tears but by shame. 'I'm sorry. I never talk of it, it makes Alexei so angry.'

He swore again, more viciously, and pulled her tight against him. She buried her face in his chest and sobbed. He held her tightly, smoothing her hair, stroking her back, whispering soothing words she could not understand in the soft lyrical language of his native land. Gradually, her sobs abated. 'I'm sorry,' she said, her words muffled. 'I've made your shirt all wet.'

She felt the low rumble of his laughter against

her cheek. Finally, she dared to look up. 'You don't despise me?'

He winced. 'I despise that wee shite of a man who did this, but you—no. How could you think that?'

'It is how he felt, afterwards. And his friends, when I would not—you know?' Katerina wiped her eyes, sitting up reluctantly. 'I should have known from the start that he had no intentions that were honourable,' she said with a watery smile. 'When he realised I'd taken his silly promises seriously, he was horrified. "Can you imagine what my mother would say?" she said, in a mocking English accent. '"I had as well bring an opera singer home."'

'Katerina…'

'No, don't feel sorry for me. He was right. That is exactly how his mother would have viewed me.'

Fergus swore for a third time. 'No wonder you were so careful to keep your distance from me.'

'In the last two years, I have kept my distance from all men.'

'I don't blame you.' He ran his fingers through his hair. 'Is that how you see me—as a trophy hunter?'

Katerina flushed. 'I told you this because I know you're not.'

'Thank you.' He took her hand, pressing a fleeting kiss to her knuckles. 'I mean it. I am more touched than I can say that you trusted me. It must have taken a good deal of courage to speak about such a very personal matter.'

'You don't think less of me?'

'Katerina, I think a great deal more of you.'

'I sometimes wish that I was more like Alexei. He takes it all so lightly. A different place, a different woman, and when it is over—well, then it is over. But I'm not like that, Fergus,' she said plaintively, 'you do believe me?'

'I do believe you.' He kissed her hand again, but then let her go, looking uncomfortable. 'I only wish I could say the same thing of myself, but I fear I've been more like Alexei than I care to admit. There have been many women and much pleasure, but not a single *affaire* which lasted beyond a particular posting. And none at all of late. It seems my appetite for war and dalliance go hand in hand.'

'Until now?'

'No.' Fergus shook his head firmly. 'I would not call this dalliance. I told you, I'm not a trophy hunter. I'm not flirting with you, Katerina. To be honest, I don't know what I'm doing.'

'No more do I,' she admitted with a sigh. 'I do feel better though. Thank you, for listening to my sad little story.'

'The story is sad, but you are not. You've survived—and how! Just look at you. You are a very brave woman. Don't make light of it.'

She shrugged, because she did not want him to see how much his words meant. 'I think I have been a lonely woman, a little. But I am not lonely today.'

He pressed her fingers. 'Nor am I.'

She leant towards him. His knee brushed her leg. She tilted her face in invitation, and felt the warm, soft brush of his lips on hers. His tongue caressed her bottom lip. She sighed, lying back on the rug, pulling him with her, arching her body against his, touching her tongue to his. She could feel the solid ridge of his arousal. She opened her mouth, pressing herself against him, and their kiss deepened. Heat flooded her as his mouth shaped itself to hers, as their tongues touched, tangled, touched again, and their lips clung, and a heavy ache grew low in her belly.

It was Fergus who broke the kiss. 'I don't want to hurt you, Katerina.'

'You won't, Fergus. How can you? This is not the real world, it's a little dream place we have made. On Saturday, you will return to your world and I to mine.' She said the words as much to remind herself as to caution him. 'You can't hurt me, Fergus, I won't let you. I promise.'

It did not occur to her that she could possibly hurt him. In many ways, she really was an innocent, Fergus thought, as he watched Katerina set out their picnic lunch on the blanket. She had taken off her close-fitting riding jacket and pushed up the full sleeves of her blouse. Wisps of her hair had come loose from her chignon. He'd likely freed them himself, when he'd been kissing her. Realising that watching her bend and stoop was hardly conducive to his recovering his dignity, he turned away to splash some icy water from the stream on to his face.

Until today he'd never thought of his life as an officer as a performance, but in a way that's exactly what it was. A lifetime of campaigning, of hard-kept discipline, hard-won respect and intense mess-room rivalry had taught him to keep his innermost thoughts and feelings to himself. Had he been lonely? He'd not thought so, until she'd told him of her own solitude, but he'd certainly never felt this affinity, this easy companionability, this distracting combination of simple liking and complex desire before. Then again, he'd never met anyone like Katerina before. Odd that they had so much in common, when they came from such very different worlds. Like him, Katerina had a taste for danger. When she was leaping about so fearlessly, so gracefully, on that terrifyingly high tightrope, her eyes were alight with excitement. He recognised that feeling. He remembered it well from studying battle plans, from readying his troops to enter the fray, and if he was honest, in the heat of battle too, barking orders, having to react to unfolding events at lightning speed, knowing that every second counted, that every decision mattered, that every move could mean the difference between life and death. The difference between balancing on the rope and falling.

There was a different and equally exhilarating rush of excitement every time he looked at Katerina, dragging him into her orbit, making him want to reach for her, touch her, hold her. It was like standing on the brink, walking a different tightrope, this time between victory and defeat. She went to his head. She made him want to lose his head. He'd never felt that before, never even come close.

The picnic they ate consisted of a selection of Russian delicacies. 'Monsieur Salois, the duke's French chef, he has to prepare a Russian banquet on Friday, and he had very few authentic receipts, so I have been assisting him,' Katerina explained. 'I could not persuade him to let me take some of the caviar and in any event it would have been a sacrilege to eat it warm, but I hope you like fish? Here is a coulibiac.'

'Your favourite, is it not?'

'You remember?'

'I remember everything you tell me.'

'Oh. Well. Yes, it is my favourite.' It was silly to be so touched by this. Katerina stared down at the food. 'These are blinis, and this is knish, which is a potato dumpling. I suspect it is too much like peasant food to be served to the duke's aristocratic guests, but *monsieur* was eager to experiment, so I showed him how to make them. What do you think?'

'Russian delicacies, made by a Russian delicacy,' Fergus said with a teasing smile. 'You really made all of this?'

'Not the blinis, which are far too thick but yes, of course I can cook. My mother taught me. Every Russian woman can cook.'

'I'm willing to bet that not a single one of the female guests at Brockmore can so much as coddle an egg. I know my sisters can't.'

'That is because they don't have to. We Vengarovs may be aristocrats when it comes to acrobatics, but we are not wealthy. We are proud of our heritage, but to your family, I think, we are little more than gypsies. No, don't deny it, for it is true, Fergus, is it not?'

He could not lie. 'My father prizes his lands before all else. The estate, the castle, that's where his heart is, and where my brother has been forced to locate his heart too. I've always been glad to be the second son, I don't share their love for the place but—yes,' he finished awkwardly, 'he'd see you as rootless. He'd not understand that there are other types of dynasties to be maintained.'

'You don't need to be embarrassed,' Katerina said, handing him a plate of beautifully arranged food, 'my father is exactly the same. There is his way—our way—and there is no other. It is not the ownership of land which is important, it is the blood, the line, the talent.' Katerina sipped at her wine. 'This is good, but it is French. I doubt even a man so well connected as the Silver Fox will be able to conjure up some excellent Crimean wine to accompany the Russian dinner.'

After they had finished the wine, they sat in contented silence watching the trout leap for flies in the stream. As Fergus saddled the horses for the return journey, Katerina tidied away the remnants of their picnic. She did even the most mundane of tasks with such grace. Her body moved as if she were held together by wires, not bones. She could bend herself backwards, sideways and round about, yet every shape she formed was fluidly achieved. She could likely wrap herself around him and hold herself there, her legs curled around his waist, maybe her hands clasped around his neck. She could rock against him. He would cup her delightful rear, just to steady her as he slid into her. If she arched her back then, she would take him higher, and he would...

He was hard again, dammit! Think of jumping

into that stream. No, even better, remember what it was like plunging into the mountain waters of Glen Massan in the spring, when the river was full of snow-melt. Or if not cold, think of pain. The agonising blast of the musket ball when it exploded into his shoulder, the white-hot pain slicing though him when the shrapnel was removed, the persistent aching throb that had kept him awake for nights afterwards. Aye, that was working. That had done the trick.

Fergus checked the stirrups and picked up his coat. Katerina was sliding her arms into her jacket. The movement lifted her breasts. They were small, but like the rest of her, perfectly formed. Fergus cursed himself again, but could not bring himself to look away. A few more days, and then she'd be out of his life for good. This thought, finally, resolved matters. By the time he helped her into the saddle for their homeward journey, he was thoroughly deflated in more ways than one.

Chapter Five

Wednesday June 18th
Brockmore Manor House Party

Programme of Events
A Morning of Strawberry-Picking
A Celebration in Honour of the
Second Anniversary of the
Illustrious Military Victory at Waterloo

Wearing her robe over her flimsy tunic, Katerina slipped out of the house by a side door and set off for the practice area. The Duchess of Brockmore's orchid house was a wooden-framed glass structure, comprised of a central block three storeys high, flanked by a low wing on either side. Though it was early, the windows had already been opened. Peeping through the central door, Katerina was drawn in by the sweet, earthy smell of the carpet of moss which acted as ground cover for the rare and precious blooms, whose heady, perfumed scent hung in the air like incense in a cathedral.

Inside, the air was humid, the paved floor damped down with water. In the high central atrium a selection of palm trees, exotic ferns and succulents soared towards the glass ceiling like a miniature jungle. The orchids were discreetly planted in small groupings set on waist-high tables around the magnificent centrepiece. The colours were breathtaking: delicate blushing-powder-pink; impossibly fragile pale lemon; tiny icing-sugar-white clusters like constellations in the night sky; huge single blooms on mossy mounds, ranging from pale blue to speckled green and poisonous purple. Like the family portraits on the great staircase, each was clearly labelled. The labels showed that they had been collected from the four corners of the world. Katerina was examining a grotesque black-tongued specimen when she heard the doors creak open.

'What's so dashed urgent, Brigstock?' The voice was testy, male and vaguely familiar. 'If we don't catch up with the others before they reach the stable block, then they'll have their pick of the horses. I don't want to be lumbered with a broken-winded nag for the race tomorrow.'

'I doubt very much that the Duke of Brockmore would tolerate any nags in his stables, broken-winded or otherwise,' the other man replied witheringly. Brigstock, Earl of Jessop. Katerina remembered him now as the man who had made such a hash of both juggling and the hoops. He had absolutely no co-ordination. She could not imagine that he would have much chance of winning a horse race even if he were riding Pegasus himself. 'Listen here, Addington, this is a bit embarrassing, but I need to ascertain your intentions regarding the Kilmun ladies.'

'Well that's easy enough to answer, old chap. Frankly I have little, if any, intentions in that direction. Blast it all, that pair have led us a merry dance from the off, and all because I happened to call Cynthia Cecily. Or Cecily Cynthia.'

A low chuckle met this remark. 'Once was forgivable, but three times, Addington? If you cared a jot, you'd have made an effort.'

'There's the rub, as old man Shakespeare would say. I'm not sure I can bring myself to care.'

Katerina was feeling distinctly uncomfortable. Hidden from sight of the newcomers by the central display of palms, she was reluctant to make her presence known. Not only would she embarrass the two men, she was horribly aware that her state of relative undress might encourage them to attempt to take advantage. She had not been aware that either of them had shown more than the tiresome but ubiquitous level of male interest she had become inured to, but she preferred not to take any chances. Shrinking against the palm tree, she had no choice but to wait until they concluded their conversation.

'So you're taking yourself out of the running then?' Brigstock asked.

'I do believe I am. Which leaves you an open field, dear boy. Which filly do you wish to capture, Cecily or Cynthia—or doesn't it matter?'

'It does matter, rather a lot actually. Would it surprise you to learn that I have been able to tell the difference between the two of them since that very first day, though I've been at pains to keep that to myself.'

'It would astonish me. Please feel free to pursue your differentiated miss, whichever one it happens to be, Brigstock. I wish you nothing but luck.'

'Much obliged. But what about you, Addington? Let us not beat about the bush, we have both come here at Brockmore's behest to make a match of it with the twins. The duke is not a man I would care to thwart. Quite the opposite. One word from him in the right ear can make or break a man.'

'Oh, you don't have to worry about me, dear boy. The duke will get his match, though not the one he planned. I've a mind to make Florence Canby an offer, though it's not settled yet, so I'd be obliged if you would keep that to yourself for the time being. Now, if you're happy we've cleared this little matter up, I really would like to make haste to the stables.'

The door closed on the two men. Never mind a hothouse, this place was a positive hotbed of intrigue, Katerina thought, as she followed them out a few minutes later, making for the walled garden. The Duke of Brockmore's schemes were clearly not all going to plan. Though some, she suspected, were closer to his heart than others. Such as those for his niece. He would be furious when Fergus informed him that particular plan had gone awry.

Poor Fergus.

Oh, Fergus.

Her stomach did a little flip. Yesterday had been one of the most delightful days she had spent in a very long time. She had not planned her confession, but though it had been painful, it had left her feeling considerably better about herself. Fergus had not condemned her. On the contrary, he thought her brave. Remembering his words made her glow. It changed none of the very hard lessons she had learnt. She was still ashamed, and she still thought herself a fool, but she did not, now, blame only herself.

Fergus. Last night, she had been unable to sleep for thinking about him. Fergus's kiss. Fergus's smile. Fergus's hands on her. Touching her. Bringing her body to life, awakening her senses. Making her crave that touch more, and more, and more. She had been lonely. In the two years since her disastrous *affaire*, she had been wary of the most fleeting contact with any man. They wanted only one thing from her, she had thought, not realising that there were things she was missing in return. Friendship. Laughter. Understanding. Ridiculous to imagine that you could come to know someone in just a few short days, but that is exactly how she felt about Fergus. She did know him, and he understood her in ways that no one else did. He was excited by the tightrope walker, but he was as intrigued by the person behind the performer, the woman behind the artiste, as she was by the man behind the regimentals, the person not the soldier.

Would it be so wrong to surrender to temptation, to go so far as to make love to him? Katerina shuddered. Her body had no doubts, but it was the strength of her wanting that gave her pause. Yesterday she had assured him that he could not hurt her, certain in the knowledge that whatever they felt for each other, it could mean nothing. Fergus's extremely modest opinion of himself was patently not shared by either Wellington or Brockmore. He would fly high in society, military, diplomatic or otherwise. Well beyond the scandalous, twilight world of a tightrope performer. And so you were right, Katerina told herself firmly, Fergus cannot hurt you, because after this house party, Fergus will be out of your life.

But until then?

She turned the corner, past the succession houses and the pinery, into the walled garden, and there he was. Until the party was over, there could be no reason at all to deny herself what she wanted more than anything.

* * *

The vaulting horse was made of leather and wood, with a carved head, a silk tail, and a fixed saddle on its back, constructed with a pommel on each side. The horse's neck had a hidden lever which could be adjusted to lie it horizontal with its back, giving the performer more room to execute his moves. Alexei had first seen a similar one in Berlin, at Friedrich Ludwig Jahn's gymnasium, and had had his own constructed to order.

Fergus was in his shirt and leather breeches, bare-footed, astride the vaulting horse, the neck of which had been lowered. His shirt was open at the throat, the sleeves rolled up. He was balancing on the pommels, the sinews of his arms like cords. He had obviously seen someone perform on a vaulting horse before. Slowly, he raised his legs and tried to swing over the pommel. His leg caught. He sank on to the saddle, but only a few seconds later he tried again, and got halfway round. He had his back to her now. She could see his shoulder muscles straining as he raised himself up and tried again, but once again his leg caught. Brow furrowed, arms shaking, he tried once more and slowly managed a full circle.

Katerina burst into applause.

His head jerked up. A smile lit his face. His eyes were so very blue. 'This is a private area,' he said in a fair imitation of her own accented English, in her own words from that first day. 'You should not be here.'

'I was looking for Keaton, the gardener,' Katerina teased.

Fergus jumped down from the vault. 'Would you like me to fetch him?'

His smile was making her heart do somersaults. She pretended to consider it, then shook her head. 'I will make do with your company, I think.'

'Because any company is better than none?'

His shirt clung to his chest. She could see the dark circles of his nipples. She reached up to smooth back his rebellious kink of hair. She leaned into him. Sweat, the leather from the pommels, soap. Her hand slid down to stroke his cheek. 'Because your company is superior to any other,' Katerina said.

He hesitated for only an instant before pulling her into his arms and kissing her roughly. Without hesitation, she kissed him back, clinging to his damp body, pressing herself urgently against him. His kisses were hungry, his hands moulding her to him, roaming over her back, cupping her bottom, his mouth hot on hers. Heat swamped her. She was mindless with desire, wanting only more, ever more. Her back was pressed against the vaulting horse now. Her hands were tearing at Fergus's shirt, feverishly seeking skin. Hot skin. Skin that rippled under her touch, the muscles beneath tensing. There was a deep gouge on his shoulder. His Waterloo wound. There was another ridge of a scar on his belly. Her robe was open. Fergus kissed her neck, the swell of her breasts in the vee of her tunic. Her heart was racing. His hands slid up her flanks, her waist, to cup her breasts. Her nipples were hard. His thumbs stroked them, making them tauten further, making her moan, sending heat sparking out, down, through her body.

She felt as if she were flying through the air. She felt as if she was only just maintaining her balance. His arousal was pressed firmly against her belly. She stood on her tiptoes, wanting it to press lower, to where she ached and throbbed. He put his hands around her waist and lifted her on to the vault, which was set low for practice, seating her sideways in the saddle, dipping his head to take one of her nipples in his mouth, through the soft fabric of her practice tunic. Katerina caught at his shoulders, wrapping her legs around his waist. He groaned. His mouth sought out hers again, his hands claimed her breasts, and their kisses made her head spin, as it did when she looked down from the most vertiginous rope. Everything inside her tensed, clenched with the effort of preventing herself from tumbling to earth, back to reality, or perhaps with the effort of willing herself to let go and soar on wings of desire. Which, she neither knew nor cared.

'Katerina.' His voice was hoarse. He was breathing as if he had completed fifty rotations of the vaulting horse. His eyes were dark, the passion she felt gleaming and reflected in his eyes.

'No.' She tightened her legs around his waist, digging her heels into his clenched buttocks. 'No. Don't stop.' She pulled his face towards her, claiming his mouth again. His kiss was desperate. She had no doubt he wanted her as much as she wanted him. All she had to do was to kiss him and kiss him and kiss him and...

'Katerina, we are in a public place, someone might see us.'

She dragged her mouth away. She uncurled her legs and slithered down from the vaulting horse. Remembering too late, much too late, where they were, she retied her robe, casting an anxious eye up to the overlooking windows. The sun made them opaque, the interiors dark with shadows. The walled garden was empty, though she doubted either of them would have noticed if someone had inadvertently stumbled upon them. This morning's strawberry-picking outing was taking place in the fields of one of the village farms. Most likely they had not been observed. They had been incredibly lucky. She could not believe they had taken such a chance.

But her body still thrummed, making its own unreasonable demands. Katerina tightened the sash of her robe. Fergus had tucked his shirt back into his breeches. He bent down to pick up his waistcoat and his breeches stretched tight across his buttocks. She dragged her eyes away, but her gaze drifted down to linger on his muscled calves, on the slender length of his bare feet. She wanted him so much.

He pulled on his stockings and boots, picked up his coat. The air was thick with suppressed passion, with stifled desire. 'You've got me turning somersaults in more ways than one.' Fergus's smile faded. 'What you told me yesterday about men pursuing you...'

'I know you are different.'

'Am I? The first time I saw you was here on the tightrope. And later that night, that performance, you were like a star flying through the night sky. I couldn't take my eyes off you.'

'But yesterday, it was the same, and I was wearing a riding habit.'

'I don't want you to think that I'm like that man who hurt you. I do want you, you can be in no doubt of that.'

'Any more than you can doubt that I want you.' Heat flushed her cheeks, but she knew that if she wanted this, the initiative must be hers. 'From the moment I saw you, it was the same for me, Fergus. I couldn't take my eyes off you. We have so little time. I would like us to—to make the most of it.'

He caught her hands between his. 'You feel it too, this—this pull between us? I am not imagining it?'

'No.'

'Katerina! My God, Katerina, if you knew how much—' He broke off. 'I do want you, but I want you to be sure. What you told me yesterday, it was obvious how painful it was for you. You can trust me, I promise you can. But I want you to be sure. I know we have so little time, but I can wait. I have never met a woman like you before, Katerina. You have no idea how extraordinary you are.'

The flowery, superficial compliments other men paid her meant nothing. Fergus's compliments meant too much. 'I think you underestimate yourself, Colonel Kennedy,' Katerina said. 'I think you have no idea of how extraordinary you could be.'

With silent accord, they left the potent atmosphere of the walled garden and returned to the house to change. When Katerina rejoined him on the South Lawn, wearing one of her simple summer gowns, she seemed pensive. They headed for the relative privacy of the lake, sitting together on the end of the jetty. 'The duke celebrates the anniversary of Waterloo tonight,' she said.

Fergus winced. 'Celebrate is not a word I'd choose. In all my career, I've never seen more carnage.'

She rested her hand gently on his shoulder, where the gouge left by the musket ball was. 'You have a constant reminder of that day, right here.'

'It's a small price to pay, for lasting peace. There are others who paid a much higher one.'

She brushed a kiss to the location of his scar. He could feel the heat of her mouth through the linen sleeve of his shirt. 'You don't like to talk of it, do you? You are not one of those men who likes to play out every move on the battlefield, or tell tales of death and glory.'

He smiled at her use of his own words, though her choice troubled him. 'That is because death is not glorious.'

'And you were only doing your duty, no?'

'Don't start imagining I am some sort of hero, Katerina. I'm just a soldier.'

'Who has made his way up the ranks without the purchase of a commission. Who has not one but two dukes so eager to have him allied with them that they have actually come up with a joint strategy.'

He shook his head. 'It's not like that. Wellington needs a man in Egypt he can trust. I happen to be waiting on a posting and conveniently available, that's all.'

'No, Fergus, it's not all! There must have been any number of postings which would have suited you in the last two years, but the point is they have not suited Wellington.'

'What do you mean?'

'I mean that Wellington has kept you tethered to that desk you hate, because Wellington knows how very valuable you could be to him. He has been keeping you waiting until the right opportunity presented itself. An opportunity for him, not you. He has not been concerned about your best interests. The only interests he serves are his own.'

Her anger confused him. Her questions troubled him. 'Wellington is my commander-in-chief,' Fergus said.

'And you have been following his orders for sixteen years.' Katerina jumped to her feet. 'For goodness' sake, how can you be so blind? You are an extraordinary man, Fergus, and Wellington knows it. He needs you a great deal more than you need him.'

The idea was ridiculous, Fergus thought. Preposterous. 'Without him behind me, I won't have a career.'

'What do you have at the moment? I'm sorry,' Katerina said when he flinched, 'but it is because

I think you deserve so much more than to serve others. What do you want, Fergus?'

'To serve others,' he replied glibly, but it did not ring true. 'You're saying I'd be better off serving my own interests, is that it?'

Katerina took his hand, pressing a kiss to his scarred knuckles. 'I'm saying that I would like you to feel what I feel when I'm on the tightrope. Flying free.'

Flying free. Was he really so fettered? Two years ago, the answer would have been an unequivocal *no*. Two years ago, he was fighting a battle for lasting peace. 'You don't know what you're asking,' Fergus said. 'I'm a soldier. It's all I've ever been.'

'And all you've ever wanted?'

'Yes.' He hesitated. 'It's all I've ever wanted.' It had always been true. Until now, that was.

The Duke of Brockmore had requested that all his guests gather in the drawing room at seven sharp, where they would have the honour of mingling with several of the heroes of Waterloo, including their own Colonel Kennedy. Said Colonel Kennedy straightened his scarlet coat and threw back his shoulders before entering the fray. After he had left Katerina, he had put the many, deeply uncomfortable questions she had raised to the back of his mind, and spent time in the chapel, in silent communion with his lost comrades. Recalling the horrific reality of those frenetic and hugely significant few days, he was now prepared to regale the duke's guests with the sanitised, glorified version crafted for public consumption.

One of his closest friends, Wellington's codebreaker Jack Trestain might have been in attendance, had he not chosen a path which set him on a collision course with the Establishment, but Fergus was pleased to recognise several other of his fellow officers among the milling throng. None of Wellington's hated artillery, he noted without surprise, and naturally representatives from the ranks of enlisted men who were the true architects of the victory were conspicuous by their absence.

The nature of the commemorations tonight was as yet unspecified. A dinner, some toasts, perhaps the dishing out of some medals, was the usual form. Brockmore had not yet made his appearance and nor, Fergus noted, had his niece. Despite their agreement to put up a front, Lady

Verity had by and large been avoiding his company, and Fergus had been happy to comply.

'Oh, my! Not only a red coat but a kilt. Colonel Kennedy, you spoil us. I hope you do not object to my saying that you have a very fine pair of legs.'

'Miss Kilmun, I would be most disappointed if you did not.'

Cynthia Kilmun tapped him playfully on the arm with her fan. Sir Timothy Farthingale appeared at his elbow, and raised his quizzing glass. 'Scarlet suits you exceeding well, Colonel Kennedy. Indeed I can think of only one other person in the room who carries it off to better effect.'

Fergus followed Sir Timothy's gaze.

'They do not call her the Lovely, Luscious Lillias Lamont for nothing, Colonel. Now then, what do you think Brockmore has in store for us? Why are the drawing-room windows wide open, do you think?'

Fergus had assumed it was due to the heat, but as he opened his mouth to say so, from outside, in the rose garden, there came a drum roll and a sudden blaze of torchlight.

The assembled company all rushed towards the windows and on to the adjoining veranda for a better view. The group standing in a halo of light consisted of four people, two on the left, and two to the right of a shrouded plinth. The Duchess of Brockmore wore a silver gown, heavily trimmed with silver and black lace. Beside her, the Duke of Brockmore's black evening dress was relieved only by a silver waistcoat. On the other side of the plinth, Lady Verity was magnificent in gold. And next to her, slightly in the shadows, stood a tall man in a tightly fitting scarlet coat emblazoned with gold braid. An ornately jewelled order lay across his chest.

Brockmore's guests peered closer, jostling for a prime spot. They began to mutter and murmur. Surely it could not be. It was not possible. Not even Brockmore could... Then the man stepped forward into the light and a gasp of amazement emanated from the crowd.

'What the devil?' hissed Sir Timothy. 'He was opening the new Strand Bridge with Prinny today. It can't be.'

Fergus eyed the haughty face and the distinctly hooked nose, feeling distinctly sick. 'I am very much afraid that it can,' he said, as the Duke of Wellington, victor of Waterloo, took out his ceremonial sword and cut the ties which held the swathes of silk in place over the plinth, to reveal a bronze bust of himself.

Alerted by the applause and cheers coming from the garden, Katerina and Alexandr abandoned their dinner and went outside to investigate. The rose garden was lit up by a circle of braziers. A crowd of people stood around a huge plinth which Katerina did not recall having been there before. There was a bust on the plinth and a man in scarlet with a hooked nose standing beside it. 'Surely that cannot be the Duke of Wellington himself?' she whispered, aghast.

Alexei shrugged. 'You would think he had erected enough statues of himself by now to satisfy even his bloated ego.'

'He is a real-life legend,' Katerina said. She doubted very much that Wellington had come all the way to Brockmore Manor merely to unveil his own statue. What else was important enough to summon him? Of course, Fergus! Brockmore must have tipped Wellington off that the campaign was going badly. He had come to rally his troops. Did Fergus know?

She looked for him and spotted him easily, as he was the only man wearing a kilt. It hung just above his knee, giving a tantalising glimpse of flesh between the plaid's edge and the top of his knitted stockings. He stood alone, on the fringes of the crowd, his arms crossed across a chest encrusted with medals. He looked—angry? They had not parted on bad terms this afternoon, but she had crossed a line with her questions. She had not intended to challenge him in that way, but they had so little time, and Fergus was so blind.

Had he surmised, as she had, that Wellington was here for his own purposes? She wanted desperately to talk to him, but she did not dare. She had, unwittingly, taken several steps towards him, when the Duke of Brockmore appeared at his arm, steering him towards the guest of honour.

'Have a care, Katya.'

She jumped. She had quite forgotten Alexei's presence. 'What do you mean?'

'That man. The Scottish soldier. You have been spending a great deal of time in his company. Retton, the head groomsman, told me you took horses out together yesterday. No,' Alexei said, 'I've not been spying. He mentioned it in passing.'

'Fergus is no libertine, Alexei. He would never—he is an honourable man.'

'He is a man destined for great things, according to those twins who follow me around like lap dogs,' her brother said. 'Look at him now, Katya, standing there between Wellington and Brockmore, twin pillars of society and two of the most powerful and influential men in Europe. Don't fool yourself into thinking he'd throw all that away for you.'

'I'm not. I don't. It's not the same.'

Alexei sighed. 'I grant you, Colonel Kennedy seems like a decent man, but you must see, no good can come of whatever it is you're doing with him. I don't want you to get hurt, Katya.'

'I won't. He can't hurt me,' Katerina said, 'because I won't let him.' She fervently hoped she sounded more convincing than she felt.

Chapter Six

Thursday June 19th
Brockmore Manor House Party

Programme of Events
The Annual Midsummer Ride
Lunch and Auction on the Village Green

When the summons came, Fergus was in the act of finishing his breakfast. Under the ever-watchful eye of Sir Timothy, attired for the first meal of the day in an eye-watering combination of puce and emerald green, he put aside his second cup of coffee and followed in Thompson's stately wake.

'His Grace awaits you in the library,' the butler intoned, throwing open the heavy double doors and stepping inside. 'Colonel Kennedy, your Grace.'

The room facing out over the south lawn was a pleasant one, the pale walls lined with high glass-fronted bookshelves. A scattering of comfortable chairs and thoughtfully placed tables and lecterns invited the reader to linger. This morning however, it was bereft of bibliophiles, and it was not the Duke of Brockmore, but the Duke of Wellington who arose from behind the massive mahogany desk which formed the centrepiece of the room.

Having spent most of the night pacing, turning Katerina's questions over in his mind, adding several of his own, Fergus was as ready for the confrontation as he would ever be. Nevertheless, his stomach was churning as he greeted the duke. He was about to spectacularly burn his boats. Rather fittingly, it was another great general, Alexander the Great, who had ordered his men to do exactly that before fighting the vastly superior Persian forces. Faced with no means of retreat, it was win or die. They were victorious. Fergus pushed back his shoulders. Onwards to victory.

Clad in morning dress, Wellington greeted him with one of his thin smiles, and ushered him to a chair facing the desk, ranging himself on the opposite side. 'I must perforce be brief,' he said, steepling his fingers. 'My time as ever is precious, and I can see from your dress that you intend to take part in this morning's race, so I will cut to the chase. I am disappointed to learn from Brockmore that negotiations between yourself and his niece have not yet been satisfactorily concluded. I am sure you don't need me to remind you how…gratified I would be if you could expedite matters, Kennedy.'

'No, your Grace, I do not.'

The duke straightened the blotter. 'And I do not, I assume, have to remind you either, that this posting to Egypt you're so keen on, is dependent upon your marriage.'

Fergus curled his fingers around the arms of his chair. 'It surprises me that you think my memory so impaired, your Grace, when you previously entrusted the most complex of orders to me without having to take the trouble to write them down.'

'You cannot possibly be thinking of refusing to take advantage of this opportunity, Colonel?' The duke moved the blotter another precise fraction to the left before fixing Fergus with his steeliest of gazes. 'Let us, for a moment, consider the consequences of failure. I do not take kindly to being let down, as you know. I would find it difficult—exceedingly difficult—to recommend you to another position, and frankly, Kennedy, languishing in the army in peacetime must, for a man of action such as yourself, be a dreadful prospect. Yet, as a career soldier who knows no other life, languish you must.'

As he had suspected, his resolve was to be stiffened by fair means or foul, the illusion that he had a say in the matter ripped asunder. Katerina had been right. Wellington was interested only in how Fergus could serve him, not how he could in any way be of service to Fergus. He bit his lip. His blood was beginning to boil but now, more than ever, was the time for a cool head.

'The scenario you paint is a doleful prospect indeed,' Fergus said carefully, 'but as you have pointed out, your Grace, I am a man of action and it is long past time that I took control of my own destiny. I do not take kindly to threats and I most certainly will not be blackmailed.'

It was the merest flicker, but Fergus had the satisfaction of seeing he had taken Wellington utterly aback. Following the duke's own favoured battle plan, he took advantage of the successful surprise attack and pressed home his advantage. 'It will pain you, I know, but the time has come to be frank. Irrespective of how good a match Lady Verity or any other of your friends' daughters may be, I will not make any offer of marriage under orders. Directly and indirectly, I have been obeying your orders as man and boy. I may at times have questioned their validity in private, but in public my loyalty to you, to my fellow officers and to my men has never once been questioned.'

'Your unblemished record, Kennedy, is one of the things which make you eminently suitable for this role.'

'Indeed, you would be able utterly to rely on me to do your bidding, because I have never done otherwise.'

For a long moment, the duke did not respond. He took a gold snuff box from his pocket and delicately sniffed. 'I have put myself out on a limb for you, Colonel, and I do not do that often. You understand that, don't you?'

'I thought I did, your Grace. What I have come to believe is that you never put yourself out for anyone, unless it is also of benefit to you.'

For all of his adult life, Fergus had held this

man in awe. He had risked his life for him, and lost the lives of countless of his men following his battle plans. He had followed him across Europe, through bitter winters and sweltering summers. He had cursed him, he had lauded him, but he had never held him in anything but the highest esteem and he had always assumed that in his own way, Wellington returned the compliment. Now, thanks to Katerina, the wool had been pulled from his eyes.

Fergus got to his feet. 'You understood me better than I did myself when you offered me the posting in Egypt. You knew I would jump at it, because you'd made damned sure I was bored enough to jump at anything. But the bigger the prize, the higher the price, is that not so, your Grace? I won't pay it. I will not make a marriage for the sake of personal advancement.'

Wellington narrowed his eyes. 'And if the price were to be lowered? If the appointment came without the requirement to take Brockmore's niece? If I allow you to choose your own—suitable—wife?'

Could it possibly be that Katerina was right about this too? If he had not heard it himself, he would not have believed that Wellington would

ever back down, even a little. Dare he push further? 'And if I choose not to take a wife at all?'

The duke closed the lid of his snuff box with a
snap. 'You drive a very hard bargain, Kennedy.'

It took him a moment to take in what he had
just heard. Another, even more fleeting moment,
to realise that it was too little, too late. 'Thank
you, but no thank you.'

Wellington's mouth dropped. 'You are turning
down my most generous concessions?'

Fergus smiled. 'Indeed I am. I am tired of being
under orders, you see.'

'But Egypt...'

'It's no longer about Egypt, your Grace.' Fergus extended his hand across the desk. 'You'll
have the formal resignation of my commission
on your desk by Monday.'

Getting to his feet, Wellington shook his hand
reluctantly. 'This is madness, Kennedy. What the
devil are you going to do without my patronage?'

'Stand on my own two feet,' Fergus said. 'You
never know, I might even learn to fly.'

Wellington snorted. 'You will more likely end
up in Bedlam. You give me no choice but to offer
you a second chance, something else I very rarely
do. You have until Monday to change your mind,

Colonel. Think very carefully before you do something both rash and irrevocable.'

The door closed softly behind him. Shaking, Fergus slumped back into his seat and dropped his head into his hands. He'd done it. His boats were well and truly aflame. There was no going back. Remorse, regret, a sense of loss, of being let down, of betrayal even, those were the things he had expected to feel. Instead, he felt exhilarated. His heart felt lighter than it had in years. He'd done it. He was free. Lord knew what he'd do now, but it would be at no one's behest save his own. He couldn't wait to tell Katerina.

A gong sounded in the hallway. Checking his watch, Fergus cursed. First there was a race to be run.

Katerina had waited in the walled garden, but when Fergus had not sought her out, she concluded that he had most likely been closeted with the Duke of Wellington. On tenterhooks as to the outcome, knowing that he was committed to riding in the race, she stood with the villagers, anxiously watching the riders line up at the start of the cross-country course. Fergus was on the same horse he'd ridden out on Tuesday.

What an age ago that seemed. His coat was buff-coloured. His quirk of hair, as usual, was standing up on end. Was he frowning? No, he seemed in surprisingly good spirits. He was standing up in the saddle now, shading his eyes with his hand and looking straight at her.

Her heart did a flip as he smiled at her. But it was too late. A flag was dropped before she could wave, and the horses were off, some at a gallop, others needing a great deal of persuasion to do more than a desultory trot. One rider set off in the wrong direction entirely.

While the duke's guests and the villagers became engrossed in the making of wagers and the partaking of fruit punch, Katerina paced, lost in her thoughts. Finally, the thunder of hooves approached the finishing line. Fergus and Kael Gage, whom she remembered from the master-class, were neck and neck. As the horses crossed the line in a cloud of dust and wild cheering from the crowd, Gage had won by a short head. Barely taking time to congratulate the other man, Fergus flung himself from the saddle, handing the reins to a waiting stable hand.

'Katerina!' He was dusty. His cheeks were flushed and his hair was standing on end. His eyes were alight. 'I spoke to Wellington this morning.'

He seemed oblivious of the other spectators. He seemed oblivious of anyone save her. Her heart gave a little flutter. 'He offered you the Egypt posting without the encumbrance of a wife,' she said.

'How did you guess?'

'I told you, you underestimate yourself. He needs you more than he will admit. Congratulations.'

He laughed. 'I didn't take it.'

'What?'

'He offered me the posting, and I turned it down. I'm also resigning my commission.'

'Fergus! But what will you do?'

He laughed again. 'Wellington asked me the same question. I told him I had no idea, which is the absolute truth. I don't know, and right now, I don't care. I feel—free. You did this, Katerina.'

'No, you did it, Fergus.'

He took her hand. 'You know what I'd like to do most, right now?'

Her heart began to beat wildly. Her mouth went dry. 'Fly?'

He nodded. 'Fly with me, Katerina? If you are sure?'

She hesitated, more for form's sake than because she had any doubts. 'I am very sure,' she said.

She took him to her room, for only she and Alexei occupied that floor, and her brother had told her he would be away all day. As she closed and locked the door, Fergus pulled her into his arms. 'Katerina...'

'I'm sure,' she said, this time much more firmly. 'But I'm also nervous.'

Fergus kissed her, his lips gentle on hers, his fingers twining in her hair. 'I'm nervous too. I've never wanted anyone the way I want you. I'm afraid I might not be able to wait.'

Katerina smiled. 'I don't want you to.'

'Oh, I think you do,' he said, his voice ragged. 'And I intend to do my very best to make the waiting worthwhile. For both of us.'

He kissed her again, and her nerves began to subside as his mouth melded with hers and their tongues tangled fiercely. His fingers rifled through her hair, tugging it free of its pins. He feathered kisses along her jaw, on the sensitive skin behind her ear, down the line of her throat, along the swell of her breasts at the modest neckline of her gown. Her flesh rose and fell rapidly as he kissed her there, his hands cupping her breasts, stroking her nipples. She moaned. She ached. Deep inside her, she began to throb.

She slid her hands inside his riding coat, smoothing her palms over his back. 'Take it off,' she demanded, and he laughed, doing as she bid him. 'And that,' she said nodding at his waistcoat, made confident by the way he looked at her, his eyes slumberous with passion. 'And this,' she said, pulling the complex knot in his cravat undone. 'And this.' She tugged his shirt free from his breeches. He kissed her hard on the mouth, before wrenching the shirt over his head, the action making his muscles flex and ripple. In the sunlight filtering through the gauzy curtains, the rough smattering of hair on his chest gleamed gold. The dip of his belly was in shadow. When he folded his arms around her, the heat of his skin made her shiver. She brushed his chest with her lips. She smoothed her hands over the breadth of his shoulders, pressing gentle kisses to the gouge that the musket ball had made, and then to the scar on his belly.

He muttered her name, his voice oddly hoarse, claiming her lips once again, his hands on the ties of her gown. It slid to the ground in a soft rustle. She would have left it there, but Fergus picked it up, draping it carefully over a chair. As if she cared. But he did. Lovely, lovely man.

She wrapped her arms around him, pressing herself tight against him. Their kisses became more urgent. She could feel his arousal, pressed hard against her belly. She arched into him, making him moan. He was loosening her corset, making shorter work of it than she ever did. It fell to the floor, unlike her gown, unheeded. Her chemise slid down over her shoulders. His lips were soft on her nipple, eliciting an aching drag that merged with the slow, insistent pulse inside her. He took his time, his hand on one breast, his mouth on the other. She closed her eyes, clutching at his shoulders, whimpering as her senses flared at his touch.

'Beautiful,' Fergus murmured. 'You are so lovely. Quite perfect.'

She was wearing only her stockings and garters. Her body was lean and supple. It was the perfect body for an acrobat, for a tightrope walker, but she had never before considered it perfect in any other way. But Fergus said so, and she believed him. Under his gaze, she felt her last inhibitions unfurl. She smiled at him, a sensual smile she had not known she possessed. 'Now you.'

He kicked off his riding boots and undid the fastenings of his buckskin breeches. His thighs were muscled. There was another scar, a long thin spidery line, on his left flank. Later, she would trace it with her fingers, as she had traced the others, wanting to memorise it. Later, she would ask him when and where. But now, he stood naked before her and she exhaled sharply. His arousal jutted upwards, the skin stretched taut, with such a silken quality.

'May I touch you?'

He nodded and took her hand, wrapping her fingers around his length. He was so hard, the skin satin-soft. Her touch was making his chest rise and fall more rapidly. His eyes were fixed on her hand, the pupils large with desire. The throbbing inside her intensified. Tentatively, she stroked him. He groaned. She stroked him again, and he shuddered.

'Wait.' He stilled her hand. 'Ladies first,' he said, with a wicked smile, as he picked her up and set her on the bed.

He kissed her again, but not on her lips. His mouth was on the soft flesh inside her thighs. When he licked between her legs, kissing that most intimate part of her, she closed her eyes, lost in the slide and stroke of his mouth and his tongue. She didn't dare imagine what he was doing. She didn't care. She was climbing higher and higher with every stroke. She was tense, tight, braced, as if on the edge of the tallest ladder, balanced on the highest tightrope. She wanted to take the first step. She wanted to prolong the anticipation. She arched under him as he licked her again, moaning, muttering inarticulately in her native language, and then it happened, she was flying, soaring, calling out his name as she climaxed, her fingers clutching at the sheets, her heels digging into the mattress, the throbbing, pulsing waves of pleasure taking her higher than she had ever been before.

As the last pulses eddied, she sat up, pulling him towards her, kissing him deeply. His naked body covered hers, burning skin on burning skin, but it wasn't enough. 'Now, Fergus,' she said.

'Are you...?'

'I am sure.'

'I'll be careful. I promise.'

'Yes, I know you will.'

He kissed her again, his hands under her bottom to tilt her towards him. The tip of his shaft nudged against her sex. He hesitated. She realised, with a shock, that he really was nervous. It eased her own tension. She slid her hands around his back, smoothed them over the muscles of his buttocks. 'Now,' she said.

He eased himself inside her slowly. She was tight, but she was wet. No pain, only an odd friction as he pushed higher, and higher still. She felt as if she were being unfolded. Sweat stood out on his temples when they were finally, completely united. 'Yes?' he asked.

'Yes,' Katerina said.

It was a rhythm she did not recall from before, it felt like nothing else, the slow push and pull of him inside her, the drag of her muscles on his, the beginning of another climb, to different heights. She wrapped her legs around his waist, wanting him deeper. He groaned. When he leaned over to kiss her, she wrapped her arms around his neck, wanting to feel all of him, skin and muscle, against her, inside her. He thrust faster. She met him, holding him, clinging to him. He thrust again, harder this time, and she met him again, urging him on with her hands and her mouth, and inside, the tension built and built. Harder. Higher. Higher. Harder. This time her climax took her unawares, a tripping fall that she could not stop, sending her spiralling, pulsing against him, pushing him over the top. With a hoarse cry, he pulled himself free to spill outside her.

She knew, as she looked at him lying beside her, his eyes glazed with spent passion, his chest heaving, his cheeks flushed, that making love to him had been an enormous mistake. She had once thought that nothing would ever exceed the thrill of the tightrope but this—this was unsurpassable. It had been every bit as wonderful as she'd imagined, but it had not been enough. It would never be enough.

Her stupid heart gave a sickening lurch. The urge to throw herself on top of him, to twine her body around him, to cling and to never let go, terrified her. Curling her toes and her fingers in an effort to stop herself acting, she lay inert at his side. She had promised Fergus that he could not hurt her. She knew that he would not, not deliberately. But without knowing, he could so very easily break her. She could not possibly risk making love to him again.

His breathing calmed. By the time he turned to her, she had managed to regain control of her feelings—though she knew that control was fleeting. 'It's getting late,' she said.

He said nothing for a long moment, studying her face, though his own was oddly blank. Only when he finally nodded, got out of bed and began to dress, she realised she had not, after all, been willing him to go. She had been desperately hoping that he would stay.

Chapter Seven

Friday June 20th
Brockmore Manor House Party

Programme of Events
Annual Midsummer Treasure Hunt
A Celebration of Russian Cuisine with
Dinner served in the Maze

The morning of the Treasure Hunt looked set to be another perfect summer's day. Sitting on the boat house jetty, Fergus watched the sun rise over the lake, turning the dawn sky from pale pink to pale blue, from the colour of Katerina's tightrope tunic to the colour of her riding habit. The gown she'd been wearing when he found her asleep in the maze had been yellow. Yesterday, he recalled, the gown he'd helped remove had been green, though not the green of her eyes, which he'd thought at first were emerald, but now he knew her better, he reckoned were a sort of mossy colour. In the sunlight, there were hints of gold around her iris, but in the height of passion, her eyes were much darker, and her creamy skin had a flush to it. Her hair, splayed across the pillow, was like fire.

The memory stirred his blood. He could not recall ever experiencing such an intense climax. Afterwards, he had felt both weighted down and light as air. He hadn't wanted to let her go. In the past, lovemaking had filled him with boundless energy, making him want to run or swim or dance or go for a gallop. Yesterday, all he'd wanted to do was stay cocooned, to hold Katerina so tightly that their skin clung, that the lines between his body and hers were blurred. And then to make love to her again.

The strength of his feelings had confused him, leaving him wordless. Afraid of overwhelming her with the fierceness of his passion, he had forced himself to lie still, to take his cue from her. But when the flush faded from her cheeks, the face she turned to him was curiously devoid of feeling. She'd made it clear she wanted him to leave, and in doing so made it clear to him that the thing he had wanted above all was to stay.

He had known, as he closed the door of her bedchamber behind him, that he was in love with her, but it had taken many hours of heart-searching before he could admit it to himself. He was in love for the first time in his life, and at the age of thirty-five, he was pretty sure it was also the last. From the first moment he saw her on the tightrope he had been drawn to her. She seemed to blaze so much more brightly than any other woman he'd met, so fearless, so passionate, so exotic, so elegantly, impossibly lithe. He had desired her then, but his desire to know more of her had taken root there in the walled garden too. Blinded by his passion for the artiste, he had not noticed his love for the woman growing. He had envied her her freedom. She had given him his.

He loved her. He loved her so much it ached. He wanted to believe she loved him. He knew she wanted him as much as he wanted her, but love? She was afraid of love. He was terrified of hurting her. Did she love him? Dear God, he hoped so. He could not bear to contemplate a life without her, though what kind of life they would have together...

Fergus jumped to his feet. First things first. If she loved him, the future was bright. If she did not—but she must. It was surely that simple.

Following a night alternating between elation and despair, Katerina was restless. After Fergus had left, she had indulged in a fit of pointless tears, castigating herself for not asking him to stay. But she knew even as she fought the urge to dress and go after him that it would be a terrible mistake. She would be unable to hide her feelings, and without any idea at all what she wanted to do about those feelings—no, no, a thousand times no.

Instead, she tried to talk herself out of it. She was not in love. She could not possibly have fallen in love in the space of a few days. In any case, how could she possibly be sure? She'd thought herself in love before, though in comparison to this, it was a mere shadow of a thing.

Wasn't that the point? No man had ever made her feel the way Fergus did. The way he looked at her. The way he touched her. The way he made her laugh. The things he understood about her that no one else did. She loved the rebellious kink in his hair and the cleft in his chin. She loved the rapt way he watched her on the tightrope. She didn't know him, she could not possibly know him after so short an acquaintance, yet she felt as if she understood the essence of him all the same.

She had paced her bedchamber, muttering to herself. It was ridiculous. It was a passing fancy. It was infatuation. It was lust. But no. It was love. She knew it was love. Real love. True love. Devastating love.

She was in love, and she was an idiot, she had finally concluded. Fergus didn't love her in return. He wouldn't have been so easily persuaded to leave, if he did. He would have stayed. He would have made love to her again. He would have told her that he loved her. He had been so very careful not to tell her anything at all, save that he wanted her. He was a good man. An honourable man. He would never tell her glib lies. So...

So Fergus did not love her. Most likely Fergus regretted making love to her. Indeed, even more likely, he was waiting in the walled garden to tell her so. It was a mistake, he would say. Or perhaps, it was delightful while it lasted, but now it is over. There was not the slightest hope that he would tell her he loved her.

Pushing aside her untouched coffee, Katerina sped down the main staircase, taking the quickest route to the gardens.

'Miss Vengarov.'

'Lady Verity. If you will excuse me, I...'

'I am so glad to have bumped into you. I have been wanting to have a private word. It will take but a moment. If you will?'

Reluctantly, Katerina allowed herself to be led along the length of the portrait gallery to a quiet alcove at the end. Lady Verity was looking particularly beautiful in white today, though she also looked slightly uncomfortable. 'The matter upon which I wish to speak is delicate,' she said. 'Were it not for the fact that I rather admire you, Miss Vengarov, and very much respect Colonel Kennedy...'

'Fergus! Has something happened to Fergus?'

'Not yet.'

Katerina's nerves were already frayed. Seeing that Lady Verity, clasping and unclasping her fingers, was obviously steeling herself, she too braced herself. 'What do you mean, not yet?'

Lady Verity smiled nervously. 'Miss Vengarov, you must understand, I would not dream of speaking to you on so personal a matter if I wished either you or the colonel anything other than good. I do not wish either of you to be made miserable. You do believe me, don't you?'

Her earnestness was undeniable. Katerina looked around, at the gallery of Lady Verity's venerable ancestors gazing down on her, telling herself she was imagining their disapproval, but she had a horrible premonition. 'I believe you,' she said hollowly.

'You love him, don't you? I saw the way you looked at him yesterday, at the race. I am not mistaken in that, am I?'

It did not occur to her to deny her feelings. She did not want to. She had no blue blood, she had no fortune, she had no pedigree that would mean a thing to Lady Verity and her family. But her feelings were true. 'I do love him,' Katerina said defiantly. 'You are not mistaken.'

'I thought not.' Lady Verity stared intently at the portrait of the first Duke of Brockmore for a moment, before resuming in a firmer tone, 'I don't know if you are aware of the interview which took place between Colonel Kennedy and the Duke of Wellington yesterday?'

'I am.'

'Yes, of course. When I saw him seek you out after the race, I did not know what had transpired, but later, when my uncle informed me why the duke left in such high dudgeon, then it became clear.'

'Fergus refused the posting in Egypt.'

'Though in the end, it was offered without strings,' Lady Verity said with a smile. 'My uncle could not credit it.'

'Fergus believes it has lost him Wellington's good will for ever.'

'On the contrary, my uncle believes it has earned him Wellington's eternal respect. Wellington told him that he'd rarely come across a man with such integrity. In fact, my uncle is sure that Colonel Kennedy's courage in standing up for himself will earn him the pick of any number of choice postings. So sure of this is Uncle Marcus that he has become more set than ever upon the match between us.'

Katerina stared at Lady Verity in dismay. 'But you were—forgive me, I was under the impression...'

'That I did not wish to marry Colonel Kennedy,' Lady Verity said. She pursed her lips. 'I will confess, just between us, that I could easily have been persuaded to accept the colonel's hand in marriage, but I could not stomach the idea of living in Egypt.'

'And now that Fergus is not going to be posted to Egypt...'

'No.' Lady Verity flushed. 'He made it clear that he was not—not inclined to take me as his wife, whatever the circumstances. A rather demoralising truth for an established beauty such as myself,' she said sardonically, 'but honest. So few men are, I find.'

'Then what—I don't understand. To be blunt, your ladyship, if you do not want him...'

'But you do, my dear Miss Vengarov, and really, to cut to the chase, you cannot have him. A liaison with a woman from your background— forgive me, but it cannot be ignored.'

If she had spoken less gently, Katerina would have been angry, would have taken umbrage at the insult and walked away. But the kindness behind the brutal truth could not be ignored. A lump rose in her throat. 'Would it really be so scandalous?' she asked pathetically.

'I think you know the answer to that question. Can you imagine the reaction in diplomatic circles, if he were to introduce a tightrope walker as his wife?'

Her words, inadvertently, were a horrible echo of the past. Katerina's heart sank to her toes. She could imagine it all too well.

Lady Verity pressed her hand. 'No matter how many excellent qualities the colonel may possess, the one thing which the Duke of Wellington will not overlook is a lack of breeding. Any public association with you would blight his career for ever.'

'Fergus doesn't need Wellington's patronage.'

'No, but he cannot succeed in a society which shuns him. And they would, Miss Vengarov.'

Lady Verity spoke crisply now, absolutely and utterly devastatingly sure of her ground. Realising how perilously close she had come to allowing history to repeat itself, tears stung Katerina's eyes, but she blinked furiously. 'My brother said as much the other day.'

'Your brother is right. You will be much happier if you stick to your own, and allow the colonel to do so too. I trust I can rely upon you to make the situation plain to him?'

'What do you mean?'

'If he is so foolish as to make you an offer of any kind…' Lady Verity said delicately.

'Clearly, you think it could only be improper. What harm do you imagine I could do Fergus as his mistress?'

'As his mistress, Miss Vengarov, the harm done would be to you,' Lady Verity said bluntly. 'Contrary to common understanding, I do not happen to believe that your habitual lack of decent clothing signifies a habitual lack of morals.'

'Oh. Thank you.'

'It makes no difference though, does it? I am in the minority. Besides, you told me you loved him. Would you be happy with such an arrangement?'

Unable to speak, Katerina shook her head.

'I can rely upon you then, to do what is right?'

'Right,' Katerina repeated dully. 'Lie, do you mean? Pretend I don't love him? Ensure he makes me no offers, proper or improper?'

'It will spare you both pain, if you do so.'

Katerina brushed away a stray tear. How ironic, in the end, that it was not Fergus who hurt her, but Fergus's rejected bride. If only she could hate Lady Verity, it would be easier. If only she could believe that she spoke out of malice. She sniffed. 'Yes, you may rely upon me.'

'I am very, very sorry, Miss Vengarov, to have caused you so much pain.'

Lady Verity handed her a scrap of lace. Wiping her cheeks, Katerina felt utterly deflated. Before that gallery of aristocratic faces, she could almost feel herself shrinking. She blew her nose vigorously and defiantly on the monogrammed handkerchief before trying to hand it back, only to have it refused with a barely repressed shudder.

'I brought it on myself.' Katerina stared at a particularly ugly wolfhound painted at the feet of the second duke. 'I suppose I must thank you for being so honest with me. I may not sound appreciative, but I am.'

'I will leave you now. The treasure hunt…'

'Before you go, I have a favour to ask of you.'

Lady Verity raised a delicate brow. There was a hint of impatience in her countenance. Having prevented the hired help from getting above herself, she was eager to return to her party. The spurt of venom gave Katerina only momentary relief. What did it matter that Lady Verity cared more for her own kind, when it did not alter the facts? 'Fergus took a great risk in spurning the arrangements proposed by the Duke of Wellington,' she said. 'I understand that he proposes to inform the Duke of Brockmore that he will not be making you an offer.'

'Colonel Kennedy wishes to spare me my uncle's wrath.'

'By incurring it himself.'

Lady Verity's cool smile faded. 'What are you implying?'

'That Fergus doesn't deserve to contend with two dukes. That you ought to take some responsibility for your own fate, just as you have asked me to take responsibility for mine.'

'If I tell my uncle that I will not have the colonel, he will be furious. You do not understand, Miss Vengarov, I have already refused several matches. My uncle is fast losing patience with me.'

'Don't you wish to be married?'

Lady Verity stared down at her hands. 'I have a perverse wish to make my own choice.'

It seemed perverse indeed to Katerina, at that moment. 'What is preventing you from doing so?'

The question elucidated an odd little laugh. 'An obstinate desire to postpone choosing?'

Emotionally drained, Katerina lost patience.

'Yet no desire at all to permit me to choose. You will admit, those do seem rather like double standards,' she said waspishly. 'Oblige me by speaking to your uncle, Lady Verity. You owe me that much. Don't let Fergus take any more blame.'

Her ladyship sighed heavily. 'It is rather annoying to discover one has a conscience. Very well, I shall do as you ask, but if it is to be before the treasure hunt, you must excuse me. My uncle has paired me with Colonel Kennedy. It seems I must find a new partner from the somewhat limited choice.'

Fergus had waited in the walled garden until Alexandr Vengarov had turned up and informed him abruptly that he was trespassing. Asked to divulge his sister's whereabouts, the male half of the Flying Vengarovs' countenance had darkened. 'If my sister has any sense, she will stay away from you.'

Fergus's fists clenched automatically. Only the realisation that Vengarov would not be warning him off unless Katerina had failed to heed a similar warning made him turn on his heel and leave. He was rewarded, as he crossed the marble-tiled reception hall, with the vision of Katerina herself descending the staircase. 'I've been looking for you.'

She jumped. Her hands fluttered to her breast. 'Fergus.'

'In the flesh, though you look as if you've seen a ghost. What's wrong?'

'Nothing.' She gave herself a little shake and joined him at the foot of the steps. 'Aren't you taking part in the treasure hunt?'

'I've a rather more important quest of my own to resolve. I need to talk to you. Come into the library.'

He took the precaution of turning the key in the lock. Katerina sat on the edge of a seat by the window. She looked paler than usual. There were dark shadows under her eyes. A good or a bad sign? He didn't want to cause her sleepless nights. At least he did—but not that kind. Lord, but he was nervous. He took an anxious turn towards the desk, picked up a brass paperweight in the shape of a lion, and put it down again.

'Katerina.'

She jumped up from her seat. 'Fergus, yesterday…'

He took her hands in his. He looked down into her big green eyes and his heart turned over.

'Yesterday, I left you because I didn't know what to say. I had no words for how you made me feel, but now I do. I love you, Katerina.'

Tears welled up in her eyes. 'Oh, Fergus.'

'I love you with all my heart.'

Her mouth trembled. 'Oh, Fergus. No.'

'But I do.' He tried to pull her to him, but she resisted. 'Katerina, I love you.'

'You can't.'

'I know it's only been a week, but I feel as if I've known you for ever. From the first moment I saw you I felt—transfixed. You fascinated me. The more I knew of you, the more I wanted to know. And yesterday, when we made love—I've never felt like that before. I love you, Katerina. I want to spend my life with you.'

Tears streaked down her cheeks. She shook her head. 'You can't.'

His stomach clenched. 'I know there will be difficulties for us to overcome. I will not pretend that I have any idea of how we will live, but if you love me as I love you, surely that is all that matters?'

He felt her shudder. The expression on her face was tragic. 'It's not, Fergus,' she said. 'If I—if I loved you...' She broke off on a sob, wrenching herself free, wrapping her arms tightly around herself. 'It would be a very poor love indeed, to allow you to give up everything. I am sorry.'

He could not take it in. He hadn't realised how certain he had been that his feelings were returned. 'You don't love me?' he said stupidly.

Katerina turned away, her shoulders hunched. 'I am sorry,' she said.

Fergus ran his hand through his hair. He felt as if he was plummeting to earth. She didn't love him. He wanted to take her in his arms and kiss her until she changed her mind. No, he didn't want that at all. He didn't want to have to change her mind. He couldn't force her to love him. No, but by heavens, he could make her bloody miserable by forcing his feelings on her.

What Katerina loved was performing, Fergus recalled. Was it that? 'You know I would never ask you to quit the tightrope unless you wanted to,' he said.

'I know.' Another sob racked her body. She turned around to face him. Her face was chalk white, her eyes huge, drenched in tears. 'I know you would never ask anything of me that I could not—that would be wrong. Please don't ask, Fergus. I can't bear it,' she said. 'I'm sorry.'

Covering her face with her hands, Katerina fled the room. Fergus fell on to a chair, feeling as if his legs had been blown from under him by a cannonball. His heart and his head were quite numb. Staring blankly into space, he was in a trance-like state when the door opened and Lady Verity entered the room escorted by the merchant, Desmond Falkner.

'Colonel Kennedy! I hope you have not beaten us to it. I believe it is contained in one of my uncle's books.' She consulted the slip of paper in her hand which Fergus realised, vaguely, must be the list of treasure-hunt clues. Getting to his feet was an effort.

'Lady Verity was good enough to partner me when Sir Timothy claimed Mrs Lamont,' Falkner said.

'Two minds are better than one, Mr Falkner,' Lady Verity said, waving a book at him. 'I have found it, and I do believe our next clue is in the portrait gallery. If we are quick, the diamond may yet be ours.'

'You will excuse us, Colonel.' Falkner made his bow and left the room, so excited by the hunt that he seemed not to have noticed that Fergus had remained quite silent.

'One moment,' Lady Verity said, closing the door behind him. 'Are you quite well, Colonel? You look rather pale.'

'I'm fine.'

'Really?' She raised her brows disbelievingly. 'Well, I have news that may make you feel a little better. I have spoken to my uncle,' Lady Verity said. 'It was pointed out to me that I was being rather selfish in allowing you to take responsibility for what was as much my decision as yours. I am not such a coward after all. Now, you will excuse me, I have a diamond to find.'

Alone again, Fergus stared at the door. What had she said to make him so uneasy? It took him a moment, but finally he realised. Ruling out the duke himself, there was only one person here at Brockmore Manor who would have had the courage to tell Lady Verity how to behave. And, he thought, only one reason she would dare to do so?

He truly hoped so.

The very last thing Katerina wished to do was attend tonight's Russian dinner in the maze, but she could think of no excuse that would not arouse Alexei's suspicions. After she fled the library feeling as if her heart might break, she had cried herself into a stupor. Knowing that Fergus loved her made it so much harder to give him up. The pain in his voice had almost been her undoing. It had taken every ounce of willpower to hold fast, clinging to the knowledge that Lady Verity was right, that Alexei was right, that there could never be a place and time where she and Fergus could be happy. She would not ruin him. She would not allow him to ruin himself. She loved him too much to do anything other than leave him but oh, how it hurt to have to do so without even the salve of telling him that his love was returned.

Her eyes were still puffy as she finished her *toilette*, but a combination of powder, and a rearrangement of her hair to fall over her face would hopefully be enough to keep anyone from guessing how she had spent her afternoon. She dreaded seeing Fergus, yet she longed to see him. How to endure the evening watching him, knowing how much she had hurt him? Far easier than to endure a lifetime knowing she had ruined him, she told herself.

Arriving at the maze by her brother's side, she was distracted by the chaos which greeted them. Surprisingly, the Duke of Brockmore had lit not only the true path, but every path. Katerina had not had the temerity to correct any of his guests as they made their way to the centre—or failed to—but she did redirect several bemused footmen wandering aimlessly around the outer reaches bearing silver salvers of rapidly cooling food. It was to be hoped that the ice statue on which the caviar was to be served would not melt in this muggy heat before the last of the guests found their way to the centre of the maze.

Atlas and his plinth had been moved to one side, a feat which must have taken a great deal of manpower, allowing the large square table to be set up in the centre. Katerina was seated between her brother and the flamboyant Sir Timothy Farthingale, who asked her why she had not worn traditional Russian dress for the occasion, and looked somewhat confounded when she informed him that she did not own such a thing. Her only decent evening gown was plain cream satin with a spider-gauze overdress worked with a simple pattern of circles in her favourite blue, and festooned with satin ribbons in the same colour around the flounced hem. Sir Timothy assured her that she looked radiant, but he couldn't disguise his disappointment as he eyed Alexei's black dinner clothes, asking plaintively why he preferred buckled shoes to the long pointed boots of the Cossack.

The rest of the guests and more of the footmen were arriving now, some of them wearing the foliage evidence of a close encounter with a maze dead-end. Her heart thudding so loud she wondered no one else heard it, Katerina waited anxiously for Fergus to arrive. When he did, he was alone, and her heart, still unable to accept the futility of her love for him, leapt in her chest, her pulses quickening. His hair was combed ruthlessly back, and in the light of the braziers, was the shade of ripe wheat. His dark evening coat showed off his broad, soldierly build to perfection. They had parted on such dreadful terms. Was he angry with her? Hurt? Did he still love her? Would he speak to her? Ignore her? She couldn't bear any of it. He had spotted her. He was heading towards her. Alexei was watching him and her brother's expression was black.

She got to her feet, half in mind to run, when an odd sound coming from an unlit corner at the centre of the maze halted Fergus in his tracks. It sounded to Katerina—but it could not be—yes, it sounded like a balalaika. At the same time, looking very unlike his usual stately self, Thompson, the duke's butler, arrived leading the lost guests, and ushered all, including Fergus, to the table. He was seated directly opposite her, between the twin sisters. The balalaika struck up again, and the unseen player launched into a jaunty tune as the duke and duchess appeared, attired in what they clearly believed to be Russian peasant dress, though no Russian peasant to Katerina's knowledge wore rubies and gold thread in their headdress. Beside her, she could sense Alexei trying not to laugh. She nudged him, but it only made him tremble more. 'I do sincerely hope that they do not intend to dance,' he muttered.

'Dear boy,' Sir Timothy replied, 'if that is something you could do—say, on the tables—I believe the good old D. of B. would be thrilled. I had no idea he was taking this whole Russian thing to heart.'

To Katerina's surprise, Alexei laughed. For the duration of the seemingly never-ending meal, the two of them talked, leaving her little to do but nod and smile occasionally. The extrovert Englishman knew a surprising amount about the world of travelling artistes such as the Vengarovs and even more surprisingly, seemed to have contacts at the Russian court, which he would, he averred, be more than happy to exploit in their favour.

Though Monsieur Salois had excelled himself, and though most of the receipts he had used had been Katerina's—or more accurately, her mother's and her grandmother's—she could eat nothing. A black cloud took hold of her. Whatever Fergus felt or didn't feel for her, her love for him was futile. It was safest and kindest to avoid him. As soon as dinner was over, she slipped away, leaving Alexei and Sir Timothy to discuss the relative attractions of vodka over whisky.

She had reached the edge of the maze when he caught up with her. 'Katerina.'

She jumped. 'Fergus. You startled me.'

'I need to talk to you.'

It was late, the sky an inky blue. In the shadow of the tall hedges of the maze, she could not make out his expression. 'I don't think there is anything more to be said.'

Fergus took her arm, leading her purposefully towards the rose garden, giving her no option but to follow him. He came to a halt in the corner furthest away from the maze and the house. The stars cast a shadowy light here. The air was heavy with the perfume from the roses. 'There is one thing you did not say today, Katerina.'

His voice was gentle. Her heart seemed to have forgotten how to function normally. A moment ago it had been fluttering and pounding. Now it seemed to stop altogether. 'What was that?'

He stroked her hair back from her face, gazing deep into her eyes. 'You did not tell me you love me,' he said, 'but nor did you say you do not.'

Her mouth went dry. She tried to look away, but she couldn't drag her eyes from his. 'Fergus…'

'If you loved me, nothing else would matter, Katerina. I know you spoke with Lady Verity. I can guess what she said.'

'No, I don't think you can. She said that Wellington was so impressed by your integrity that you could have your pick of any posting. You have not ruined your chances, Fergus, you have given yourself more choices than you could ever hope for.'

'Yet all I hope for, all that matters to me is one thing. I love you, Katerina.'

He loved her. Her heart soared, then plummeted. 'Fergus, Lady Verity is right,' Katerina said urgently, 'it would be such a scandal, I would ruin you.'

'And if you are not by my side, you will make me miserable. Katerina, my love, my dearest, if I cared about the things they do—ambition, influence, money— then I would have offered for Lady Verity. But I don't. All I care about is you. You are all I need to make me happy. I want you to be my wife, to be by my side through thick and thin and everything else that life may throw at us. I love you.'

'Fergus, I am not fit to be your wife. You know you were not the first man I...'

'And you were not my first woman, but I want you to be the last. The only. If you love me?'

She could deny it no longer. 'I do. Oh, God, Fergus, I do. I love you so much.' The words brought such relief that her doubts fled. 'I love you.' She threw her arms around his neck. 'I love you every bit as much as you love me. More. Much more.'

He laughed. 'Not possible. I can't believe it. No, I can. Earlier...'

'Oh, Fergus, I am so sorry I hurt you.'

'To spare me pain. Foolish Katerina. The only pain would be losing you.'

'You won't ever lose me now. I won't ever let you go.'

'You won't have to.'

'But there will be such a scandal. We have a saying in Russia. "When love whispers, reason falls silent." How are we to live?'

'Hush.' He kissed her slowly, lingeringly. 'Tomorrow, we'll think about that. Tonight all I care about is telling you I love you.'

'And showing me?'

He laughed, picking her up in his arms and holding her high against his chest. 'And showing you.'

Yesterday, when he had made love to Katerina, he had not known that he had truly been making love. Tonight it was different. Tonight, he knew he loved her, and she loved him. Love flavoured their kisses, giving them a new sweetness, a drugging tenderness, a different heat. This was not the first time for them, but neither was it the last. There was all the time in the world to touch, and to stroke, and to kiss. To cup her breasts, and her delightful *derrière*, to explore the soft flesh of her thighs, and the quivering muscles of her belly. There was all the time in the world for her to touch him too, and to kiss him and to stroke him, her fingers sending waves of heat through his blood, making him ache to enter her, giving the anticipation its own quivering tension.

He murmured her name over and over as he kissed her. Her breath became faster, morphing into the softest, most arousing of sighs. There would be other times, when he would gather her in his arms, have her twine her legs around his waist, as he had dreamed, but for now he wanted to worship her, to show her how much he loved her.

Her kisses became deeper, and her touch became surer, and as he stroked into her, felt her tense and tighten, he felt his shaft tense and tighten in response. He entered her as her climax took her, riding on the pulsing waves, shuddering as she clenched around him, as she said his name, her fingers digging into his back, her heels into his buttocks, driving him harder, faster, hurtling him into a new world, clinging tightly as he flew higher than he had ever flown before.

Chapter Eight

Saturday June 21st
Brockmore Manor House Party

Programme of Events
Annual Brockmore Midsummer Games
The Midsummer Ball

'You're awake.'

Katerina sat up, pulling the rumpled sheet over her naked body. 'You didn't leave.'

'I couldn't.'

'We'll create a scandal if you are discovered.'

'I've been thinking that I'd rather like to create a scandal,' Fergus said, joining her on the bed.

'What kind of scandal?' Katerina asked, though her attention was only half on his words. Fergus was already aroused. Looking at him, she felt the answering tingle in her blood, the awakening pulse inside her. He pulled the sheet away and rolled her on top of him. 'What scandal?' she asked again, with considerably less interest.

'It can wait,' he said, kissing her.

They made love again, slowly and patiently at first, before building to a frenzied climax, hearts pounding, chest on chest, their skin sticking with sweat, their fingers entwined.

'What scandal?' Katerina prompted him, when their hearts had slowed and the sweat had dried.

'A great big scandal that no one can ignore, that will have everyone in the world talking about us, not just the Duke of Brockmore's guests.'

She laughed, but eyed him nervously. 'That sounds dangerous.'

'It is. That's one of the attractions.' Fergus kissed her lingeringly, before rolling out of bed. 'Horses and guns,' he said, beginning to dress. 'Horses and guns, and planning, and manoeuvres. The tools of my trade. It never occurred to me that they had more than one use.'

Laughing at her confusion, he kissed her again. 'I am tired of my world. I am tired of being hide-bound by convention, and I'm tired of being predictable. I want something new—something completely new. I want something dangerous and exciting. I want us to make our own world, Katerina.'

The gleam in his eyes was infectious. 'How would we do that?'

'A circus,' he said with a dramatic flourish. 'A spectacle so dazzling that it will make Astley's Circus seem like a mere sideshow. We will become the toast of America.'

'America!'

Fergus grinned. 'Our new world. Our land of opportunity. You said you wanted to go there.'

'I did. I do.' Katerina clapped her hands. 'Alexei has always wanted to go too. You do wish Alexei to be part of this, don't you Fergus?'

'That is up to Alexandr. I don't want to have to watch my back every day for the rest of my life.'

Katerina chuckled. 'He does pride himself on his knife-throwing skills. A friend of our father's taught him. But seriously, Fergus, you need not worry about my brother. He wants only for me to be happy. No, that is not wholly true. If you give him the opportunity to dazzle new, bigger audiences—no, Alexei will not be the problem.'

'I am pleased to hear it.'

'Yes, but, Fergus, such an enterprise as you

are imagining will cost a great deal of money to establish.'

'And it will earn a great deal of money once it becomes successful. That is where Sir Timothy comes in, my love.'

'Sir Timothy Farthingale?'

'Don't let that gentleman's foppish dress mislead you. He would be an excellent backer. He has sound business acumen, and a reputation for achieving the impossible. Don't underestimate him.'

'Indeed, he certainly dresses like a performer.'

'He may attend our opening night, but I do not anticipate him doing anything else save provide the funds.'

'It will be a huge amount of work to set up, Fergus.'

'Enormous. I'm imagining our circus on the Roman scale rather than the Russian one.' Fergus took her hands between his, smiling down warmly at her. 'What do you think, can we do it?'

'I believe I once said to you that you are an extraordinary man, Fergus Kennedy. I think you can do anything you wish.'

'*We* can do it, together, my darling. What have I said to make you cry?'

Katerina sniffed. 'I never dreamed I could be this happy.'

'Nor did I.' Fergus kissed her lingeringly once more, before tearing himself away with a sigh. 'We must catch Sir Timothy before these blasted games begin. Will you meet me in the library in an hour? I must get back to my room and exchange my evening clothes for something more suitable.' He rolled his eyes. 'Farthingale may prove more amenable if I appear in my kilt.'

Katerina giggled. 'Then there would be two of us in the room who would not be able to take our eyes off you.'

'The only eyes I'm interested in are green, and if you don't stop looking at me like that…'

'Go.' Katerina wrapped the sheet around herself. 'Go. We have the rest of our lives to look at each other, but only one chance to catch Sir Timothy.'

The ballroom of Brockmore House had been transformed for the Midsummer Ball. Stars twinkled from the dark-blue gauze which hung in swathes from the ceiling. Exotic potted ferns and dwarf trees stood in clusters, giving the impression that the forest had crept indoors from the grounds. Lanterns were hung at regular intervals. The subtle scent of pine wafted in through the terrace doors, which had been thrown open, and where Katerina stood nervously by Fergus's side. Below, on the South Lawn, one of the Kilmun ladies could be seen dancing with one of the male guests to the music of a hidden orchestra.

'Cecily, I believe,' Fergus said, after a moment. 'It seems Brigstock has made his match. The duke will be pleased on that score.'

Katerina edged closer to him. 'But it won't compensate for the match he had his heart set on. Fergus, I'm not sure it's a good idea for me to be here. I don't belong.'

He took her hand, tucking it firmly into his arm. 'Here in fairy land?' he said, waving at the ballroom. It did indeed seem to have acquired a magical quality, for the ladies had taken the duchess's theme to heart, and were decked out in gauzy gowns, tiaras, and spider-web lace. 'I can't think of anywhere more fitting for two people hovering between worlds,' Fergus said. 'Besides, if things go as Lady Verity seems to be planning, the duke will get his nephew-in-law.'

Katerina eyed the tall, extremely thin man

standing by Lady Verity's side. 'Surely he cannot be her choice?'

'Well, he was her partner of choice for the treasure hunt. I believe they found the diamond in the orchid house together. It looks like they may have found something else besides.'

'But he is so—I can't believe she prefers that man to you.'

Fergus laughed. 'Thank you, my love. He is, however, extremely rich, and extremely influential. Perhaps Lady Verity sees something in him which you cannot.'

'I hope so,' Katerina said, looking sceptical. 'I hope she is not simply clutching at straws.'

'I would like to think that she's following our example, and taking her fate into her own hands.'

Thinking of the long hours of discussions they had had earlier, Katerina's stomach fluttered with excitement. 'We are taking a very, very big chance.'

'One that could make us very rich.'

'That is what Alexei said. I told you he would not need much persuading to accept you.'

'He almost bit my hand off,' Fergus said, grinning. 'Where is Alexandr tonight?'

'At the dance in the village, preening himself

with the fair maidens who cheered his knife-throwing prowess at the games this afternoon.' Katerina chuckled. 'I suppose you will wish to add that to our list of acts, Monsieur Grand Circus Master.'

Fergus laughed. 'I'll concentrate on what I know for the moment.'

'Horses and guns.'

'Re-enactments, with real soldiers.' Fergus's expression turned serious. 'My friend, Jack Trestain, was Wellington's famous code-breaker. Now, he spends his life exposing the things Wellington would prefer remained hidden. The soldiers who have no jobs. The soldiers' widows who have no pensions. We can help these people, find them gainful employment, and in the process create a spectacle like no other.'

'And so you will be an officer again, only without the bloodshed.'

'And you, Katerina, are you willing to be an officer's wife? I have asked you twice now, and I don't believe you've actually said yes.'

She stared at him, wide-eyed. She had not thought her heart could absorb any more happiness, but it seemed it could. 'Do you mean it? You really want us to be married?'

'I love you. All I have to offer is the hope of a glittering future, but with Sir Timothy's backing, my management, and your talent, I know we can do it. America is where the future is. A new country, where we can make our own destiny, our own rules. We can make our own dynasty too. Take a chance with me, Katerina. Marry me.'

'I can think of nothing I would like better.'

Inside the ballroom, the orchestra struck up for the first official dance. If Fergus and Katerina had looked through the window, they would have seen Lady Verity bestowing the honour of her hand on Desmond Falkner. They would have seen Jessamy Addington dancing with Florence Canby, and Cynthia Kilmun standing disconsolate to one side as her sister danced for the second time that evening with the Earl of Jessop. They might have noticed the Duke and Duchess of Brockmore eyeing the other various couples on the floor with a mixture of pride and disappointment. They would not have seen Sir Timothy or Lillias Lamont, for after a long day discussing his circus venture with Fergus and Katerina, Farthingale had decided that he and that luscious lady were in need of a rather more adult form of entertainment.

But they did not see any of this. They were, shockingly, locked in one another's arms, and kissing in the most indecorous of ways. 'I love you so much,' Katerina said.

'How much?' her betrothed asked with a wicked smile.

'Spirit me away from this fairy land, and I'll show you,' she answered.

At which point, they retired, to dance to their own particular tune. And with that, the curtain is discreetly lowered on the Brockmore Midsummer Party.

* * * * *

THE DEBUTANTE'S AWAKENING

Bronwyn Scott

For Evelyn,
independent bookstore owner extraordinaire.
Thanks for making Good Book Café a great
place where readers and writers can meet.

Chapter One

Saturday June 14th, 1817
Brockmore Manor House Party

Programme of Events
Welcoming Party in the Drawing Room
Exhibition by the World-Famous
Russian Acrobat Troupe
The Flying Vengarovs in the Ballroom

This was the house party of the Season? Miss Zara Titus stood in the archway of the Duke of Brockmore's elegant blue, ode-to-the-sea drawing room and surveyed its occupants with what may have well been a hint of disdain in her gaze. After all, it was so very hard to hide one's true feelings all the time and the truth was: she'd rather be anywhere else than here. In fact, up until three weeks ago, she'd never dreamed she'd *need* to be here. Then Viscount Haymore had broken their long-standing betrothal and everything had changed. Even her. Not just who she was but what she wanted. She'd gone from being successfully betrothed and anticipating a Christmas wedding to suddenly being a three-Seasons debutante with no husband in sight.

This party was supposed to rectify that. *If* she allowed it. The old dreams no longer suited her. In the wake of Haymore's defection, she wondered if they ever had. She had new dreams now, dreams of independence where she chose the path of her life and who, if anyone, she walked that path with. This party posed a danger to those fledgling dreams.

Oh, the party looked innocuous enough—all the usual players in all the usual places: Lady Verity Fairholme, the duke's niece, at the centre of the room, surrounded by her beaux, and arranged portrait-perfect on a large hassock, having no doubt selected her cream gown with its blue trim to complement the room's decor—a strategy Zara noted her rival often used to gather attention; Miss Florence Canby dressed in white sitting by the open French doors, gentlemen hovering about her who would say they had drifted over because it was cooler, but who in truth were probably there because of the 'unconfirmed' rumours from the Westcott ball that Florence would indeed kiss a man and a bit more in the garden if she had enough champagne. No wonder the girl was here—she needed to marry fast.

Like you, Zara's conscience prompted. *You are no longer different than these other girls.* They might not be as pretty, but they were just as wealthy, just as highly placed in society and, for whatever reasons, just as in need. Zara pushed the negative thought aside. That was the old Zara talking, the old dreams reasserting themselves.

It had been rather humbling to realise how much she had prided herself on that betrothal, how much she'd unconsciously defined her self-worth by it and now it was gone, all because Haymore had found his true love and it wasn't her. Losing Haymore had hurt, but growing pains always did. This party would be the first test of the new Zara's resolve and the power of her new dreams—dreams crafted by her, for her, not given to her by a set of well-meaning parents.

Zara's gaze quartered the room to take in the rest. There were other well-known, expected guests: Jeremy Giltner, Douglas Brigstock and Jessamy Addington, all known protégés of the duke; the newly inherited Lord Markham and his sister Catherine, who was getting a late start on her Season after a year of mourning; the pretty Kilmun twins, Cynthia and Cecily, who lingered near Verity; shy Miss Ariana Falk and her dragon of a mother; Mr Melton Colter, who had a terrible habit of graphically discussing horse breeding at dinner. It was a traditional assembly of London's *haut ton*, each guest carefully selected by the duke. But only the most naïve would think this gathering was innocent.

Anyone who was anyone knew what went on here. This was where the most prestigious matches of the year would be made—nay, not merely 'made'—to say matches were *made* minimised the party's significance. This was where the most prestigious matches of the year would be *orchestrated* by the Silver Fox himself, the Duke of Brockmore and his Duchess. These were not ordinary marriages, they came with plums: prime diplomatic postings, estates, seats in Parliament, military offices. The Duke could make a man's career. He could establish a woman in a life of wealth and comfort, position her to become one of London's leading hostesses. Anything was possible as long as one married appropriately according to the duke's dictates. To do otherwise was unthinkable. By attending, guests were agreeing to play by those rules.

Zara Titus wanted no part of it. She did not want to marry a man she'd known for a week just to save face. Of course her mother, the unflappable Viscountess Aberforth, felt otherwise. In her opinion Brockmore's was exactly where they needed to be in order to show the *ton* Haymore hadn't jilted Zara, that the break was indeed mutual if not slightly skewed to Zara's benefit. Zara could do far better than the viscount and she had a week to prove it by effecting a betrothal to a man of better rank and wealth. It was all Zara had heard for the last three weeks.

'Chin up, shoulders back, gaze to the left, make eye contact with our host,' her mother coached in firm undertones beside her as Brockmore himself moved forward to greet them, stately and sleek with silver hair that gave him his moniker, a man still in his prime despite his fifty-two years. 'Breathe in and exhale…'

With a smile, Zara finished silently in her mind, flashing the room a dazzling one without second thought. After three years, she knew the routine by rote and carried it out effortlessly. It was the routine of a woman who was confident in herself, in her beauty, in her ability to captivate a room as if it was her due. For three years she had done just that. Only it had never really mattered. Everyone had known she was destined to be Haymore's bride. Now it mattered. In ways her mother would not expect. Her mother would be quite exercised to know the thoughts running through her usually dutiful daughter's head. Zara meant to rebel against all of it: the rules, the expectations, the stifling propriety that said good girls did what they were told, never thought for themselves, never experienced life for themselves.

She might be furious with Haymore for having deserted her—it was embarrassing no matter how Haymore had let her father shape the news of their betrothal 'broken by mutual agreement', but she would not sell herself in marriage simply to avenge herself on Haymore. Marriage was for ever. Scandal was for a few weeks until something else came along to take its place, and something would. London thrived on rumours.

She'd learned a lot about herself in the three weeks since Haymore cried off. She'd learned she hadn't really loved Haymore, only the comfortable idea of him and even then only because she'd known nothing else. She'd learned she was strong. She'd faced down the initial wave of speculations. She'd learned too that she liked her freedom. Haymore had been chosen for her almost since birth.

Now she had a choice if she was brave enough to make it. Haymore had been brave enough. Why shouldn't she be? Why shouldn't she taste a little of life's pleasures instead of having everything decided for her? She would choose if she married, who she married and when. She would choose how her life would be spent and where even if that meant away from London society.

'How exciting, darling, to think your husband is in this very room at this very moment,' her mother whispered as the duke neared. 'Perhaps the dashing Mr Giltner or young Lord Markham?'

That was exactly what Zara was *very* afraid of. She doubted a man who would let her eschew convention and live freely was in this room—arguably the most proper drawing room in England. This room wasn't a field of opportunity, as her mother liked to portray it. It was a trap waiting to devour her.

The sinking feeling Zara had fought ever since they'd turned down Brockmore's mile-long, oak-lined drive became a full-blown pit of anxiety as the duke bent over their hands, all graciousness, giving no acknowledgement that he knew precisely why they were here. 'Miss Titus, it is a privilege to have you here.' A privilege? Is that what the genteel scrambling for a last-minute invitation was called these days? Zara was well aware her own highly connected father had called in a few favours to arrange this. The guest list had been set months in advance.

'Let me introduce you, although I am sure you know almost everyone.' The duke had a fatherly hand at her back, ushering her towards the groups of people gathered about the room, while her mother walked on his other side, looking sophisticated, calm, and above all else, supremely pleased to be here, as if life hadn't been turned on its ear. Perhaps her mother *was* pleased to be here. It was all a game to her mother and the duke, they were all living chess pieces to manoeuvre around society's board.

Zara was done being a pawn. This week would be about rebellion. The more her mother liked something, the more Zara would resist. In the end, she would taste something of freedom and her parents would understand she'd be making her own decisions from here on. The lesson would serve all parties.

'You know my niece, of course.' The duke beamed as they approached the hassock. How could she not? The two of them had been in direct competition to be the *ton*'s leading beauty for years now. But Zara smiled and kissed Verity's cheek, exclaiming over her gown as if they were the best of friends because that's what rivals did. They moved on to greet the Downings, Catherine and Richard, the new Lord Markham. That was when she felt it, or rather *him*.

A man was watching her, his eyes following her as she moved from group to group, making it hard to concentrate, hard to pretend she was unaware of his attention. By the fourth group, she gave up and hazarded a glance about the room. She found him immediately. He stood with the rather eccentric Timothy Farthingale and the prudish merchant, Desmond Falkner—the only two guests who were here for business, not matrimony.

He was bold in looks and demeanour. He was tall next to the shorter men, his dark hair pulled back in to a sleek tail to reveal the strong bones of his face and piercing dark eyes. With the right clothes and setting he might easily pass for a pirate. Here among the assembled proper, he was positively feral. He made no move to cut his gaze away. Instead, he smiled broadly when their eyes met, confirming what Zara already knew. He was no gentleman.

He wasn't merely looking at her, he was *undressing* her with his eyes. Zara felt an urge to fan herself that had nothing to do with the actual warmth of the room. She resisted on principle. She would not give him the satisfaction or the acknowledgement. Zara leaned towards the duke. 'Who is that man?' She indicated the stranger with only her eyes, careful to keep her tone neutral.

The duke smiled kindly and patted her hand, exchanging a look with her mother. 'Merely a guest, my dear. Hardly anyone for you to worry over.' The message was clear; He was precisely the sort of man her mother wouldn't want her to meet. He was to be ignored. That made him the perfect place to start.

The duke's words were entirely the wrong thing to say to a girl who had no intentions of ending the week with a husband and every intention of exercising a little independence. The man in the corner was suddenly much more interesting than he'd been a few moments ago. Now, he'd become positively intriguing. Zara discreetly flipped open her fan. A little acknowledgement might be in order after all.

Chapter Two

Kael Gage recognised a cat-and-mouse game when he saw it. He and the striking woman in the butter-yellow muslin were initiating a subtly aggressive flirtation, each of them seeking to command the other, their roles switching from pursuer to pursuant with a motion of the eyes and the flick of a fan from across the room.

It was his turn to answer and he would do so with a calculated move. He would wait and make her wonder if he would indeed respond. There was no need to rush over immediately. To do so would concede early victory and put him in her power as a man she could manipulate. It would not enhance his appeal. A woman liked nothing as much as the man she couldn't have. Likewise, a woman lost interest in a man who was too easily won. Near unattainability was key.

Kael turned his attentions back to the conversation between Falkner and Farthingale, which had its own engaging value, Falkner in his dark, puritanically plain clothing questioning the business practices of the flamboyantly garbed Sir Timothy Farthingale, but there were practical reasons too for not approaching his lovely butter-gowned flirt just yet. To do so while she was in the duke's company *and* her mother's would be to court rejection outright.

He didn't need to be a mind-reader to know what the duke was whispering to the pretty brunette right now, or to know the meaning behind her mother's brief, shrewd glance in his direction. Kael smiled in their direction, indicating he was aware of their polite censure and that he didn't care a whit. During his ten years on the town, he'd fought three duels of honour—two with pistols which meant he'd faced mortality at twenty paces at dawn, one of the more frightening things a man could do. He would not be intimidated by a matchmaking mama's stare and a duke's whisper.

Still, whatever they whispered to his flirt was undoubtedly true. That he was no good; he fraternised with the wrong sort of women—opera singers, actresses, jewels of the *demi-monde* and a certain kind of experienced *ton*nish woman. He couldn't deny it. He did more than fraternise with them. He seduced them, bedded them, found physical pleasure with them. But a lot of men did that, even married ones. What was probably less forgivable in their eyes was that he had no prospects. His family tree was a stump with broken branches everywhere. His grandfather had been an earl with a prolific ability to produce reckless sons—seven of them, in fact, only the heir still living—but a less prolific ability to generate income which had left six of those careless sons to fend for themselves, his own father included.

As a result, Kael had his good looks to recommend him, but not much else except a small horse farm in Sussex. It meant he was fit for a squire's daughter or a gentleman farmer's girl—a lesson that had been drilled into him since he was eighteen; the fine debutantes of the *ton* might flirt with a man like him, but they'd never marry him. It had been a hard lesson for an eager grandson of an earl to learn, no matter how pretty the face delivering it.

Now, at the age of thirty, he knew very well for a fine diamond of the first water like Miss Butter-

Gown, he was persona non grata, which served to make him contrary. It made him want to play the game all the more, just to be contrary, simply because he could. From the flick of her fan, she did too. She was restless. It was there in her gaze, hidden behind that confident smile of hers as she moved from group to group, and in the defiant tilt of her head that she couldn't quite hide. She didn't want to be here. How very interesting. Most women would kill to be here. To find someone who would not, was intriguing. It made her different, it made her stand out. It made him want to know her. What sort of woman would willingly eschew this opportunity?

This was shaping up to be quite the entertaining house party. He'd not expected it. This was not his usual venue. He'd merely come as a means of getting out of London, all too happy to be Jeremy Giltner's guest. The city had become rather 'hot' for him at present in a way that had nothing to do with the weather.

Kael waited until after the acrobatic display by the Flying Vengarovs that evening to make his response. It had been a scintillating performance, leaving spirits high and imaginations aroused.

Perhaps exactly what their host intended, Kael thought with cynicism. The Silver Fox did nothing by accident. Katerina Vengarov had been nearly naked as she'd navigated the tightrope strung across the ballroom high above the floor, igniting all sorts of fantasies in the male mind, while her chiselled brother had likely made the same impact on the female population.

Kael's particular quarry slipped from the ballroom on to the terrace, cheeks flushed from the heat and maybe more. She'd been restless all night. He'd watched her at dinner; her eyes too bright, her laughter too forced. No one else would notice, it would be beyond their imagination to conceive of someone *not* wanting to be here. But it was not beyond his, especially now that he knew who she was. Miss Zara Titus. He'd asked around, discreetly of course. Haymore's intended, or should he say 'unintended'? Rumour had it, the split was mutual. But Kael had his doubts. What was politically correct was often not exactly the truth, but a polite rendering of it. The chit was beautiful, captivatingly so with intelligent hazel eyes, piles of satin-shiny coffee-coloured hair and a body that did a dressmaker proud. He'd seen her in two gowns now, each one showing her to be more stunning than the last. Haymore must have been out of his mind to let her go. Then again, he'd heard rumours about Haymore too. It wasn't beyond the realm of possibility.

Kael counted to five and began to make his way towards the doors, sidling out into the cool night. He found her easily in a far corner of the veranda, the silver of her gown giving her away in the moonlight although her posture clearly indicated she wanted to be alone. Ah, defiant *and* restless. A potent combination and one he understood. He'd been defiant and restless since he was twenty and Miss Ella Davison had informed him she was far above his reach no matter how much she liked his kisses. It had only become worse in the intervening decade.

He leaned against the stone balustrade overlooking the gardens and gave her an assessing smile, letting his eyes hold hers with a brazenness that would have sent a shy miss like Ariana Falk running for the shelter of the ballroom. 'So, you're Miss Zara Titus, the jilt.'

Her green eyes narrowed but held. Her response was even and neutral, but he noticed her gloved hands tightened almost imperceptibly on the balustrade. She didn't like the term. 'What a terrible thing to say.'

'What an *honest* thing to say,' Kael drawled. 'It's true, after all, isn't it? You jilted Haymore. Why shouldn't we speak plainly? The name's Gage, by the way. Kael Gage.'

She straightened, her eyes firing delightful little sparks of emerald flame. 'You assume I want to know.'

He chuckled. 'Oh, you do.' He flicked his gaze to the fan dangling from her wrist. 'You all but invited me out here.' He reached for her hand, drawing circles on her palm through the fabric of her glove as he gave her a smouldering glance through lowered eyelids. 'I know what you want, Zara.' He lowered his voice. 'We were made to fly. Why do you think our "esteemed" host invited the acrobats? To set the mood rather blatantly, to stir our senses, to challenge our grasp of the possibilities that await us.' He brought her palm against his cheek and placed a kiss at its centre, feeling her pulse catch in her wrist. 'You want to fly. You were *made* to fly.'

'With you?' Her tone was aloof. Her body was not. There was interest in her eyes as she took him in and that interest betrayed the direction of her thoughts.

'Absolutely with me, with a man who knows what you need.' Kael raised his eyes to hers, his meaning naked in his gaze. She was already wondering what he might show her. Zara Titus had spirit.

'What is it that you think I need?' She angled her head coyly, the streamers of light from the ballroom catching the tiny diamonds at her ears, a subtle reminder that she was indeed a woman far above him in station.

'To be kissed and perhaps more.'

'By a man I hardly know?' She made no move to pull her hand away, making it clear she was not challenging him, but daring him. Her body had inched slightly closer to his, her lips had parted and, by Jove, he was tempted to take that invitation, to prove himself. The night was quiet about them except for the crickets in the bushes. It was easy to forget there was a ballroom of people a few yards away. Their privacy was an illusion. He'd do well to remember that. If they were seen…well, it was far too early in the game to risk such a thing.

'Don't you think it's better that way?' Kael

prompted, fuelling the flames of her defiance. 'No expectations beyond the here and now, no plans beyond the week.' He gave her a half-smile and released her hand, stepping away. It was always best to leave them wanting more and he was confident the seed was planted. He'd issued his invitation. It was up to her to accept it, to decide what she wanted to do with it. He gave her a last bit of encouragement. 'To fly is your destiny, Zara. A woman such as you can hardly seek to escape it. You'll see. Resistance is futile.'

What was he doing, seducing an innocent under the duke's matchmaking nose? Kael tossed back a healthy dose of Brockmore's excellent and expensive brandy conveniently left in decanters in the gentlemen's chambers. This was the height of madness and he ought to know. He'd been party to plenty of madness in his day. It was insanity enough to seduce Zara Titus; a virgin, a daughter of a peer, and a wealthy heiress. To do it at a party specifically designed to create marriages was a whole other level of crazy. This party would usually be off limits to him. This was rarefied air he was breathing to move in such elevated circles. He was a lowly horse breeder. These guests were the richest, the most powerful people in England. The girl was off limits too. She was the sort of woman who would claim everything a man had, body and soul, the sort of woman a man couldn't afford to fail. He'd already failed one important woman in his life. The precedent was set. He couldn't possibly make a woman like Zara Titus happy in the long run. It wasn't in his scope of capabilities.

He poured another glass and swallowed it down. And yet, even knowing better than to pursue her, he couldn't resist the allure of her confidence, of her beauty. He couldn't resist the temptation of waking her to passion's joys. The curiosity behind her innocence drew him, appealed to him, even as the consequences for what he was about to do terrified him. But only, his wicked conscience reminded him, if he was caught.

Chapter Three

Sunday June 15th
Brockmore Manor House Party

Programme of Events
A Tour of the Gardens for the Ladies
Al Fresco Luncheon at the Lake Summerhouse
Boating to Follow
Cards and Conversation

'Miss Titus, I believe this basket is ours.' Richard Downing politely, *decorously*—compared to the other excited shouts around them as baskets were discovered—held up the picnic hamper bearing their names from the long table set up inside the summerhouse on the lake.

Zara managed a tight smile. It wasn't his fault. Richard Downing could not possibly know the amount of panic those seven simple words engendered. It appeared her mother's instincts were right, or had her mother known all along? She was intended for Richard Downing, the new Lord Markham, or Jeremy Giltner and his parliamentary ambitions. She'd been seated between them at dinner last night and now Markham was being given a chance to stake his claim.

What about *her* claim? It wasn't that she hated Markham. What she hated was that no one had consulted her. It had been assumed she'd be thrilled with the match—either of them—as if husbands and wives were interchangeable parts; anyone would do as long as they had enough money and rank. Shouldn't marriage be more than that? Shouldn't *she* be more than that?

The tender shoots of rebellion she'd nurtured for weeks began to put down roots. If she meant to rebel, she had to do it soon or it would be too late. She would end up married to Markham and leading the life her mother had planned for her since birth—a safe life, a secure life, lived under the gaze of the *ton*.

Resistance is futile. Zara heard Kael Gage's mocking laughter in her mind, as she took Lord Markham's arm. She did indeed feel that way. Things were happening too fast. It was only the first full day of the party, but already it was clear the duke had matches in mind for his guests, herself included. Today's picnic was an opportunity to try out those matches and see how they suited.

She and Markham wound their way through the throng of guests crowded about the table, all eager to find their baskets, and perhaps eager too to see what destinies the baskets held. Futures could be made or lost at this meal. *Yours too*, her conscience gave her one final push. Her decision was made. Rebellion had to start now. It wasn't fair to Markham to lead him on, to create the impression she wanted to be his marchioness. Really, when she thought about it, she was doing him an enormous favour. Any other girl at the party would consider him quite a catch. She just wasn't looking for a 'catch'.

Outside the summerhouse, small white canopies filled with picnic blankets to accommodate two or three couples dotted the shoreline, making for a very festive appearance that matched the spirits of the guests. There were bursts of surprised laughter and exclamations as people grouped up to claim spaces. Zara surreptitiously looked about for Kael Gage, wondering who would be sharing his basket and feeling an irrational twinge of jealousy. Would it mean anything? Surely, after last night's conversation with her, he wasn't here for a bride.

A pretty brunette waved in their direction and Markham acknowledged her with a nod. 'Perhaps we might join my sister and Jeremy Giltner, Miss Titus? Unless there are others you'd like to sit with?' Markham added, picking up on her distraction. Unfortunately, she had not been as surreptitious as she thought. But Markham was too much the gentleman to mention her inattention. She should *not* be looking for Mr Gage. He was wicked and he would tempt her to wickedness too if she allowed it. *Should* she allow it? It would certainly be one way to rebel and wasn't that the point? Her rebellion wouldn't get very far if she didn't start thinking beyond the rules.

'Sitting with your sister would be fine.' Zara favoured Markham with another smile to make up for her lapse. A lady never gave a gentleman the impression she'd rather be somewhere else, or with someone else. Just because she was rebelling didn't mean she had to be rude. She had a plan, after all. She would be polite, but not encouraging.

They had no sooner settled themselves under a

canopy with a rather unusually rigid Jeremy and a quiet Catherine when a voice booming with bonhomie intruded. 'Giltner! Old man, there you are. Might we join you?'

Jeremy rose and beamed, looking relieved at his good fortune. Apparently the notion of eating alone with two potential brides and one of their older, titled brothers, had sapped some of his typical *savoir faire*. But one man's saviour is often another's devil. Kael Gage ducked beneath the canopy and helped a blushing Ariana Falk find a space on a blanket as a blush of her own began to haunt Zara's cheeks. Just because she'd been looking for him didn't mean she wanted to sit with him. Gage could have sat anywhere. How dare he come over here after the way he'd importuned her on the veranda last night!

How was she supposed to sit through lunch giving Lord Markham a polite cold shoulder while Kael Gage sat across from her, his eyes conjuring hot reminders of his mouth on her palm, his words vivid and provocative in her mind? But there was no way out now. Baskets were being unpacked, conversations begun, introductions made and her mother was sitting one tent away with other matrons at tables, keeping a discreet but close eye on the proceedings. The viscountess was pleased over Markham's attention.

Lunch was delicious—cold chicken sandwiches, wheels of cheese and apples, with chilled lemonade for the ladies and ale for the men, the perfect summer menu for a warm afternoon. Conversation flowed easily between the six of them, moving from Jeremy Giltner's politics to Markham's estates, the men politely, discreetly, auditioning themselves. Except for Gage. He contributed to the conversation, but made no effort to put himself on display. Then again, he didn't have to.

It was rather hard to concentrate on civil conversation when there was Kael Gage to look at. Today, he wore tall boots and tan riding breeches, a full-sleeved white shirt with stock under a patterned waistcoat the colour of summer grass. He was dressed much like the other men and like the other men, he'd discarded his coat out of deference for the weather. So what set him apart? What kept her eye wandering in his direction? Maybe it was the broad shoulders, unleashed from the confines of a coat, the long legs shown to muscled perfection in well-fitted breeches.

Or maybe it was the hair, gathered once more into a dark fall, pulled back from his face to reveal those eyes with their secret laughter, as if he found them all amusing and showed it the way *she* wished to but didn't dare.

'Miss Titus? Do you have a question?' Kael leaned forward, a wry grin on his face, suggesting he knew she was staring even if the others didn't.

She hated being caught out, but she would make him pay a little for his poor manners. 'I was wondering, Mr Gage, where do your interests lie? Are they in politics with Mr Giltner or with your estates like Lord Markham?'

'Only two choices, Miss Titus?' He speared her with a hard gaze. He understood what she had done. It hadn't been particularly nice of her. If it had been anyone else, she would have felt guilty. 'If so, I would choose neither estates nor politics. I prefer investments.'

'You're in luck then, Farthingale has a prime opportunity cooked up and word has it, he's here looking for investors.' Jeremy Giltner contributed excitedly. 'I was thinking of buying in myself.' Jeremy shot a look at the tent where Farthingale sat with the duke and duchess, turned out in eccentric splendour. 'The man can't dress, but he's got a Midas touch when it comes to money.' He cleared his throat. 'But enough about business. I am told there are to be berry parfaits for dessert in the summerhouse. Miss Downing, would you like to accompany me?'

Ariana Falk looked wistfully at the summerhouse, implying she'd welcome an invitation to dessert too, but Gage made no move. Lord Markham shot Kael a questioning glance in an attempt to prompt him into action. None was forthcoming. Finally, Markham got to his feet. 'Miss Titus, Miss Falk, perhaps you would like to come with me for parfaits?'

'Or perhaps, Miss Titus,' Gage drawled, his eyes on her, 'I could persuade you to take a turn around the lake with *me*? I know I'm too full to eat another bite without some exercise.' He was daring her with his gaze. She ought to say no. The old Zara would. She caught herself. *Think beyond the rules*. She'd not come to this party intent on doing what she *ought*, but what she *wanted*. Her mother would have a fit. That decided it.

Zara got to her feet and shook out her skirts.

She was going to do it—she was going to go walk about the lake with a man the duke and her mother didn't want her to meet. Still, this had to be managed with more finesse than Kael had managed his request or people would talk. 'If it is acceptable to Lord Markham, I should enjoy the exercise.' Markham seemed to hesitate, torn between honouring his invitation to Miss Falk and leaving her with Kael Gage, who might be suitable company for other men but was perhaps questionable company for the Miss Tituses of the world. 'Please, you and Miss Falk go on,' Zara urged. 'I wouldn't think of denying either of you the treat on my account.'

'Neatly done, Miss Titus.' Gage spoke quietly from behind her as Markham and Ariana moved out of earshot, his nearness surprising her. She hadn't heard him rise. 'You've dispatched the last of them so now we can be alone.'

'How dare you put me in that position!' Zara hissed.

'What position would that be?' His hands closed over her arms where the puff of her sleeves ended and her skin was bare, his voice low at her ear. 'Missionary? Woman on top? Stallion to mare? Do you have any idea what I'm talking about?'

'There's no way a lady can possibly answer that, Mr Gage, without impugning herself one way or another.' His hands on her were giving her delicious shivers even in the heat.

'*Touché*, Miss Titus. I see your tongue is a sharp weapon. Perhaps I might teach you some other, more pleasant uses for it besides cutting a man down to size.' His hand dropped to the small of her back. 'Shall we? The lake awaits.'

The exercise Gage referred to turned out not to be a walk, but a boat. Several other guests had availed themselves of the rowboats and the lake was full of merrymakers as gentlemen showed off their talents with the oars, yet another opportunity to audition themselves as potential mates. 'It's to be Markham for you, then?' Gage asked as he manoeuvred their boat through the busy traffic of the lake. He was quite good with the oars, his skill evidencing the muscles of his arms. Too bad he couldn't row with his shirt rolled up, or even off, came the forbidden thought. It was not the thought of a well-bred young lady. But maybe it should be. Perhaps the duke should consider *that* in his auditioning process. Estates and finances were only part of what made a good match and arguably not the most important parts. A girl didn't have to go bed with those.

'It's to be no one for me,' Zara responded sharply. 'Coming here was my mother's idea, not mine. I have no desire to throw myself into a hasty marriage just to prove I have one up on Haymore.' It felt incredibly cleansing to say the words out loud.

Gage chuckled. 'You'd better tell Markham that. I think he missed the polite hints at lunch.' He turned their boat, veering towards the little island in the centre of the lake. 'It won't work, you know, your little plan to encourage but not encourage. Markham is too much the gentleman. He'll think your coolness is part of your virtue.' She'd come to that conclusion over lunch, but that didn't mean she liked Kael Gage throwing it in her face.

Gage laughed. 'Rebellion is harder than you thought, isn't it? It has to be an outright declaration of independence and that makes it risky. There's no going back once it is done.'

'Is that a warning or an invitation?' They had made their way to the back side of the island and they were entirely alone. The water was quiet here, undisturbed by the splash of oars and the shouts of boaters. She should not be out with him, not here where no one could see, and yet his words resonated; rebellion could not be halfway. Rules must be broken or she would end up engaged to Markham, her defiance coming to naught. She understood. He was daring her to declare herself, testing her resolve to see whether she was all bluff.

He grinned, his eyes crinkling at the corners as he rowed towards the shale beach. 'You decide.' There was another factor too—rules or not, she *wanted* to be out here with him. Not just for rebellion's sake, but for hers. His touch roused her, the audacity of his words excited her, and yet she could not simply embrace that excitement with abandon. There would be consequences. Was she ready for them?

Gage pulled off his boots and took off his stockings. He nodded her direction. 'You might want to take yours off too. I'm *not* carrying you to shore.' 'Shore' was only a few feet away, but there would be a small amount of wading required.

Zara narrowed her eyes. 'Are you here hunting a wife, Mr Gage?'

He gave a loud guffaw. 'Hardly. I'm not the

marrying type, Miss Titus.' He lowered his voice and waggled his dark brows. 'Does it disturb you to think we have something in common?'

'No.' Zara was all coolness as she reached for the lace of her half-boot. 'I'm relieved, actually, because asking your intended to take off her stockings and shoes is not the most romantic way to get under her skirts.' There. That should shock him. She was feeling worldly and rather pleased with her sophisticated set-down. It would pay him back for that comment about positions earlier and prove she wasn't afraid to play his naughty little games.

Gage folded his arms across his chest and leaned back in the prow of the boat, considering her with dark, hot eyes. 'What do you know of getting beneath skirts, Zara?'

She blanched. The old Zara was not entirely vanquished and she was well aware her ploy had completely backfired. She had not repelled intimate conversation, but invited it, and from a man who knew no boundaries when it came to civility or its antithesis. He arched a dark eyebrow. 'Did Haymore get beneath your skirts? Is that why the two of you "mutually" cried off?'

Her cheeks heated. 'That's backward logic.

If he had, do you think we would have broken our betrothal?' This was the oddest conversation she'd ever had—discussing sex and her former fiancé with a man she barely knew. It was a scandal in itself. She had never entertained such thoughts about anyone, not even Haymore, before, but now Kael had her thinking all nature of wickedness. 'It would have been all the more reason to stay together.' She could hear the mortification in her own voice. She hated it. She wanted to sound assured, a woman capable of rebellion, capable of making her own choices.

'Not if you didn't like it. Then, it makes perfect sense,' Gage suggested. 'Life is a long time to be with a man who is no good in bed.'

That was outside of the pale. Zara grabbed her shoes and stockings in one hand and stood up, rocking the boat dangerously with her sudden movement.

'Zara!' Gage grabbed either side of the boat with his hands, trying to steady it. 'Do you want to land us in the water? It might be a bit hard to explain both of us coming back wet.' Ah, so the rogue did have a tiny bit of social conscience, after all.

'It can't be any harder to explain than your last

comment!' She stepped out into the water, skirts in one hand, shoes in the other, the water coming up her calf. 'Only a cad would make such assumptions.'

Zara strode towards the beach, water splashing, the shale hard beneath her bare feet, but she didn't care. He was outrageous! And he was exciting. Maybe the person she wanted to get away from was herself. She could hear him splashing behind her. His hand closed about her arm. 'Only an honest man would make such assumptions,' he corrected. 'Why shouldn't you try out the goods before you buy them?' he challenged. 'Why shouldn't a woman have a taste of what awaits her?'

She made the mistake of looking at him. Her face gave away too much. 'Hah!' he crowed. 'You think so too, you just don't want to admit it.'

'You are a scandal.'

'Do you mean that as fact or censure?' His eyes glittered, his voice was low, his words private. 'It's hard to get a read on you, Zara. Are you truly scandalised or do you only *believe* you should be?' His mouth, his body, were just inches from her and she pulsed with the knowledge of it. His finger traced her lips. 'I think such plain speaking excites you. I think *I* excite you.' His eyes lingered on the mouth he'd traced, his words a whispered murmured before his mouth covered hers. 'And you, Zara, excite me.'

Chapter Four

Zara Titus *was* exciting. Kael ran his tongue along the seam of her lips, encouraging, coaxing her to open. He felt the slightest of questioning hesitations, proof that Haymore certainly hadn't kissed her with any amount of proficiency. Who kissed with their mouths shut? Zara wouldn't, now that she knew better.

Her mouth opened beneath his, eager, her untutored hunger intoxicating, perhaps even defiant, wanting to prove to him that she could match him. She couldn't, of course, she hadn't an ounce of his experience and yet *this* was what made her exciting—she was a woman who yearned for that experience, yearned to tap her own sensuality. Untried though she was, she was not afraid of her body's physicality like so many other purebred misses. He'd seen that confidence in her smile, in the cut of her gowns—simply but exquisitely tailored to show off the contours of her body instead of hiding them behind ruffles—he'd not been wrong about the cues of her clothing. A woman dressed her truth, just as she kissed it. He'd not been wrong the other night. Zara would demand a man's all, an appealing and terrifying prospect altogether.

'Put your tongue in my mouth, Zara,' he instructed, nipping at her lower lip with his teeth. 'Taste me.' She would be a delight to tutor, to awaken. She was ripe for rebellion, ripe for whatever earthy pleasures he cared to introduce. There were plenty of pleasures that didn't require the breaching of her maidenhead. He'd leave that intact for Markham.

'Would you like me to bite you too?' Zara's voice was husky as her tongue traced the outline of his lips in a teasing, flicking motion that had him imagining that tongue on another entirely male body part. Haymore had missed out. His Zara was a fast learner. That made her dangerous, that and her innocence. If they were caught, it would be a disaster. And yet the thrill drove him to continue.

'Bite me, lick me, suck me,' Kael murmured

at her ear, his own tongue beginning a flicking caress inside the curve of her ear. 'I am yours to command.' Would Markham know what to do with her? Markham was nice enough, but nice sex had never inspired anyone. She would be wasted on the likes of him.

Water lapped at his bare feet, reminding him they had to move further into the island. Zara's skirt would get wet and it was deuced hard to kiss without hands. He had his hands free, but she didn't. Her hands were holding shoes and skirt hems. He wanted them to hold him, wanted her to cradle his face when she kissed him, wanted those hands to roam free on his body to feel what he was made of.

Kael moved them away from the shore and selected one of the paths leading to the interior. There were other reasons too to step into the island, reasons like the risk of discovery. He'd fled London because there'd been a 'small' indiscretion with a lady whose virtue was questionable, but an angry brother who was not. Said brother had made London rather uncomfortable of late. It would hardly do to commit the same *faux pas* under the esteemed Duke of Brockmore's roof after the duke had so generously looked the other way.

Not only that, but Zara wasn't his usual sort of woman. Discovery would have consequences. She wanted to be rebellious, not married, certainly not to a man she hadn't chosen. She would hate being forced. If she was going to marry anyone, it should be a man worthy of her in rank and position, a man like Markham. She'd already established she wasn't interested in such a man. At present, she was still reeling from Haymore. But some day, she would be interested again. When that day came, she would no doubt look back at her interlude with him and recognise it as foolish.

'Oh, look! A little cottage,' Zara exclaimed. The interior of the small island was full of tall trees and maintained paths, all of them directing the adventurer to the island's centre. In her excitement, she tugged on his hand and drew him forward.

The cottage was open, as Gage suspected it always was, and Zara couldn't resist going inside. It was a single, simple room containing a bed, a table, two chairs, a small cupboard and a fireplace. Gage chuckled. The duke was a devil still, in his middle years. The intentions of the

cottage were obvious. This was a place for secret trysts very few knew about other than the
duke and duchess. The old Silver Fox was a romantic at heart.

Zara moved about the little room, hands trailing over furniture, gaze distracted. He let the silence linger, waiting for her to speak, waiting to
see what she'd do next. She stopped next to the
table and met his eyes. 'What was that down at
the boat?'

Kael crossed his arms and leaned against the
doorframe. 'What would you like it to be? An
invitation to pleasure? A caution against sharp
tongues? This is your rebellion, Zara. If you mean
to rebel, you have to do more than give Markham
a cold shoulder.' That got her ire up. Her chin
tilted, her arms crossed beneath her breasts. Did
she have any idea how alluring she looked when
she was defiant? He wanted to pull off her hat
and take out every pin from her perfectly arranged hair until it tumbled over her shoulders.
He wanted to see her mussed. 'Do you know
what I'd like to do right now?' Kael growled,
pushing off the door.

Her eyes narrowed, watching him stalk towards

her. Her tongue wet her lips. 'What?' She wasn't afraid. She was aroused.

He untied the blue ribbon of her hat and tossed it aside, his eyes holding hers. He would start slow, with liberties she'd likely allow. 'I want to take down your hair.' He slid one pin free, then another and another until the pile of it came loose, falling over his hands, satiny and smooth. He raised a length to his nose and inhaled, eyes open, never leaving hers. Lavender—a lady's scent—and sage—earthy, faintly lemony, not nearly as innocent as the lavender.

'And now?' Her words were a mere whisper. 'What now?'

'Now, I want to push you up against the wall and kiss the hell out of you.' His voice was rough and hoarse as he pushed his hands through her hair, framing her face between them, his body taking them to the wall, his mouth coming down hard on hers, and she took him, tongue and all.

Her arms were about his neck, her body answering the press of his. He moved his hips against her, letting her feel the rock-hard solidness of him. Her moan filled his mouth. She was a vixen, this beautiful untried woman, although he doubted anyone would believe the untried part if they could see her now, her hair about her face, her lips swollen from his kisses, his bites, her eyes wide and wild. He kissed her again, his hand curving over the swell of her breast, the flat of his palm feeling her nipple tighten beneath the fabric, beneath his touch. She arched into him, impatient.

'Touch me, Zara.' He took her hand, guiding it to where the core of him jutted hard against her abdomen. She did not shrink from the blatant intimacy. Her hand closed about him through his trousers and his body raged. She didn't need any more encouragement. Her hand traced him, moulded him. He had his mouth on her again, allowing himself a few more moments in this heaven–hell of pleasure before he had to stop it, before he had to get her to commit. He was seldom surprised, but Zara Titus was far more exciting than he'd even imagined.

'How does rebellion feel, Zara?' He touched his forehead to hers, struggling to get his breathing under control. He'd not thought he was that far gone.

Her hazel eyes were dark. 'Unlike anything I've ever felt before.' There was honesty in the throaty response. The experience might have overwhelmed a more timid miss, but she had mastered it, even revelled in it.

'There is more pleasure to be had, Zara. I meant it. I am yours to command. I can show you more, give you more,' he murmured his temptation. He wanted her to say yes. 'I can show you things Markham would never dream of. But you have to decide how far this rebellion goes.' He twisted a strand of her hair around a finger.

'I think it's already been decided.' Zara gave a shaky laugh. 'We've—we've…' she stammered, looking for words. 'We've done so much.'

'And no one saw a thing,' Kael finished. 'Everything you've done today doesn't count. Nothing you did with Markham, everything you've done with me, *none* of it counts because no one saw.' He stepped back and scooped up her hairpins. 'It's the old-tree-falls-in-the-forest argument. If a virgin puts her hand on a man's cock and no one sees, has she really done it?'

Her eyes flared. She didn't like the crassness of his comment. Kael took her hand and cupped it, pouring her hairpins into it. 'Put your hair up, Zara, and put your hat on. I'll wait outside.' She could choose, of course, to keep her hair down and signal to all and sundry they'd got up to some mischief, but she wouldn't. Not today. She might be willing to kiss a scoundrel in private, but she wasn't ready to own her rebellion. Yet. The question was, would she own it before it was too late? Markham might be nice, but he was shrewd. Markham knew how to close a deal and so did the duke. Zara had five days. He'd match her step for step, but how far was she willing to go?

Zara had put her hand on a man's penis. She had put her tongue in his mouth. He had put his hand over her breast, his mouth had done decadent things to hers, and, none of it had been rebellious? It had certainly been glorious. So glorious, in fact, that dinner paled in comparison.

Under other circumstances, dinner would have been dazzling. Brockmore had set up a long table outside on the veranda, flowers and candles running the centre of it. The evening had cooled to 'pleasantly warm' and the menu was entirely self-contained; from the flowers on the table to every dish served, everything was produced or raised on the Brockmore estate. It was quite an accomplishment, but so was this afternoon. How was she supposed to think about the meal when all she could focus on was the man sitting across the table from her?

Kael Gage, like the other men, had traded his casual boating attire for the dark evening clothes of a gentleman. This might be the country, but it was still the duke's house and the Silver Fox was a stickler for propriety at dinner. Everyone dressed. But Zara didn't think any male present could compete with Kael, not even Markham who sat beside her. Perhaps it was only natural to feel that way since the incident at the lake. They had kissed one another, touched one another. Whether it was rebellious or not, it had certainly been enlightening, exhilarating. She had not imagined a man would feel that way— so hard, so hot, so *alive*.

'Miss Titus, how do you find the fish?' Markham asked. 'I am told it was caught in the river on the duke's property where the gentlemen will be fishing on Tuesday.'

'It's very fresh,' Zara managed, taking a bite in the hopes it would redirect her thoughts. The effort was only marginally successful. Would Lord Markham feel the way Kael had? Would Markham ever take off her hat and pull down her hair with a fierce, almost primal look in his eyes? Would Markham ever ravage her against a wall?

'There are a lot of fresh things at dinner, I've noticed,' Kael said from across the table. Zara felt her cheeks heat at the innuendo she might be one of those fresh things. He was trying to draw her out, trying to make her say something rash.

'Yes,' Markham replied with stiff politeness to the interruption. 'Everything tonight comes from Brockmore's estate. It's a very impressive feat.' He directed his next words at Miss Falk, who sat beside Gage, looking lost and perhaps intimidated by the masculine force at her side. 'My apologies, I did not mean to interrupt.' It was a neat rebuke, as Markham hadn't been the one to intrude. Kael ought to be talking with his dinner partner, not eavesdropping on conversations held across the table.

'I do hope I did not err in leaving you with Gage this afternoon.' Markham said in low tones once Kael returned his attentions where they belonged. 'It was a rather impossible position and Miss Falk was out of her depth. I don't know what the duke was thinking to pair her with Gage.' There was an undercurrent of anger beneath his words. Zara couldn't help but glance over at Ariana. Her blonde hair and blue eyes gave her the look of a porcelain doll, a look enhanced by the fragile structure of her bones. Delicate was exactly the right word to describe her. Honourable men like Markham would feel compelled to defend a woman who looked like that.

'She is a far too delicate specimen of womanhood for a man of Gage's attributes.' Carried away by his chagrin, Markham caught his *faux pas* too late. He reached over and squeezed her hand in apology where it lay in her lap. 'I did not mean to imply, Miss Titus, you are not delicate. You are in, fact, the very flower of womanhood, a rose among daisies.' She could not imagine the nice, warm hand that squeezed hers on her breast, where it would probably be very 'nice' as well, touching her gingerly lest he shock her sensibilities with his base urges. He might even apologise afterwards. Such lukewarm efforts did not appeal. She'd *liked* the aggressive glide of Gage's palm over her nipple, the somewhat rough squeeze of his big hand as he'd cupped her. Did that mean she was not delicate? Probably.

'Of course not, Lord Markham. I didn't take the comment as such,' Zara assured him with a smile. Markham was usually a very collected fellow, not given to misspoken words and the need for apology. A foot *sans* shoe made contact with her ankle beneath the table and began to work its way up her skirt. She fought the urge to jump. She didn't need to look to know the foot belonged to Kael and he was trying to provoke a response. But two could play that game. She slid her foot out of her slipper and walked her toes up his calf, more than gratified when he had difficulty swallowing his wine.

The next course came and she pressed her advantage, taking a rather wicked bite of fresh asparagus, but Kael merely grinned and when no one was looking, mouthed the words, *not rebellious.*

And it wasn't. She had yet to declare her independence to anyone but herself; Markham was tongue-tied in her presence, a sure sign he had staked his hopes on making this match, and Kael Gage had his foot up her skirts. Things were getting serious. She had to get serious too.

Chapter Five

Monday June 16th
Brockmore Manor House Party

Programme of Events
Masterclass in the Acrobatic Arts to be
held in the Ballroom
Expedition to a Mystery Beauty Spot
Musical Evening with Recitations and
Recitals from the guests

The girls were all giggling by the time Zara arrived at the acrobatic exhibition the following morning, each of them dressed in split skirts for easier mobility and excitedly ogling the gentlemen across the ballroom. The gentlemen too had stripped down for the activity, an act that required more courage from some of them than others. Her eye went immediately to Kael, who wore breeches splendidly, showing off well-muscled calves as he stretched in warm up. But others like Melton Colter could be kindly characterised as 'slender' in build.

Katerina Vengarov gathered the women around her and began offering instructions. The ladies would be allowed to attempt some juggling while the gentlemen would get to try tumbling. Zara thought tumbling looked like more fun, all that twisting and turning of one's body, and testing one's strength. Only Colonel Fergus Kennedy and Kael seemed to be having moderate successes. In fact, it looked like so much fun, she was having trouble concentrating on her juggling. She dropped the balls yet again.

Katerina hurried over with a laugh. 'Miss Titus, you have to pay attention to your skittles!' In a low voice she added, 'And less attention to the fine men over there, although I know it can be hard.' Katerina gave her a conspiratorial glance and Zara noted Katerina's own gaze drifted towards Colonel Kennedy more often than not. 'Which one is yours?' Katerina gave her a friendly smile.

'Oh, none of them are mine,' Zara said, flustered at the bold question.

Katerina bent to pick up the skittles. 'Surely one of them is? Don't be shy, we all know the purpose of this party.'

It would be easy to confide in this pretty Russian girl, but Zara didn't dare. Who knew what tales might get carried to the duke's ear; the girl was in his employ. Zara opted for her tried-and-true strategy of another smile. A smile could mask so many things. 'Perhaps there's one or two I might consider.' Zara said with an air of mystery. It seemed to satisfy Katerina.

'Well then, I will leave you to your "juggling", as it were.'

Juggling didn't hold her attention for long. Verity Fairholme was having far more success and Zara's competitive nature couldn't stand to be so obviously bested by her long-time rival. She found it more interesting to watch others. Colonel Kennedy had come over to compliment Verity only to receive yet another cold shoulder, an apparent repeat of last night's brush-off during cards. Jeremy Giltner's posturing indicated he was spending most of the time pretending not to know Catherine Downing was looking at him.

Zara let her own eyes do some drifting of their own back to Kael, who was doing a trick called a round-off which required his body to do a turning handstand in motion. His shirt had come out of his waistband, showing off the firm muscles of his abdomen. He caught her stare and grinned. He put a hand to his head, discreetly miming a headache and pointed to her, nodding his head towards the open doors leading outside.

Ah, she was to feign a headache and excuse herself. Brilliant. Zara smiled her response and headed over to murmur her apologies to Katerina before slipping out the French doors and into the gardens. Kael joined her ten agonisingly long minutes later.

'I'm not interrupting your fun?' she queried, scolding him a bit for having taken so long.

'*You* are my fun.' Kael caught her about the waist and swung her around in a circle. She gave a gasp of surprise. No one had swung her about since she was a little girl. 'Besides,' he said, setting her down, 'Alexandr Vengarov is a show-off, not a teacher. He's more interested in preening before the ladies.' Kael snorted. 'He doesn't have a chance with any of them, if that's what he's after. I'm not sure it is. I think he just likes being admired by anyone.'

'Why wouldn't he have a chance? I am sure a

lot of girls find him attractive. You aren't jealous, are you?' Zara teased. Kael had been rather hard on the Russian acrobat and Zara felt compelled to take up the standard on his behalf.

'It's not so much about him as it is the ladies present,' Kael clarified. 'They're all practical sorts at the end of the day. They might admire his body from a distance but that's all.' There was derision in that comment directed at the girls who wouldn't break the mould of delicate womanhood for the sake of adventure. The realisation emboldened Zara. Frankly, she wanted to break the mould. She *wanted* to please Kael, to be wild for him and for herself.

'I hate moulds. I detest being crammed into one, like being stuffed into someone else's clothes.'

Kael's hands rested at her waist, unwilling to release her. 'Is that why you came out here? To break some moulds?' He gave her a wicked smile, his voice low in sensual invitation. She knew what he wanted her to say.

Zara tried some daring of her own. She wrapped her arms around his neck, revelling in the ease with which she touched him. 'I came out because I wanted more of yesterday.' It was true. She wanted more of the adventure he'd offered her. How liberating it was to speak her mind without worrying about offending someone or showing herself in a poor light.

'Not here.' Kael whispered. 'Come with me.'

It turned out the Duke of Brockmore's estate was brimming with buildings one could sneak off to: a pinery, an orchid house, the boathouse, the summerhouse, the carriage house by the stables and, of course, that delightful little cottage on the island. They opted, however, for the maze.

'Aren't you afraid we'll get lost?' Zara laughed as Kael led her through the turns.

'Would you mind?' He was flirting with her and she loved it. No one, not even Haymore, had flirted with her before. Good girls were too delicate for teasing.

'I wouldn't mind being lost, but I *would* mind being found.' If they had to call out to be rescued, there would be no explaining why they were in the maze together. It would be one way of settling the question of her future. She studied Kael's broad shoulders. Would the duke make her marry Kael if they were caught? Would Kael do it? He wasn't the sort to play anyone's puppet. Ruined reputation or not, he didn't strike her as a man who would marry a girl just because someone told him to, even if that someone was a duke.

A shiver went through her. If that was true, then Kael Gage was the most rakish man she'd ever been in contact with. Her reputation was in real danger when she was alone with him and yet she was not afraid. She definitely didn't feel fear when she was with him. She felt excitement. She liked being with him.

'Don't worry,' he assured her. 'It's all right turns to the centre. We should almost be there.' On cue, the centre of the maze came into sight, decorated with a giant statue of Atlas and a bench to view the artwork from.

'How did you know it was all right turns?' Zara asked. She would have been hopelessly lost.

'It seems like something the duke would do.' Kael grinned. 'A subtle reminder that he is always "right", just like Atlas here is no doubt meant to be some symbolism of the duke's power. He carries the weight of the world on his shoulders.' Kael made a wide gesture with his arms and laughed.

'That's a fairly arrogant interpretation of things.' Zara wandered the perimeter of the centre, looking up at the statue, aware that Kael had stopped by the bench and followed her with his eyes. He was not bothered by her argument. He merely shrugged and mounted his defence.

'The duke is a fairly arrogant man. Everything at this party is designed to have us jumping at his behest. Think about it, it's all like a labour of Hercules, all of us jumping through hoops in order to be able to claim our prize. We began with the conversational trials, if you will, at the boaters' luncheon—our first opportunity to test the waters. Today was the physical trials, in case you didn't guess. How often do you get a sanctioned opportunity to appear in dishabille in front of the female guests at a house party? Tonight, the musicale will be an obvious test of genteel talent for male and female alike. The week will be full of such trials. All the activities are designed to showcase attributes someone may want a spouse to possess.'

'Are you always this cynical?' Zara stopped her perambulation of the little square in front of the bench where Kael sprawled.

'I'm always this *honest*.'

Zara cocked her head and offered him a coy smile. 'All right, let's test your hypothesis. Why did we tour the gardens and the stables then, separately?'

'That's easy.' His dark eyes danced. 'There is always the reminder to each of us that the duke is the one with the power. Why was the theme for last night's dinner "The sustainability of the Brockmore estate"? I assure you, it *wasn't* done without purpose.'

'I knew the party was all matchmaking, but I'd never thought of all those details being so deliberately designed.' She suddenly felt naïve, she who had thought she'd so expertly navigated the *ton* for three years. It was quite a web the duke had spun. She reached for Kael's hand and pulled him up. 'I didn't come out here to talk about the duke. I believe I mentioned already that I came out here because I wanted more of yesterday.' An escape from that intricate web of matchmaking, a glimpse of what freedom could bring, what it could *feel* like.

Kael's hands were at her hips, a position that was becoming welcome and familiar. She liked the feel of his hands on her. 'You are a greedy miss, Zara Titus.' He laughed, obliging her with a kiss. She took advantage of having him in dishabille to run her hands beneath the loose folds of his shirt, feeling the hard planes of his body against her palms.

'We can do more than this, Zara.' he whispered against her ear as her hands moved over the flats of his nipples. 'We don't have to settle for stolen kisses and the press of clothed bodies. Come with me this afternoon. Skip the mystery tour and we'll make our own. Meet me at the pinery after lunch.'

She answered before she could think. 'Yes.'

Lunch was something of a trial all its own. Zara hated, positively *hated,* watching Kael with Ariana Falk. It was the third time they'd been paired together and it did make Zara wonder. Was Kael really here just to escape some unpleasant situation in London? Did he entertain hopes of snaring Ariana as a bride? Was she merely an attraction on the side while he pursued something more serious with Ariana? Jealousy stabbed hard when he handed Ariana her dropped napkin. Was he meeting her in secret too? All these questions made it difficult to concentrate on Markham's attentions. Markham was disappointed to hear she wouldn't be on the mystery tour. But that was nothing compared to her mother's concern. Zara didn't think she'd ever convince her mother to go on the tour without her. 'You can keep an eye on Markham,' Zara finally suggested. The idea that her mother could somehow be her representative in pursuit of Markham won the day at last.

Being bad certainly took a lot of work. She was, horror of horrors, *sweating* by the time she reached the pinery. Kael was already there, waiting in the humid interior. 'Trouble with your mother?' he drawled knowingly.

She was hot and the remark made her prickly. It made her sound as if she were a child tied to her parent's apron strings. *Which you sort of are.* She didn't care for the reminder even if it was true. 'I was concerned *you* might have trouble leaving Miss Falk,' she snapped.

Kael seized her around the waist and drew her close, his mouth pressing hard to hers, his words a primal growl. 'There is only you, Zara.'

They did not stay at the pinery. Instead, they sought a cooler sanctuary along the river. 'I found a swimming hole on my morning ride,' Kael announced proudly. 'Just perfect for a hot afternoon like this.'

The entendre was not lost on her and she shivered in spite of the heat. Kael wasted no time in pulling off his boots and socks. He dragged his shirt over his head and tossed it aside with easy abandon, comfortable in the baring of his body. He turned towards her, letting her look her fill. 'Zara, I don't mean to swim in my clothes.'

Zara gave him a coy smile. 'Good. Neither do I.'

Chapter Six

He loved it when she talked like that, showing him the bold woman inside the lady. Kael held her eyes as he shoved his trousers over his hips, revealing himself fully to her as her gaze travelled the length of him, stopping to rest on his core. Her hazel eyes went wide with appreciation and he felt uniquely pleased that she found him so well endowed. It had been a long time since a woman had looked at him in fascination. There was something empowering and potent about being a woman's first. He'd forgotten how that felt.

He hadn't been a woman's first anything for quite a while, in part because the sort of woman he consorted with hadn't had firsts for ages and in part because innocence was a messy business. He didn't have time for tears, regrets or unfulfilled expectations—mainly marriage proposals that failed to materialised. Experienced women knew the rules, innocent girls did not. Zara Titus was somewhere in between—innocent most certainly, but not unapprised of the rules. It made her exciting. How far would she go?

Kael crossed his arms over his bare chest. 'Now it's your turn.'

She gave him a coy smile. 'You'll have to help. Dresses are not as easily discarded as trousers and shirts.'

He took up a position behind her, his fingers working the laces of her gown. He had the dress off in record time. This disrobing was not a seduction. He wanted her in the water as quickly as possible. She did hesitate once her dress pooled at her feet, her fingers stalling on the lacy straps of her chemise.

Kael dropped a kiss on her shoulder. 'Don't be skittish now, Zara. You will be beautiful to me, have no worries.' He helped her with the undergarments, his hands encouraging hers until she was naked too. Zara turned slowly, shyly, to face him, but there was boldness in her too. She made no effort to hide herself with crossed arms or discreetly placed hands. Kael sucked in his breath, his voice hoarse as he took in the round fullness of breasts, high and firm, set atop a trim torso that flared into softly curving hips and surprisingly long legs. 'Venus rising from the sea could not be more lovely.' Zara Titus was gorgeous in her gowns, but out of them she exceeded stunning. When was the last time a woman had stolen his breath? It seemed to be a day for firsts.

Kael drew her to him, taking her mouth in a kiss, their bodies naked against one another at last. He lifted her in his arms and carried her to the water. 'You do know how to swim, right?' he murmured as the water rose over his thighs and tickled the cascade of her hair hanging over his arm.

She laughed. 'Yes. Lucky for you.'

He set her down, steadying her until her feet found the silty river floor, and then he executed a shallow dive and swam away. She shouted her disappointment after him and he laughed. 'If you want me, come and get me.' To his great pleasure, she dove into the water and came after him. This was what he wanted—to play, to have some fun with her, and once they were relaxed and cool, they would play a different game.

They swam and splashed, and occasionally

shouted when they dunked one another. They tried the rope that was tied to a sturdy tree branch, Zara screaming her delight the whole time. 'I've never done anything like that!' She laughed as she came up sputtering from her drop. 'Let's do it again.' She raced him up the bank, winning handily after elbowing him in the gut. They swung on the rope until the river bank was slick with muddy footprints.

'Oof!' Zara slipped in the mud, going down hard, her rather lush rear end, which he'd been judiciously watching go up and down the bank, landing in a puddle. Kael laughed. It was a mistake. 'You think it's funny?' Zara looked up at him. 'Do you think *this* is funny?' She flung a handful of mud at him, catching him in the chest.

It was war then. She scrambled to her feet, inelegantly clawing her way to the rope swing, evading his hands as he grabbed for her ankles. But she couldn't escape him for ever. He caught her in the shallows and the mudslinging continued until they were both a mess.

'Pax!' Zara cried, shaking mud off her hands. 'We both need a bath.'

'We're in the perfect place for it.' Kael set down his muddy ammunition. 'Truce, Zara.' He held out his hand and drew her out into deeper waters, watching the water climb up her legs, cover her to the waist. 'If I was a painter, I'd call this Venus submerging.'

She wrapped her arms about his neck and laughed, her eyes dancing. 'I'd call it Poseidon seducing a water nymph. Or on second thought, maybe I'd just call it "the mud bathers".'

'I like the first one better. More flattering.' Kael grimaced. 'Mud bathers? Really?' Whatever they called it, it was the most erotic bath he could recall taking, probably because *she* was bathing him.

Zara cupped her hands to scoop up the water and make a shower of it over his head after he'd taken a dunk to get off most of the mud. She ran her fingers through his hair, catching any chunks of dirt, her hands moving on to his chest. She scrubbed in circles, her palms running over his nipples and down his torso to his hips, his body coming alive in the wake of her stroke. Every place she touched was alight and eager for more. 'I love your hands on me,' he rumbled against her ear. 'The only thing I could love better would be my hands on you.'

He was seducing her now, no woman would

mistake it for a simple bath, not the way he dripped water over her breasts, the way his hands lingered in her hair or the way he carried her to shore and laid her on the blankets. And she was ready for it, he saw the desire flicker in her eyes. The afternoon had been marvellous, a wicked adventure. To swim naked with a man was daring beyond imagining, but her body was primed now for something more and, heaven help him, so was his, but the choice had to be hers.

Kael stretched out, naked and long beside her, his head propped in his hand as he drew circles on her belly. 'In the maze, when you told me we could have more than stolen kisses, I had no idea you meant swimming nude,' she prompted, her voice husky.

Kael laughed, his dark hair dripping a slow rivulet on her breast. 'What a leading comment, Miss Titus. One would think seeing a naked man wasn't enough for you.' It would have been more than enough for any of the innocent misses back at the party.

'What if I said it wasn't?' Her face turned towards him, her tone serious, her eyes a dark green and full of desire. 'What if I told you the sight of you only makes me want more.'

Kael groaned a warning. 'Careful, Zara. I am no saint.'

Their eyes met and held. She was in earnest. 'I don't want to be careful. I've been careful my whole life and look what it's got me. A broken engagement and a scandal, the two things a "careful" girl is supposed to avoid. As for saints, Haymore was supposed to be one and we all know how that turned out.' There was remorse and anger in those words.

'How did it turn out, Zara? The real story, not the one society has been told?' Kael asked, his voice quiet. She might not have loved Haymore, but his desertion had marked her. 'The best way to move past something is to tell someone,' he said when she remained silent. 'Whatever it is, it will be safe with me. I don't tell secrets.'

Zara sighed, her face turning upwards again to the sky peeping through the leafy boughs of the trees. 'It's not even that big a secret. He cried off because he loved another.' She huffed out a breath. 'There's nothing wrong with that. He came to the house and asked to speak with me. He told me he wanted to be honest. He couldn't marry me because he wanted to marry someone else, a Miss Elise Brighten, who lived near his family's home in the country. They'd grown up together and their feelings had turned from friendship into something more. He said it wouldn't be fair to marry me under the circumstances.'

'He was right,' Kael put in quietly. 'Why would you want a man who wanted another? Who viewed you as nothing more than a duty?'

'That's what I tell myself. I should be grateful Haymore was so thoughtful. He saved us from a life of misery.' Zara shook her head. 'But it's not completely fair.'

'How so?' Kael played with her wet hair, combing a strand with his fingers.

'He loved *her*. He didn't love me. Why couldn't he love me?' Her voice rose, a little shrill before she brought it under control. 'I'm pretty, I'm rich and well connected. I'm everything he was supposed to want in a wife. I'd been *raised* for him, like a prized cow.' The hurt was starting to show, maybe for the first time.

'You are not a cow,' Kael soothed. Haymore was an absolute fool not to love her with her passion for living, for swimming naked in the summer, for slinging mud patties and jumping off rope swings. There was so much more to her than a pretty face. 'Do you know the expression "love is blind"? Have you thought about what it means? It means love doesn't care about those things, about money or titles or looks. Love chooses indiscriminately. We can't help it.' It wasn't necessarily an answer to her question. It was quite beyond him why Haymore didn't love her. He pressed a kiss to her cheek. 'If I was Haymore, I'd love you.'

She shook her head, not quite believing him. 'It's easy for you to say, you've never been thrown over.'

Kael stilled. 'Who says I haven't been jilted?'

'Why would anyone not want you? You're handsome and amusing and, well, you know. You have a way about you that makes a girl crave your company.' She was blushing, her teeth catching her bottom lip.

'Crave my company, eh?' He flashed her a brief smile. He'd never told anyone about that one romantic disaster. That rejection had been personal, it had stung. Just as Zara's had and perhaps it would ease her pain if she understood she wasn't alone. His smiled faded. 'You will be surprised to know, then, that I was jilted once too. Let's say you're right and I am handsome and have a way with women, and what else was I? Amusing? Let's say I am all those things. Now let me tell you, they weren't enough, not for the girl I loved. She needed more. She needed money, and a title and fine gowns, none of which I can offer a wife.'

'I'm sorry.' Zara's brow creased in sincere regret. 'I didn't mean to joke earlier.' Her hand moved idly on his chest. She tossed her dark hair back and looked at him with her head cocked, a smile starting on her lips. 'It would be enough for me, Kael. I don't need a man with a title, with a lot of money. A handsome, amusing man would be quite enough, a dream actually.'

Kael smiled. 'It's nice of you to say so.' It was kind of her to offer the words, but she couldn't possibly mean them or understand them. She'd been raised to privilege and whether she thought she had them or not, Zara had expectations. She'd never had to do without things. In the long run, she'd tire of having to help Cook with the meals or seeing to some of the housework. And she'd tire of him, the man who had brought her so low. But his heart was safe this time, as it was every time he took a high-born woman to bed, because now he understood what he had to offer and what a woman really wanted. They were not the same thing.

He moved over her then, kissing her nose, her jaw, her mouth, her breasts, the trail going lower, his tongue tasting the river water on her skin. He blew against her navel and her body arched ever so slightly in appreciation. His hands framed her hips and he put his mouth on her mons, blowing softly into her damp curls, a soft sound of satisfaction escaping her as she breathed his name.

'Kael.' Had any piece of wickedness felt as good as his mouth against her? Somewhere in her mind, she knew she ought to be appalled, a man's mouth on her most private area. But there was no shame in this. This was heaven indeed, to feel the summer breeze drift over her, warm and soft and to feel the echo of it in her lover's breath.

'Open for me, Zara,' he whispered and she did, feeling the caress of his tongue on her, in her, as it slid over the tiny, hidden nub. She did moan then, it was not a sound that resembled soft satisfaction now, but pleasure. That pleasure mounted with each touch, each stroke. How had she not known such a feeling was possible, that her body was capable of *this*? She felt worldly and innocent all at once. She was greedy for more. Her hips rose to meet him, encouraging his efforts and he gave them until the intensity overwhelmed her and all she could do was cry her release to the summer sky.

It didn't take Zara long to realise the problem with pleasure was that it was addictive. Once had, one would always want more. She lay against Kael's chest, her head lodged at the notch of his shoulder as if it was made for that place. Her hand played idly on his chest. 'Is it like that every time?' She was drowsy—too sleepy to worry about being proper or modest.

'Technically, it can be. Every woman has a pleasure centre.' Kael sounded drowsy too.

She laughed. 'But not every man is skilled in waking it?' She sighed against him. 'I never knew it had a purpose. Hmm. I wonder why no one ever tells you such a thing. It's far too fabulous to be kept a secret.'

'Perhaps the fabulousness is the reason no one tells you.' Kael's voice was full of humorous exaggeration. 'Can you imagine what parties would turn into if debutantes knew? Every alcove would be filled. It would be a scandal.'

A thought came to her. 'Do you have an equivalent?' It would be sad to think such pleasure was only available to females.

Kael's eyes challenged her. 'You can stroke me into release.'

'I can?' Zara smiled, her hand slipping between them. It closed over the length of him, hot and pulsing beneath her touch. She watched his eyes catch fire and she began to move, her hand running the length of him slowly at first, deliberately, feeling each inch of him; the long ridge, the tender tip. His body tensed and her stroke quickened as he arched.

'Zara, you're going to kill me!' The words came out through gritted teeth as he bucked. She felt his body tighten and gather itself, watched him give a violent jerk in her hand, becoming a living fountain in her grip.

'Oh, my…' she breathed, cognisant that she'd witnessed something beautiful and powerful. It was by far the most intimate experience she'd ever had, rivalling even what Kael had done to her. 'That was amazing.' It occurred to her that perhaps it was amazing because holding a man during his crisis was indeed extraordinarily intimate, but maybe it was amazing too because of what they'd shared.

'It certainly was.' He chuckled and found the strength to sit up, but despite his joke, his eyes were solemn. It had moved him too, maybe even frightened him, something she would not have believed possible, but that was before she'd heard his story. He'd loved once, given his all once to a woman and been found lacking. It threw what she knew of him into sharp relief. He was a rogue out of necessity, out of the need to protect himself. It was far easier to seek affairs with those who would not demand his emotional availability only to trample on it later. They were far less risky too.

She understood, in her own way. Haymore was like that: safe, not risky. Haymore had been comfortable, not asking too much from her. He had not challenged her emotions. When he'd left her, he'd left her exposed. The loss of Haymore had forced her to challenge her assumptions and to embrace new ideas, even if they were bound not to be popular. Her life was on the line. 'We're alike, you and I,' Zara murmured the thought as it came to her.

'Hmmm? How's that?' Kael sounded dreamy, content.

'We're more vulnerable than people realise, all

they see is the strong outer shell. They don't see what matters, what lies beneath the clothes, the façade of confidence.' She sighed. 'Not even my parents see it.'

Kael played with her hair, a soft soothing gesture as they exchanged secrets in the late afternoon. 'You'll have to tell them then, before it's too late.' She shook her head against his shoulder.

'They'd have a fit, especially my mother. She'd probably fall over on the spot.' Zara gave a wry, short laugh. She couldn't imagine doing it, but she'd have to if she ever meant to be truly free. Freedom was hard. She hadn't realised how hard until she'd embarked on this course. It made the man beside her all the more impressive. He'd eschewed convention and survived it. She could too.

They lingered by the swimming hole for a while longer, lying in each other's arms in silence, letting the breeze blow over them, letting their bodies dry, letting their minds forget they had to go back. 'I could stay here for ever,' she murmured, snuggling against him. 'I would never have to dress for dinner again, never have to impress a room, never have to be the most beautiful girl at a party.'

'Don't you like those things?' Kael asked, raising his head to look at her.

'My mother likes those things,' Zara clarified. 'Do you know what I want? I've not told anyone. I want to live in the country and ride astride, in trousers. The other girls in London would laugh if they knew.'

'Then they're not real friends,' Kael consoled.

Zara gave a laugh. 'I never thought they were. A girl like me doesn't have friends, she has rivals.' She paused, thoughtful. 'How do you do it, Kael? How do you let go of all of this and follow your own path?'

He was slow to answer. For a moment, she thought he wouldn't. 'Zara, you took a great risk in coming here today,' he began. 'Was it worth it?'

She rolled to her side and levered up on an arm to look at him, wanting him to see her when she spoke. 'Yes. I would do it again.' It had been worth it, not just the physical exploration of a man's body, but the exploration of a man's soul. Not just any man's soul, but his. The soul of Kael Gage.

He smiled, his dark eyes soft and thoughtful when they looked at her. 'Then remember how you feel right now, remember how you felt today, whenever it seems easier to give up your dreams than to fight for them.' He covered her hand with his. 'Zara, *this* is what freedom feels like and it is worth the price.'

Zara nodded, emotion threatening to choke her words. No one had ever spoken to her like that. There were depths to this man and they intrigued her even beyond the physical pleasure he could offer. She could lie here for hours, listening to him talk about life, about what mattered. Whatever else happened, Kael had given her a great gift today; he'd shown her a piece of himself and in doing so he'd shown her part of herself as well. Most of all, he'd shown her she was not alone.

Chapter Seven

A summons to the duke's study was waiting for him in his room when Kael got back. The promptness of it struck him as a little eerie. The summons was already on his pillow and his hair wasn't even dry yet. It made him wonder how many eyes the duke had on his property. It also made him wonder just how much the duke knew.

Kael made his way to the study, following the map that had been left in all the bedchambers so guests would feel at home. He mentally selected and discarded opening lines. How did he want to start this conversation, since he wasn't sure if this summons was about the swimming hole or if it was simply the duke calling in his marker for allowing him to be here? Kael decided on flattery. Flattery never hurt and it almost always helped.

The duke's private study was set at the back of

the house and commanded an outstanding view of the wide south lawn and the lake beyond it. Kael noticed this because the duchess was sitting in front of the windows and her presence had drawn his immediate attention. He had not expected her to be here. He went to her straight away and bowed over her hand. 'I must thank you again for your hospitality.' He took the opportunity to flirt with his eyes. Even lovely women of a certain age appreciated a man's attention and the Duchess of Brockmore was definitely that.

'You're very welcome. We have plenty of room.' The duchess politely acknowledged his flirtatious efforts, but nothing more. There would be no help from that quarter.

The duke rose from his seat behind the imposing mahogany desk and came around the front to casually lean a hip against it. He gestured to a chair and urged Kael to take a seat. 'We're glad you are enjoying yourself. However, it is your first time with us and we wanted to make sure you were aware of certain nuances that make this party unique.' The duke smiled kindly, but Kael wasn't fooled. The duke might fancy himself the fatherly sort, but no one else did. 'Everyone here is intended for someone else here.'

The duchess took over smoothly. 'We merely provide a neutral place for these couples to meet and to enjoy activities together in order to decide if they do indeed suit one another.' That was an understatement. Kael thought her description better fit a zoo where one had a chance to see the species in their natural habitat.

The duke cleared his throat. 'As her Grace has said, everyone is intended for someone. That includes Miss Zara Titus.' Now they were getting to the real issue. His blue eyes held Kael's, less fatherly than before. 'It has come to my attention that you have been spending considerable amounts of time with our Miss Titus.' That made it pretty clear whose protection she was under.

Kael crossed a leg over his knee and leaned back in his chair, waiting. 'Yes, I have. She's a delightful, beautiful woman who captivates any number of men.' He shifted in his seat. His body still throbbed with the reminder of how she'd 'captivated' him this afternoon.

'That may be.' The duke gave him a polite smile. 'But she is intended for one man and that is Lord Markham.' His words were loaded with steel.

The duchess broke in. 'Mr Gage, it's just that

young girls are very impressionable, easily confused. Her mother was most aggrieved. You need to know that Miss Titus is extremely vulnerable right now.' Kael fought back a snort. Zara? Vulnerable? Hardly. If they'd seen her at the swimming hole, vulnerable wouldn't be a word that came to mind. On the other hand, it was probably best they hadn't.

'What if she doesn't prefer Markham?' Kael asked, his challenge surprising Brockmore. The man was not used to having his decisions gainsaid.

Brockmore offered him a tight smile of patience. 'As men of experience, it is our job to make sure she does. Markham is an excellent choice and, in years to come, she'll be thankful the choice was made.'

Some women might. Not Zara. He'd only known her two days and he knew that much was true. Kael kept his tone cool. 'What about Jeremy Giltner? Is she to be given no choice at all?'

'Giltner is better suited to Catherine Downing, Markham's sister,' the duke explained. 'He aspires to be an MP and there's a seat open in Markham's borough. Who better to take it than the marquis's own brother-in-law?' The duke smiled, clearly pleased with the arrangement. Why wouldn't he be? Kael could see the advantages. The match would give the duke another seat in Parliament to influence and a marquis in his debt. 'Giltner is over the moon about it. When they return to London, their match will be touted as the romance of the Season, a whirlwind affair.' The duke winked. 'Constituents love a good romance. This will endear the already charming Mr Giltner to the people all the more. Who knows, maybe some day he might make higher office.' It was a cautionary tale and a bribe all at once. The duke had the power to force one's hand. Kael felt a primal urge to protect rise, not for himself but for Zara. He didn't want Zara forced.

The duchess rose with a fond look for her husband. 'Now that's settled, I must go and check the menus for supper tonight. Please excuse me.'

Brockmore waited until his wife was gone. It was time to get down to business, man to man. 'It *is* settled, isn't it?' Brockmore asked bluntly. His wife would be disappointed if it was not. 'May I have your word that you'll leave Miss Titus alone?'

'I am not one of your aspiring protégés,' Gage replied with a degree of insouciance that surprised him. No one denied him, hadn't denied him for years. 'I don't need your plums. I can do as I please.' Gage gave him an assessing stare that rivalled one of his own as the man began to pace, laying out his argument. 'I am already ruined by society's definition—a man with no prospects beyond a gentleman's modest horse farm in Sussex. There is nothing you can take from me. Neither is there anything you can give me. I have no ambitions like Jeremy Giltner.'

Gage had nerve, Brockmore would give him that. At the moment, Gage thought he had bested him. The duke fought back a smile. He'd let the man savour his victory for a minute. It wouldn't last longer than that. Gage had made a mistake if he thought he had nothing of value. Everyone had something. Still, he was impressed with a man who would stand up to him so boldly. Perhaps there was more to Gage than met the eye.

Brockmore crossed his arms. 'Let's be blunt, Mr Gage. Every man has something to lose and you do too. I know about your sister, Adeline. I know that she doesn't see anyone any more, literally.' He watched the shock move across Gage's face before the man could master it. He hated doing it this way, hated seeing Gage realise his efforts had failed, but a man like Gage had to be dealt with the way an alpha wolf dealt with mavericks in a pack.

He knew from his own research how hard Gage worked to keep his sister private, separate from his life in London and safe. For the most part, Gage had been successful. Few people knew he had a sister. It explained why Gage's rather scandalous behaviours never touched her. No one knew it could or should. To all but a few who knew him, Gage was a lone wolf with no real family. Even fewer knew about her disability. A fever had stolen her sight over the last two years. She was completely blind now.

'My sister is well, your Grace.' Gage was tense now, watching, waiting for him to strike, alert that something was afoot, but he was not entirely on the defensive yet. He wasn't afraid to fight, which was admirable even if it was annoying. The duke was used to people crumbling at the first sign of pressure. 'My sister walks to the village, she works with all her charities. She is quite self-sufficient.'

'I am sure she is,' Brockmore said congenially. 'Thanks to you. You can create her self-sufficiency with your income and your nearness.

She lives in your home, doesn't she? You pay her bills? It might be a bit harder to help her sustain that independence should you be exiled to France.' He had Gage cornered. This should be the end game, but Brockmore found himself wondering what the man would do. Gage had surprised him thoroughly already.

'If I don't leave Zara Titus alone, you will exile me from England?' Gage paraphrased coolly.

'I am not entirely heartless. You do have a choice.' The duke held up his hands and gave a chuckle. 'If you ignore my dictates and publicly compromise Miss Titus, you could always marry her. Markham would be disappointed, but perhaps I could find Markham another. I would make it worth your while; a match for your sister, a financially secure gentleman who can provide her the servants she needs to live her self-sufficient life.' It was the one thing Gage was unable to provide for his sister—a match. Brockmore studied him, watching for signs of defeat and acceptance; a slouch of the shoulders, the lowering of the eyes.

But Kael got to his feet, his gaze direct and stormy. 'I am not going to sit here and be bribed into complicity.'

'Come now, it's hardly a bribe. Consider it a wedding gift. Don't tell me the idea of marrying Zara yourself hasn't crossed your mind. She's rich and you need the money. She's beautiful and well connected. You can't pretend she doesn't tempt you and you certainly tempt her. You might as well maximise your take and get something for your sister as well out of it.'

Brockmore waited, counting a long ten seconds in his head as silence stretched between them. 'You want to tell me to go to hell, don't you, Gage? You want to tell me that you're no man's puppet.' He gave a rueful smile. 'But you can't. You have something to lose after all. It's one thing to burn bridges for yourself, especially if you're a man. But it's another thing to burn bridges for someone else, especially if that someone is Adeline.'

Brockmore pushed off his desk with a fatherly smile. It was all settled now, as he knew it would be. 'I see we understand each other, Gage. It's a good man who looks out for his sister.' He clapped a hand on Gage's shoulder, ushering him towards the door. Gage was interesting, but his allotted time was up. There were other men to massage into compliance waiting to be seen.

Brockmore smiled and lowered his voice. 'One more thing, Gage. No more swimming holes with my female guests. You were lucky today. You won't be again.' He winked. 'I have eyes and ears everywhere, Gage.' At the door he paused, his hand still on Gage's shoulder. 'Are you racing on Thursday? I hear your stallion, Merlin, is a prime goer.'

'I thought to,' Gage replied neutrally.

'You should. There are prizes that might interest you: breeding rights with my stallion or a pick of new foals next year.' Brockmore smiled. Gage couldn't quite hide the light of interest in his eyes.

Brockmore watched him leave. The party was certainly getting interesting. The Titus girl was perfect for Markham and Markham was doing his part. But Zara didn't seem to be reciprocating with the predicted enthusiasm. Her mother had assured him Zara would do the practical thing, but after the last few days, Brockmore was no longer sure she would. She seemed attracted to Gage, who was entirely unsuitable for her, but he could change that. Zara's own father could change that. A few words in the right ears and Gage could be respectable. Her dowry would make him wealthy. Then again, perhaps it was just Gage's image as an outsider that drew her in at the moment. How deep did her attraction run?

Brockmore chuckled to himself and signalled for his next appointment. This was an intriguing little game he'd set in motion by giving Zara Titus a choice. Would she pick Gage or Markham? Would Gage play the game? If he did, the rewards would be great. In his opinion, Gage couldn't afford not to play, but then again, Gage had shown himself to be his own man more than any man here. Brockmore winced and amended his thought. Except for Fergus Kennedy, who was proving to be a downright independent pain in the arse. Their last exchange had bordered on angry and he was not looking forward to their next. Matchmaking was getting harder every year. Maybe he was getting too old for this. He laughed at the thought. Never. This was what he thrived on: the business of love.

Her mother was angrier than she let on. Zara saw it in her movements as she paced the floor of the bedroom. The usually calm Lady Aberforth was *furious*. 'You were with *him*!' Of course that was her mother's biggest concern, not that her daughter had lied to her, but that she'd been with an unsuitable gentleman. Zara secretly thought if she'd sneaked out to meet Markham, her mother wouldn't be carrying on. Then again, Markham would never agree to such a thing.

Zara sat on the bed, looking at her hands and feeling embarrassingly like a recalcitrant five-year-old caught stealing biscuits from the kitchen. She couldn't deny it. Her hair was wet. She'd thought to dry it when she'd returned, but her mother had been waiting for her. 'Yes, I was with him.' Why deny it? She didn't want to. Kael's words, 'the price is worth it', were still strong in her mind, the feel of his hand over hers as he'd talked of the beauty and price of freedom. In her heart, she knew Kael would be proud of those five words. They were her first public assertion of rebellion. Now, someone knew what she'd been up to.

Her mother stopped pacing and drew a deep breath. She faced Zara, her expression hard. Her tone was matter of fact. 'What do you know of Mr Gage? Nothing! Because there is nothing to know, nothing worthwhile. While you've been out playing, I've been gathering information. Brockmore tells me he owns a small horse farm and a cottage in Sussex. He is a horse breeder, a minor country gentleman, Zara.' She said the words with horror as if he carried a contagious disease. 'You have been dallying with a man who might as well be a *commoner*.'

'He didn't tell me.' Zara smiled dreamily. A horse farm sounded heavenly. Why hadn't he told her when she'd mentioned how much she wanted to ride? 'I love horses.'

'Of course he didn't tell you,' her mother spat out. 'It's so embarrassing to admit to it. He probably thought you would have nothing more to do with him. And rightly so.' The viscountess's eyes narrowed, her hands on slim hips. 'He is so far beneath you, Zara, his unsuitability should be obvious. He's not one of us.'

'That is unfair!' Zara snapped, her head coming up. She would take her scold for disobedience because, while it had been worth it for an afternoon alone with Kael, it was simply true. She'd broken her word and lied to her mother about her headache. But she would not sit here and let her mother malign Kael. 'Just because he doesn't have as much money as we do doesn't mean he isn't a good man.'

Her mother gave a harsh laugh. 'Stop being

naïve, Zara. Do you know why he's here at all?' It was a rhetorical question only. Her mother went on to provide an answer. 'He's here on the duke's good graces, as a favour to Jeremy Giltner. This is nothing more for him than a repairing lease from London because of potential scandal.' Zara caught her mother's knowing sideways glance. 'I'm sure he didn't tell you that either.'

Her good feelings, her strength and conviction were starting to deflate, just a little. She stiffened her resolve. She would not let her mother crack her defences so soon, but it was hard to dispel doubts. What else hadn't Kael told her? 'What does it matter, it's not as if he's offering to marry me.' But what if he did? There would be more afternoons lying naked at the water's edge talking about life, not worrying about propriety. There would be more pleasure. He would be hers to look upon always, a man who encouraged her to chase her dreams, to take the invitations life offered, and he would look at her with those dark eyes the way he had today.

'That's right, dear, it doesn't matter, because it's over.' Her mother's declaration cut into her thoughts. She sat and took Zara's hand in her own, her tone softening. Zara knew what came next—the guilt. If anger and a scold failed to cajole an apology from her, this was her mother's second line of defence. It was a pattern Zara knew well over the years. It was also usually successful. Her mother would be surprised. For the first time, she would not capitulate, not to anger, not to guilt. Freedom would be stronger than both. It had to be. *You have to tell them before it's too late.* Kael was here with her, in her heart. She could be strong. No matter what he was or why he was here, he'd given her that.

Her mother drew a long breath. 'All right, my dear, you've had a little excitement. Kael Gage is a handsome man with a certain reputation. Your attraction to him and your curiosity are understandable. But it ends now. You were lucky you weren't caught today by anyone who would expose you. What if you had been? Is Gage prepared to offer for you? You just said yourself that he isn't. Even so, is that what you want? To throw yourself away on a man who can offer nothing after your father and I have given you everything? What can he possibly give you?'

Pleasure, understanding, awakening not just to passion but to herself. Today was not the day to make that particular argument, not when the imprint of Kael's touch, his mouth, were still fresh on her body, his words still burning in her mind. He could give her pleasure and she could give him the same. Her face gave her away. Her mother huffed.

'I know what you're thinking. No, don't roll your eyes at me, young lady. You're going to listen. You've had a few kisses, a few hot moments and he's got his hand into your bodice. You're thinking love, or what passes for it with a rogue like Gage, is enough to conquer the world with.'

Oh, good heavens! Zara's cheeks were on fire. This was absolutely the most embarrassing moment ever. It was even worse than the time her mother had explained her menses to her. Her mother, a viscount's wife known for her exquisite manners, parties and social diplomacy, was using phrases like hot moments and hands getting in bodices. What did her mother know about getting hot? Oh—oh, no, no, no. Now it really was worse! *Did* her mother know? Zara couldn't imagine her mother doing any of the things she'd done with Kael.

Her mother was not finished. 'Physical pleasure is not enough to make a marriage on. It will not feed you or clothe you, but it will, without a doubt, burn out and leave you with nothing.' Her mother's tone turned harsh. 'One must have a great deal more in a husband than skill in bed.'

'Mother!' Zara gasped.

'I'm sorry, Zara.' Her mother smiled and reached out to touch her cheek. 'I've shocked you. Remember, I was your age and in "love" once too. I know you're struggling over Haymore and wanting things society doesn't allow you. You are vulnerable. You want to make decisions, but you're not equipped to make them, not really. This is when you need to let yourself be guided by those who know what's best, not just for right now, but for twenty years from now, thirty years from now.' She squeezed Zara's hand. 'It will work out in the end. I know, I've been there. My parents saw me through and we'll see you through.'

'If there isn't love, what is there?' Zara challenged. She didn't want to disappoint her parents, but for the first time, it was more important she didn't disappoint herself.

'There's respect and it's a sight better than what passes for love any day,' her mother said sternly. 'Markham will give you plenty of that, Zara.' He would. Her mother was right. But he would never inspire great passion in her, never bring her to a shattering release that left her boneless, never swim naked with her in a river on a hot summer's day.

That was the problem. After today, she knew what she was giving up if she settled for Markham. Kael Gage had ruined her for 'nice' men, in theory. He might as well do it in practice. Her mother would be disappointed to learn of that decision. This conversation had been designed to warn her away from Gage, to remind her how unsuitable he was, and what her responsibility was, all with the intent of driving her towards Markham. But just the opposite had happened. It had solidified her resolve to hold on to Kael and whatever he offered for as long as he offered it, even if it was only for five days. Zara did not think her mother would appreciate the irony.

Chapter Eight

Wednesday June 18th
Brockmore Manor House Party

Programme of Events
A Morning of Strawberry-Picking
A Celebration in Honour of the
Second Anniversary of the
Illustrious Military Victory at Waterloo

Wellington was here! Zara and her mother entered the grand blue marine-themed drawing room on the stroke of seven to find that most of the guests were already assembled, everyone agog with excitement. Not even the extreme warmth of the room could wilt their enthusiasm. Zara had to admit to some small desire to see the famed hero of Waterloo, too.

This was the anniversary of Wellington's great

victory and the duke had arranged a special celebration, complete with requisite heroes. The volume in the room steadily rose, everyone eager to talk with the officers Brockmore had invited to take part in the celebration, many who would stay for the remainder of the house party.

Zara scanned the room. Wellington wasn't among the guests yet. Kael Gage was, however, looking resplendent in dark evening clothes, his hair pulled back in its usual fashion and a diamond stick pin winking in his cravat. Even in a room full of dashing men and uniforms, he managed to stand out. Her pulse raced just looking at him and she'd seen him only a few hours before. They'd spent the day together hunting strawberries at the picnic, much to her mother's chagrin.

Nothing short of outright rejection would appease her mother at this point and that was something Zara could not give her. There was a definite, growing tension between her and her mother since the 'discussion' Monday. A quiet tug of war had ensued. Whenever her mother manoeuvred to have them spend time with Markham, Zara pushed back. She'd made it clear to her mother today that if she had to sit with

Markham at lunch, she'd be picking berries with Kael afterwards and she had.

Zara smiled a little to herself. They'd done more than pick berries and it reaffirmed that her choice was the right one. If Kael could only be hers for a short time, she wanted all she could have of him. But it had also played a torturous game with her psyche. What if she could have more than three more days with him? After all, what did this rebellion mean if it only lasted the party? A future with Kael was a dangerous path for her thoughts to take, indeed. She knew she was setting herself up for disappointment. She hadn't forgotten that not all was perfect. He had not told her about his farm, or about London. He might kiss like sin, but he had secrets and they must be considered. But still, the temptation to disregard them was great.

Footmen circulated through the room, offering iced champagne to guests in crystal glasses while other footmen opened the doors to the veranda and the rose garden beyond. Zara took a glass, appreciating the coldness of it against the heat raised by thoughts of Kael. Suddenly a hush took the room and everyone turned to stare out of the doors. Torches were lit, one by one, illuminating the figures. Wellington was there, Brockmore and his duchess on one side of him, Verity Fairholme on the other. Everyone applauded. Brockmore raised his hand to signal for quiet and opened his mouth to speak. Another mouth whispered at her ear with a far more interesting message.

'Does the duke's pomposity know no limits? This is quite a coup to steal Wellington away on the Waterloo anniversary,' Kael whispered irreverently, his hand going to the small of her back in an intimate, possessive gesture. 'I wonder how many statues he had to commission to get Wellington here.'

'Just one.' Zara laughed. In the press of people eager to move forward towards the doors, she'd been able to move away from her mother's watchful eye, which was fixated upon the rose-garden display. 'I heard rumour he's going to unveil a statue tonight.'

'I'd like to unveil something a little more alive.' Kael drawled. 'Care to meet me in the pinery after dinner?' It was becoming 'their place', where they always started their adventures.

She nodded and felt him drift off before his attentions could draw her mother's eye. The pinery would be perfect for what she intended. Just the thought of what she had planned brought a tingling heat to her core. Tonight, she would seduce Kael.

She was so caught up in the anticipation of 'dessert' she'd nearly missed Wellington's reveal of the bust. Just moments later as Markham came to lead her into dinner, she couldn't have told anyone anything about the specifics of the statue. Neither could she have told anyone what had been served for dinner, although she was acutely aware of how *long* the formal dinner was.

Markham tried to draw her into conversation with discussion of the elegantly painted ceiling depicting the four seasons and the continents, but she managed only superfluous replies. 'You would, of course, be able to have any kind of painting you wanted at Daunton,' he said, mentioning his family home. 'It's a beautiful house, but it needs a woman's touch. It hasn't been updated since my great-grandmother took it over in 1750.'

She favoured him with a smile and a demure downward cast of her eyes, the appropriate response to such a compliment and what it implied when uttered by a gentleman. 'I've heard many good things about Daunton, my lord.' She had, courtesy of her mother. Daunton had one of the finest art collections in the north of England, an excellent stable patterned after Chatsworth, and exquisite gardens. There were heirlooms galore: china from the Elizabethan era and silver that dated back to Henry Tudor.

Markham smiled, his brown eyes crinkling in friendly appreciation. 'Your interest in my home does me an honour.' Zara would have sworn she could feel Kael bristling from across the table.

Kael was fuming by the time he reached the pinery. His emotions ranged from anger at Zara—how dare she flirt with Markham!—to anger over his own impotence to do anything about it. How could she *not* flirt with Markham, reeling the wealthy lord in like a fish? And why shouldn't she? Beyond their own more intimate flirtation, what did he have to offer her that could even compete with Markham? What did he *want* to offer her?

Marriage swam to the fore of his thoughts. In the past two days he'd come to question the wily duke's motives for planting such a seed. Had the duke done it to tie his hands, a piece of reverse reasoning in the belief that a marriage offer would drive him off? Or had Brockmore done it to prompt him to action, did Brockmore really want to see him offer for Zara? This was all Brockmore's fault. He hadn't allowed himself to think in terms of marriage until the duke had prompted such an idea.

But now that it had taken root, he was having a deuced difficult time shaking it. Not because of the benefits Brockmore had outlined, but because of Zara herself. He wanted her, not her dowry, not her family's connections. Just her, her passion, her enthusiasm for living, the wildness in her heart that yearned to match his. When she'd said she wanted nothing more than to ride horses, his soul had sung. What a life they could have. If she meant the words. If she understood all she'd be trading. Perhaps she did and perhaps she wasn't as ready to give it all up as she professed. Markham was still on her string as she'd demonstrated tonight at dinner, a back-up plan. Or maybe *he* was the back-up plan. Maybe he was too arrogant assuming even that. Maybe he wasn't part of any plan except a daring virgin's exploration into sin. He didn't want to believe that, but experience said he shouldn't put it past her. It hadn't been past Ella Davison so many years ago.

His blood had fairly boiled watching her with Markham yesterday and today, no matter that he had got the better part of her afternoon and he would definitely have the better part of her that evening.

The door to the pinery opened, letting in a draught of cooler evening air to mingle with the smell of hothouse pineapples, sweetness with the sharp. Zara stepped inside, her cheeks flushed. She'd looked stunning tonight in a white-silk gown with a wide scarlet sash about her waist in homage to the heroes and to Wellington. A delicately framed ruby pendant hung about her neck, a subtle reminder of her wealth. She would expect to always wear gems. He would not be able to provide them.

'At last! Oh, it's warm in here.' She fanned herself and then began to roll down her gloves, pulling one off and then the other. 'I thought I would never get away!' Her eyes sparkled with mischief as she moved towards him, gloves in hand as her arms wound about his neck.

'Perhaps you didn't want to get away,' Kael said cuttingly, his exasperation getting the best of him.

Her exuberance faded. 'What does that mean?' He could feel her stiffen at the rebuke.

'Am I supposed to simply sit across the table from you while you and Markham discuss your future at Daunton?' He pulled out of her embrace. 'The two of you were so cosy tonight, already discussing plans to redecorate.' What would she think of redecorating his twelve-room cottage when she could be redesigning the majestic Daunton with its heirlooms and big airy chambers? Daunton probably never got hot in the summer or cold in the winter.

'Are you jealous? Am I supposed to ignore him?' Zara was incredulous, but not cowed. Even in the dim light, he could see she was ready to defend her choice.

'Yes, and, yes!' Kael raged, his fist coming down on a work table. The pottery jumped. 'You are hedging your bets, Zara. You say you want to be free, to make your own choices, but you don't. In public you are on Markham's arm, hanging on his every word, but it's me you run to in private, it's me you sneak off to see in the bushes, in the pinery.'

He could feel her body go still. Her voice was steely when she spoke. 'Is the issue really me owning my freedom? I don't think it is. I think the real issue is you, Kael. You want to claim me publicly and you can't.'

She might as well have slapped him in the face with those long white gloves of her, so thoroughly had she thrown down her own gauntlet. 'You won't allow me to, Zara. You are too afraid of what it might mean.'

'So are you. By the way, I'm curious. What *would* it mean, Kael?' He thought he saw the arching of a dark brow, the quirk of a wry, sad half-smile. 'That's what scares you most, isn't it? What if this thing between us meant *something*? What if it *had* to mean something?'

It was the first time since Ella Davison he was entirely out of his depth with a woman. She had hit the nail of truth soundly on the head. *What if it had to mean something?* She couldn't possibly guess that it already did, that the possibility of meaning something had kept him up two nights now.

'Zara, be careful,' he warned, pushing his

hands through his hair. His anger was starting to ebb, replaced by frustration. These were questions they couldn't and shouldn't answer. He never wanted her to know about the deal the duke had put to him. 'What do you think happens in three days?'

She was quiet for a while. 'I don't know.' They were stepping closer to one another as their fight left them, each of them recognising they weren't really fighting about Markham. They were fighting about all the uncertainty that lay between them.

'I'm sorry, Zara. I didn't want to quarrel with you, it wasn't my intention when I invited you out here.' But that had been before dinner, while memories of their afternoon were still strong in his mind, before he'd had to endure three hours of watching her and Markham, watching a prelude of what her life would be like if she made the practical choice, and it had hurt most unexpectedly. 'We only have four nights left. I don't want to spend them at odds with you. Just tell me, do you want to spend them with me? If it's Markham you want, we can stop this right now.' They would *have* to stop it.

Zara set her gloves down and closed the remaining distance, her body coming up against his, her arms returning around his neck. 'It's you I want, Kael, even if we don't know what happens next. *You* are the reason I came out here.' She kissed him then, long and slow on the mouth as the sound of fireworks filled the night sky outside and he began to forget his insecurities, his lack of rank, his lack of extraordinary wealth. Only the press of her body against his mattered. But nothing compared to what she did next.

She drew his hand between her legs. He could feel how warm and damp she was through the delicate thin summer silk of her gown. 'I'm ready for you, Kael. I want you tonight, all of you, not just your mouth or your hands, but you, inside me. If we only have three days, I want it all.' She levered herself up on a potting table and spread her legs, encouraging him into the vee of her thighs.

Not even a monk could resist such an invitation. When had he ever been so blatantly seduced? His throat was dry. Before Monday he might have said yes, he might have granted her wish because it was his wish too—their wishes alone with nothing to interfere. But that was before the duke and his damnable dare. If he took her now, and the duke's dare-cum-offer ever became public, she would never trust him. She would think he'd engineered this to set himself up. 'Zara, I can't.'

She kissed him softly. 'Why can't you?' she teased, pulling on his lip with her teeth.

'I just can't. Trust me, Zara.' They needed to settle some things between them first. He needed to settle some things for himself like what he could offer her. If he took her and she didn't marry Markham, he would be responsible for her. She would need to decide in truth if that could ever be enough. He wanted her to choose without the spectre of lost virginity between them. There was a loud burst of noise over the roof of the pinery as the fireworks moved into their finale. He took her hands. 'Not tonight, Zara, although the saints know I'm tempted.'

'Tomorrow?' Zara pressed. 'I can wait one more night.'

'Maybe.' He helped her down from the table. 'You go out first.'

Kael didn't leave the pinery for a long while after she left. His thoughts were still raging, only now not with anger but with possibility. Zara stoked all nature of fantasies in him. Why shouldn't he have it all? Why shouldn't he have her? Why should he let his past dictate his future?

There was a race tomorrow, with the prize being first pick of Brockmore's excellent foals next spring or use of the Brockmore stud for one year, a gorgeous thoroughbred stallion proven at Newmarket named Excelsior. Kael knew what he'd pick if he won: the stud. He had two excellent mares, but no breeding options for them at present. To breed with Excelsior could be the start of something great for him, a chance to finally grow his farm.

Kael thought about his grey hunter, Merlin, strong and steady and fast. He would show excellently in the field laid out for tomorrow's midsummer ride. Whatever else he lacked in fine worldly goods, Kael had never lacked for a good horse. Would Merlin be enough?

Something white stood out in the dark. Zara's gloves. He picked them up and put them in his pocket as he passed. There would be no incriminating evidence left behind of their rendezvous. But she would have to decide soon if she would acknowledge him, a thought that both thrilled and scared him. So much hinged on that public recognition.

Damn the duke for giving him hope. Marry Zara and give his sister a future. Win the race and give his farm a future. It would be hard to sleep knowing that tomorrow, everything could change.

Chapter Nine

Thursday June 19th
Brockmore Manor House Party

Programme of Events
The Annual Midsummer Ride
Lunch and Auction on the Village Green

By Thursday, the tone of the house party had definitely changed. Zara sat among the crowd of guests and villagers in the stands along the starting line of the race, watching the horses line up for the annual midsummer ride. Did anyone else feel the mounting pressure? There was an ominous tension in the air that was owed to more than the oppressive grey clouds overhead and the humid stillness of late morning. In the next three days, fates would be decided. 'Auditions', as Kael would put it, had shifted to something more aggressive. If the first days of the party had been about testing the potential of certain matches, the last three were about closing those deals.

Some matches seemed inevitable and obvious like Giltner and Catherine Downing, but there was competition in other arenas. Melton Colter insisted on vying with Jessamy Addington for Florence Canby's affection, and Verity Fairholme had apparently re-thought the cold shoulder she'd been giving the handsome colonel if Wednesday's Waterloo celebrations had been any indicator, while Brigstock was paying marked attentions to one of the Kilmun twins.

Even the activities had ratcheted up a notch to reflect the change in the party's tempo. Activities had moved from low-key outings involving ruins and picnics to more competitive displays. The midsummer revels, which would span the remainder of the party, began today with the ride and culminated in the midsummer ball Saturday night—ostensibly a chance to celebrate the success of the party.

When all this was over, what would her fate be? On one hand, she was only three days away from escaping Markham's intentions. Three measly days! Surely, she could hold out. On the other hand, there were only three days until she was thrust into the unknown and the remainder of the Season. What would become of her in August when the parties were over and everyone went home? Her more conservative, practical side counselled minimising her odds. She should take Markham's offer when it came and be done with it. But that was not the decision the girl who continued to sneak out with Kael Gage would make. *That* girl would not settle for a polite marriage devoid of any true passion.

Zara shifted her position, craning her neck, to get a better look at Kael, mounted on a sleek grey stallion. He looked utterly at ease amid the other horsemen. There were fifteen riders in all, seven of them from the house party, another seven from local gentry and one from the village. Fergus Kennedy was among them, of course. As an officer, he had no choice but to ride. The ladies would have been gravely disappointed otherwise. Markham was there too on a stunning chestnut, no doubt an expensive thoroughbred, and Jeremy Giltner on a strong-chested bay recently acquired from Tattersalls for this very race.

In the spirit of chivalry and fun, a few of the

men had tied favours about their arms. She noted Mr Giltner sported a blue ribbon very similar to the one Catherine Downing had worn to dinner last night. 'Brockmore will be pleased,' her mother murmured quietly on her right. 'The Downing chit is an exquisite catch for Giltner, more than he could have hoped for on his own.' Her meaning was plain. Left to her own devices, Zara too could not hope to do better than Markham. And yet, she continued to sneak off and pursue illicit pleasures with Kael Gage, a man with no obvious prospects.

At the starting line, she saw Kael reach into his pocket at the last moment and pull something out, long and white: a glove. Twin bolts of heat and worry shot through her as he tied it about his upper arm. It was an extraordinarily intimate gesture. He glanced her way with a brief nod and her mother stiffened. Zara prepared herself for a scold.

'I do wonder how long Ariana's mother will allow this nonsense to go on, or Brockmore for that matter,' her mother said *sotto voce*. 'Gage has been after Ariana, then you and then back to Ariana, when he's not a suitable consideration for either.' Only then did Zara realise that Ariana and her mother stood behind them. Her mother thought it was Ariana's glove. Zara knew better. It was one of the pair she'd left behind in the pinery when they'd stolen out of the Waterloo festivities, but this was no act of chivalry. Gage was pushing her for a public declaration. But why?

There was no time to contemplate motives. The starter stepped forward, his voice carrying over the crowd. 'Gentlemen, on your marks, go!' The flag dropped and the racers surged forward, horses bunching together as they vied for position. Already, Kael's grey was pushing through the pack, looking to establish his lead, Markham and Kennedy moving with him, but the race was cross country and long. There would be plenty of time for the lead to change and plenty of opportunity.

The course itself was a two-mile circuit that would start and finish on the outskirts of the village. From her vantage point, and with the help of a spyglass, Zara could see the entire race from the stands. She raised the spyglass as the horses approached the first jump, an oxer with a three-foot spread. Kael and Kennedy along with Markham and Giltner made up a lead pack very clearly now.

Zara held her breath. Whoever took the jump first would have a chance to establish a lone lead. It looked to be the colonel, bent low over his horse's neck, but Kael would not concede. He took the wide jump alongside the colonel, the two horses clearing the oxer simultaneously. It was glorious and dangerous. As they landed, she saw Kennedy shoot Kael a bewildered glance; half-admiration for the daring manoeuvre and half-censure. The move had been risky. A less competent rider could have caused an accident. But the scold was lost on Kael. He kept his gaze straight ahead, his dark hair flying. He edged Kennedy out of the hedge jump by two strides and soared, his horse's belly not even scraping the greenery. Kennedy came soaring back, but the tone of the race was set: Kael to lead, Kennedy to catch and fall back once more.

They approached the third obstacle, a brick fence. It was high and Zara's grip tightened on the spyglass. Kennedy was slowing, checking his mount's paces to make sure the horse took the wall safely, but Kael was barrelling towards it heedless of finesse, caring only for speed, relying only on his horse's strength, his face a study of grim determination as he cleared the wall.

He was riding neck or nothing now. A man only rode that way if he had something to lose. Or something to win. This was about more than the breeding rights offered as a prize. And then she knew. Somehow, this was about *her*. He wanted to win her, whatever that meant, and in those moments she wanted it too, as if victory could bind them together, as if failure to achieve that victory would keep them apart.

The riders were nearing the finish line. She no longer needed the spyglass. The crowd rose. Around her, people began to cheer, urging their favourites on. Hooves thundered as they came. Markham, who had been riding a very close third, made a last-minute surge, his expensive thoroughbred lathered but thriving on the eighth-of-a-mile flat sprint before the finish. What the horse lacked in jumping strength, he made up for it in speed. Her breath caught. Not Markham! It was suddenly vital that Markham not win. For a moment he pulled alongside Kennedy and Kael, but Kael would not tolerate the challenge. The grey surged once more, shaking Markham for the last time, but not Kennedy. How to shake Kennedy?

In a last-minute miracle, the grey's stride

lengthened, his head extended, his neck long. It was enough. Kael had won. Zara exhaled, wiping sudden tears from her eyes. It was silly to be emotional over a country race, but in her heart she knew it was much more than that. Kael's gaze found her in the crowd of people exiting the stands. Their eyes held, she smiled and his face split into a grin. She could not go to him, as much as she wished it. She could not stand by his side like Verity Fairholme or Catherine Downing, who was clutching Jeremy Giltner's arm and beaming as if he'd come in first, not fourth. No, this gaze would be their celebration and in those fleeting moments, the race became a metaphor for everything that mattered.

Well-wishers surged around Merlin, reaching up to shake his hand. He didn't dare dismount. He would be mobbed. In the excited press, Kael was grateful for the stable boys that held Merlin's bridle. He returned the congratulations, adrenaline rocketing through him, what a race! But his eyes were on the watch for Zara. There! He caught her stare, revelled in the wide, exuberant smile that took her mouth. In that gaze he saw what he was looking for: she understood. She knew this victory was more than crossing the finish line first.

The duke came forward with the large, silver cup, making a speech about breeding rights before the trophy presentation and reminding everyone to enjoy the box-lunch auction on the village green in half an hour. 'All proceeds go to our church to support the vicar's nephew's mission in Africa, so bid big. Now, on to what matters,' the duke joked, raising the cup up. 'This year's winner of the Brockmore Midsummer Ride is Mr Kael Gage.'

Kael took the cup and held it high over his head, his legs tight around Merlin as the crowd roared its approval. Just this once, he was a king and his kingdom was within his grasp.

The crowd dispersed gradually. Kennedy, with Verity Fairholme on his arm, came over to congratulate him, followed by Markham, who looked at him with sharp eyes. 'I want to offer my compliments now. I won't be staying for the lunch, as entertaining as it appears. I have business to discuss with the duke.'

A little of his kingliness slipped away. Markham was warning him. He might have beaten Markham to this finish line, but there was another finish line Markham had in mind. For that matter, so did he. This was an important victory, but it was not the only victory he had to claim.

'You were brilliant. Crazy, but brilliant.' Zara settled herself on a blanket beneath a spreading oak tree, his at last although it had cost him a pretty penny. This would be the most expensive lunch he'd ever eaten. But it would be worth it, to have Zara to himself even if his bid had earned him a look of censure from her mother and another look from the Countess of Monteith, Ariana Falk's mother. He was used to it. In general, mothers didn't like him much. Today, though, he could get away with it. He was the champion and he'd won the bid on the lunch fair and square.

The auction lunch was ingenious and he clearly saw the duke's hand in it. It was quite a democratic move, a chance for men to declare themselves publicly for their choice, or for the more daring, a last-ditch effort to stake a claim. That had been the case for Addington and Colter in their squabbling bid over Florence Canby's lunch. Addington had won. For his sake, Kael hoped the lunch included champagne. For the price he'd paid, he deserved a few kisses. From the pleased blush on Florence's cheeks, he'd probably get them too.

'I think the vicar will be able to convert the whole of Africa from the money raised on your lunch and Florence's alone,' Kael joked, sitting down beside her. It was hard not to stretch out and recline, but they were surrounded by the crowd even if they were alone on their blanket. It was another ingenious arrangement on the duke's behalf. Last-minute claimants could certainly announce their intentions, but there would be no opportunity for stealing a march on other competitors by compromising one's prize.

'You're avoiding the topic,' Zara scolded him, opening the picnic hamper and pulling out ham sandwiches. 'You were brilliant and crazy. You still are.' She was serious.

He didn't pretend ignorance. His own tones modelled hers, solemn and quiet. This was the next step. He'd rehearsed this over and over in his head while he'd lain awake last night anticipating today on all fronts, not just the race. 'I think you and I disagree in our definition of "crazy". Is it crazy to wear my lady's token? Kennedy had one, Giltner wore Catherine's ribbon. I was not alone. Or do you mean it is crazy to bid on my lady's lunch? I thought that was the purpose of the game.'

Her green eyes flashed. She leaned forward, her voice hushed. 'Am I your lady, then, Kael?'

'Are you, Zara? I have declared myself privately and publicly. Now it's your turn.'

She turned stony. He felt her withdraw from him, saw the polite cool mask she wore so often in public. 'Forgive me if I am confused. You were the one turning me down last night in the pinery. I'm not sure I know what it means to be your lady.'

He held her eyes, his hand reaching out for hers where it lay in her lap. He wanted to touch her when he asked, wanted to remember this moment for ever, for better or for worse. 'Last night, I turned you down because I wanted to be sure I could offer you more than a few nights of pleasure without any promises.' He'd taken women to bed without promises before, but Zara was different. She deserved to know that now. 'You make me want to be different, not just a man who loves and leaves, but a man who can invest in a relationship in all ways.' He hadn't been that man for a long time, if ever. 'When I'm with you, I feel like I'm worth something. I want to feel that always, so I'm asking you to marry me, Zara Titus. To be my lady for ever, publicly, not just in the night.' He squeezed her hand, stalling her answer. 'But hear me out. You need to know what I can offer you and what I can't. I don't want your answer right now. Think about it because it is the rest of your life and mine.'

She was utterly still as he began. 'I have a twelve-room home in Sussex, a minor gentleman's home. My sister lives with me. She is blind. She may live with me for ever.' He was *not* offering for Zara because of the duke's deal. Neither would he throw his sister at the first suitor the duke arranged, because her happiness, his happiness, and Zara's happiness was not for sale to the Duke of Brockmore or anyone. He'd been very clear with himself on this point in the wee hours of the night.

'In addition to the house, there is a stable and there are some tenants from whom I collect modest rents. We are self-sufficient. I can afford some time in London every year. You needn't fear that we're paupers. But we are not wealthy, not like you are. I have hopes for the stable. I have good horses, two mares especially, that I can now breed to the duke's stallion next year.'

He stopped. There was something unreadable in her eyes. 'Is that all you can offer me, Kael?' she said quietly.

A chasm opened beneath him. Was she refusing him or prompting him? But to what? To where? His voice was hoarse. 'Those are things that I can offer you. I've told you we are not rich.' This couldn't be happening, rejection all over again when he'd convinced himself this time would be different.

Her free hand covered his, her voice far steadier than his. 'Yes, Kael, those are *things* you can give me. They are acceptable to me in their own right. What else can you offer me? What can you offer me of *yourself*?'

Kael swallowed, the knot in his stomach releasing. He smiled just for her. 'I will give you my affections, my love, my loyalty and my fidelity for the rest of your life. I would give you my very soul, Zara, except you already possess it.'

Her eyes were shining now and he hated the next part, but he couldn't let her romanticise their future. 'There will not be yearly instalments of new gowns sewn in the fashionable style. There will be no jewels. There is no money for excessive luxury or servants. I have four servants, two of whom work out of doors. My butler is my valet. The housekeeper handles the cooking and the house.' It was a far cry from Brockmore or her family home where there was never a shortage of footmen to wait on the table or to fetch a shawl.

He feared she would simply shove his concerns away, tell him it didn't matter. But it would matter, a year from now, ten years from now. To her credit, Zara nodded. 'I understand. You do me a great honour in proposing, in *wanting* me to be your wife, your partner. But you do me an even greater honour in respecting my choice and in giving me the information with which to make that choice. I will take it *all* under advisement.'

He'd stripped himself naked emotionally for her. Now there was nothing to do but wait.

Chapter Ten

Kael Gage slept entirely naked. It was the first fact that registered when Zara stepped into the last room on the left side of the corridor. Either out of habit or out of deference for the heat, Kael lay on his side atop the sheets, curved buttocks on display in glorious repose. Zara's breathing hitched, realisation hitting for the first time as to how momentous her decision was. *This* was the point of no return and she'd been moving towards it all week. These last steps were not taken with recklessness or rebellion, but with her future in mind.

She should be nervous; she was slipping into a man's room at a house party to answer his marriage proposal in the most sensual of manners possible and without parental approval. This was not a decision her father and another man had made for her, or a decision that her mother had coached her towards. What she was about to do was all the more momentous for it and yet all she felt was a great sense of calm. This was Kael and this was right. It was one in the morning, thirteen hours since Kael's proposal, and her answer was yes. It had been yes the minute Kael had finished asking. But he'd never believe it or accept it if she didn't follow his rules on this.

Zara stepped towards the bed, a smile on her face. This glorious man was all hers. She let her robe fall and slid beneath the covers beside him, as naked as he.

Kael was having the most delightful dream. Zara was beside him in bed, her hand on his phallus warm and inviting as her body stretched out alongside him. Best of all, she was naked. He had no idea what had happened to her nightgown, but he didn't care. One didn't have to care in dreams. She stroked him, her mouth on his in a sweet, tempting kiss, her words soft. 'Kael, wake up.' Not a chance. He didn't want to wake up, but the sweet siren beside him was insistent. In the end, he could deny her nothing. His eyes opened in the dark and he grinned. 'You're here after all. I feared I would wake aching and alone I'm only half-right.' He drew a deep, satisfied breath and sighed, savouring the sight of her beside him in bed before he had to play the gentleman. 'But this is considerably more dangerous than a dream, Zara. Dreams have no consequences.'

She leaned into him and kissed him, on the cheek, the brow, the nose. 'I am ready for them, all of them, Kael. I've come with my answer to your question. It is "yes", and I mean to seal our deal with something more than a kiss tonight.'

There was no doubt she was in earnest. Every inch of her naked body pressed up against his attested to it. It would be easy to simply accept what her body and her words offered. Normally he would, but this was Zara and there was too much at stake. 'Did you tell your mother?'

'No. Did you tell your sister?' Her hand slid up his phallus, making him shudder.

'No, but it's not the same. She's not here, for one. Besides, it's not her decision.' He ground the words out, but barely.

'Exactly. Whether she's here or not, it's not

her decision any more than it's my mother's decision,' Zara argued, her thumb teasing his tip in a delicious, languid caress. It was becoming less important that her family like him by the moment. He wouldn't hold out long against these rebuttal techniques.

'I don't want to alienate you from your family.' It would be bad enough that he was taking her from the life she knew. There was nothing he could do about that. He could not preserve her lifestyle.

'Are you doubting my judgement?' She propped her head on her hand, all her glorious hair falling to one side, her eyes glinting like sharp green shards in the lamplight. 'It very much sounds as if you are.'

'No, I'm questioning mine. I never dreamed a woman like you would want a man like me.'

'That is a very dangerous statement, Kael Gage. What sort of man is that? Do you mean to tell me you go around proposing to high-bred virgins all the time?' She was not entirely joking and his answer was serious.

'No, you're the first. The only,' he clarified. Ella Davison had not let him get that far. There would be no one after Zara. He'd never wanted a woman this way before—to possess her body and soul, to know that she was his. How was it possible she'd got to him so fast? When he'd seen her in the drawing room, restless and defiant, when he'd rowed her to the lake island, he'd merely meant to awaken her, to give her what she hungered for. Perhaps there was truth to the adage to let sleeping dogs lie. But then, he would have missed so much. He would have missed *her.*

'And the rest? A woman like me?' She was half-flirt, half-offended lover. 'What is that exactly?' She squeezed his balls. Oh, she was making him pay, exacting exquisite retribution for his caution.

'Lucifer's stones, Zara, you're going to kill me!' He groaned, arching slightly against her. 'You know what I mean: beautiful, stunning, from a high-born family, wealthy,' But it was more than that. He'd had a hundred women or more from genteel families, but none of them possessed any real moral quality or demanded anything from him beyond physical excellence. He whispered the last, hoarse with need. 'Untouched, pure, for me alone.' Would she understand how much that meant to him? Zara had chosen him, she, who could have chosen anyone, a man like Lord Markham who possessed noble qualities and a fortune to go with them.

'I want you to touch me…' she breathed against his neck '…I want you to be the only one who touches me, for ever, for always, Kael.'

He couldn't fight his body and her logic. He'd asked, she'd accepted. Why did he resist? Why did some part of him hold back as he rolled her beneath him? But he knew—he'd never allowed himself to be completely happy and it was hard to start now. He knew how to live with regret and incomplete dreams. He didn't know how to live with perfection. He would have to take this new world one night at a time. *That* he could do.

He kissed her hard to banish doubt, to affirm their decision. This was not a choice for one night of pleasure, but for a lifetime of them. His hand lifted a breast to his mouth and he took it, his tongue laving her nipple, his teeth nipping until she moaned.

Her legs opened about him, letting him lever himself between them, letting him come home. He belonged here with her like this, they fit so wonderfully together. He pressed himself to her entrance, teasing her, feeling her. She was wet. He pursued, thrusting in, wanting to be gentle, but finding no need. She was ready in both mind and body. She responded, pressing her hips against him, inviting him, taking him. He wanted to be taken, wanted to be sheathed. He felt her stretch and give, and he was there at last, completely within. He stilled and waited for her to adjust, physically, mentally to his presence. Then they began again, together this time, picking up a rhythm all their own.

She arched against him and he grunted, swept up in her unbridled enthusiasm as much as he was carried away by his own physical response. This was wild, uncharted passion and his body revelled in it, driving him onward. He felt her body tighten, felt the approach of his own point of no return, unsure he could wait for her, he was too far gone, blissfully and uncontrollably so. He tried to warn her, prepare her in incoherent words as his body gathered and exploded. He needn't have worried, she was there with him at the end, her legs wrapped fiercely around him, holding him close as the climax rocked them.

Her eyes were wide, her breathing fast as she looked up at him. 'Oh, God, Kael, what was that?'

He grinned, his hair falling over his face. 'That, my dear, was for ever.'

She smiled. 'I like the sound of that. Very much.'

Chapter Eleven

Friday June 20th
Brockmore Manor House Party

Programme of Events
Annual Midsummer Treasure Hunt
A Celebration of Russian Cuisine with
Dinner served in the Maze

'Lord Markham is undecided.'

The duke's words fell in the quiet of the study where Zara sat with her mother, taking a private breakfast with Brockmore himself, Friday morning. Zara found the pronouncement quite optimistic. If Markham was undecided, it certainly helped Kael's case, one he'd have to make very soon now that things were decided between them. The thought brought a smile to her face. No doubt, her mother did not view the news with the same equanimity. But she gave nothing away as she played with her croissant. Chef Salois, the duke's French cook, made exquisite croissants and served the richest of hot chocolates, but this morning it appeared her mother had little appetite for them.

Zara could see her mother was already scheming how best to play her reaction to the news. 'I don't understand his reticence,' her mother said coolly. She could not appear to be desperate or disappointed even if she was both, and even if the duke knew how important a match for Zara was this week, preferably one with Markham. Giltner had been a reserve, a back-up measure only. That he had gone to Catherine Downing had been no real loss.

The duke gave a shrug. 'Who can say what goes on inside a young man's head?' He turned to Zara. 'Markham certainly is interested. However…' the duke paused here and gave her a meaningful look '…he feels you do not return his regard to the same degree whereas Miss Falk is more amenable.'

'Miss Falk!' Her mother did not attempt to hide her disdain.

The duke explained patiently, unfazed by her

mother's comment, 'Markham has made it clear he will leave here with a match. He must. He needs a wife at Daunton. He cannot delay. It will be Ariana or Zara. He is waiting for a sign.'

Zara's mind raced. This was a boon! The path to Kael was becoming wider if she could use it. Perhaps even the duke could be an ally to persuade her mother. Beside her, her mother pasted on a smile, her next words dangerous. 'If Zara does not take Markham, who do you suggest?' Of course her mother would word it that way. Never would she let it be said that Markham had decided not to take Zara. If he chose Ariana, her mother would make sure everyone understood it was because Zara had simply let him go. 'Colonel Kennedy, perhaps? Or Brigstock? Surely he'd prefer Zara to the Kilmun girl.' It was positively dizzying how fast her mother had partnered her off again.

The duke shook his head and Zara felt herself breathe again. 'Not the colonel. There is much unresolved there, I think. His path may not be the one we hope for him. And Brigstock? Would you really throw your daughter to a man whom she doesn't know, Helene? I don't think she's spent more than five minutes in his company the entire week.'

'Who else is there, Brockmore?' Her mother's voice was edgy, worried. 'Certainly not Farthingale or that prudish chit he's cozied up with this week. I will not stoop to that level just to see Zara married. Farthingale is a bastion of bad fashion. Money can't buy looks in his case.'

Zara had had enough. Now that she knew the direction of this conversation, she wanted a stake in it. It was her future after all and she'd been fighting for it all week, discovering it. 'Kael Gage. I could marry him.'

The duke leaned back in his chair, hands steepled as he studied her, assessing her recommendation with shrewd eyes.

'The upstart? The uninvited rogue? Zara, you can't be serious. We have talked about this.' There was warning censure in her tone. 'We will not consider such a match.'

'We don't have to consider it, only I do,' Zara said hotly, watching her mother's face pale at the insult.

The duke leaned forward. 'They have been spending a lot of time together. *A lot.*'

'No, Marcus. Zara is young, impressionable

and the last three weeks have been very difficult.'
Oh, this was interesting now. Her mother and the
duke were using first names. If she hadn't such a
heavy stake in the outcome, Zara would be fascinated by the interplay. She doubted anyone else
at the party would dare to call the duke by his
Christian name. But of course, her mother and
the duke and his wife had all been on the town
together in their youth.

'It's more than that, Helene,' the duke said
softly, but did not elaborate. 'Gage isn't a bad
choice if she cares for him. He has a small horse
farm and he's kind to his sister. If Zara takes
him, I'll see to it that his sister marries a nice
gentleman farmer and your husband is powerful enough, he can make Gage respectable.' He
paused. 'Love is no small consideration, as you
well know, or have you forgotten Richland?' He
smiled gently, his eyes crinkling at the corners
as he rose and began to pace.

'Marcus. Don't,' her mother cautioned, eyes
narrowed. But the duke would not be stopped.

'Zara, when we were young, your mother had
a suitor. Richland was mad for her.' He shot her
mother an aside. 'I thought you were mad for him
too. I was surprised when you picked Aberforth.'

'My parents preferred Aberforth,' her mother replied quietly. 'It turns out they were right.' Her words were for Zara 'Your father has given me two children and a life of luxury and prestige.'

'And passion, Helene? Has he given you that?' the duke enquired boldly.

She gave the duke a withering look. 'He has given me something more valuable, Marcus. A girl is entitled to her fling, perhaps, as long as it is discreet and does not jeopardise her opportunities.' Zara felt her mother's gaze on her. 'His Grace wants to appeal to the emotion of romance with that memory, but I suggest you see it as a cautionary tale about young foolishness, a foolishness you can avoid, my dear girl. Markham is not lost yet.'

Her mother smiled at the duke serenely as if they had not tussled, as if her own daughter had not contradicted her in front of another. 'Must we decide today? Perhaps this could be delayed.'

'I am afraid we must,' the duke said slyly. Zara had the sense he was pushing for something. 'The treasure hunt is this morning. I am pairing couples together, as an opportunity to solidify the matches before the ball. I want Markham to be reassured.'

The viscountess rose. 'Pair her with Markham, give him the sign, then. Markham will not regret it.'

The duke rose, his eyes fixed on her 'And you, Miss Titus? What do you prefer?' Only a duke would gainsay her mother. Her heart beat fast. This was her moment. What was the duke playing at, pitting her against her mother? She couldn't worry over that. She could only do what was best for her and for Kael.

'I prefer Kael Gage, your Grace. Thank you for asking,' she said evenly although she trembled inside.

Her mother immediately overrode the declaration. 'You must excuse her, Marcus. Zara knows a girl must be practical, more practical even than a man when it comes to marriage. She will see reason.'

The duke smiled and bowed, his gaze enigmatic. 'We'll see if she does. Care to wager on that?' The moment of truth was here, or if not here precisely, rapidly approaching and Zara was ready for it.

At the stroke of ten, the duke entered the drawing room and held up the list, a gesture that signalled for silence. All the guests lowered their voices to excited whispers. No one would dare miss this gathering, some standing together with who they hoped their partner would be, others, like she and Kael, standing circumspectly apart.

The distance didn't bother Zara. She and Kael were together in all the ways that mattered. An enormous sense of calm had come over her when she'd left the duke's study. What was done could not be undone. She liked knowing that. There was security in the knowledge that she was Kael's and he was hers. It did not mean there weren't some rough patches to be navigated, but they would navigate them together.

Zara smiled to no one in particular. It was a beautiful morning. The doors were open to the rose garden, catching the cool late-morning breeze and spirits were high. The treasure hunt itself was a much-enjoyed annual Brockmore tradition, the prize always something grand. This year it was to be a raw diamond and the hunt would last well into the afternoon. But it was more than the hunt and the good weather that inspired the levels of excitement in the drawing room. The party would end tomorrow night. The time for offers was drawing near and the duke's list of partners, chosen by him alone, was an un-official seal of approval. In short, it mattered who one was paired with. Would the duke honour her wishes or her mother's?

The duke cleared his throat and smiled fondly at the guests, his eyes laughing at their impa-tience. 'The teams for the treasure hunt will be as follows: Verity Fairholme and Colonel Kennedy, Mr Giltner and Miss Downing, Mr Addington and Miss Canby.' The list went on. Zara was only half-listening. 'Miss Titus and Lord Markham.'

Her mother gave her a tiny nod of approval, the faintest hints of a self-satisfied smile twitching her lips. Zara saw red. Her protest to the duke meant nothing if she did not back it. To the rest of the guests, she was Markham's. She shot a look across the room at Kael, his eyes dark with emotion when they met hers. She saw the insecu-rity there—would she stand up for him now that it mattered? To walk off with Markham would nullify her acceptance of Kael's proposal and it would nullify her protest in the duke's study. Kael crossed his arms. He was waiting for her to make her move, here in front of everyone. The duke shot her a challenging look. He was waiting too.

Zara's palms were sweaty. She'd been wrong

last night. The whole week had been leading her to this: a declaration of freedom, to be brave as Haymore had been brave when he'd broken with her to reach out for what he wanted. She understood fully what it must have cost him to face her and declare *his* independence.

Zara let her gaze lock on Kael's. She would need his strength for this as she called out in a clear voice the fateful words, 'Your Grace, I think there's been a mistake.'

Her voice carried over the instantly hushed room. People stared. The duke didn't make mistakes. There was no going back now. Zara pushed forward towards the duke, aware every eye was on her. 'Lord Markham should be with Miss Falk, I believe. Perhaps your ink has smudged?'

The duke gave her a lingering look, his eyes sharp. 'Ah, yes, Miss Titus, I see that is the case. My apologies, everyone. Markham and Miss Falk.' Then he clapped his hands. 'You are free to disperse. The first clue is being distributed now by the footmen and good luck to all.'

The diamond was a powerful lure. No one was inclined to linger and the drawing room emptied quickly. Zara stood frozen. What she had done started to swamp her with a sense of the surreal.

She had let Markham go and with him all that she'd been raised to know and expect about her future.

'Go after him, Zara. Undo what you've just done. Beg him if you have to.' Her mother's voice cut sharply through the room, tinged with panic, which said something considering her mother was regarded by London society as unflappable. Nothing bestirred her feathers, not even Haymore's desertion had unseated her calm. But this had pierced her armour.

Zara drew a deep breath. 'No.' On her periphery, the duke gave a gesture to the footmen to shut the doors. There would be no exiting to his office or wherever these sorts of negotiations were managed. Maybe they weren't managed anywhere. Maybe no one said no to the duke. Her chin went up a fraction. Maybe she was the first who couldn't be bought? She and Kael. She liked the sound of that. Any moment he would step up and take her hand and he would validate that she spoke the truth, that he shared her feelings. She waited but he didn't come to her.

She looked around, spying him. He stood immobile as if he were a hunter not wanting to scare off prey with sudden movement. All of him was still except for his eyes, which were alive and burning like brands.

'Zara, explain this to me.' Her mother had her by the arm, leading her towards a grouping of chairs. 'Markham is waiting for a sign.' The duke crossed the room to join them, perhaps to act as a proxy for her absent father. Regardless of capacity, he was not *her* ally, not any more. Like her mother, he was a game player.

'Then Lord Markham has one, Mother. He is not my choice. I will not give him a sign to the contrary and lead him on with false hope,' Zara answered bravely. Kael moved at last to her side. She reached out a hand towards him and made her arguments. 'I understand how important it is that I marry this Season, Mother, and I understand the purpose of coming here was to make a betrothal to replace Haymore's broken one. That *will* come to pass, just not with Markham.' She felt Kael squeeze her hand. It would have been easy for him to speak the words, to take this burden from her, but that would have defeated the purpose. She understood now why he'd waited to come to her until she'd spoken. If she didn't stand on her own now, she never would. 'I will marry Kael Gage. *We* have decided it.'

Her mother's cool glance slid over Kael, not quite derogatory, but one that certainly did not contain approval before it returned to her. '*You've* decided?' The viscountess cocked her dark hair, her eyes sharp. Her shock had passed. Perhaps the duke's game in the study had given her fair warning this was coming. 'Is that what you think, Zara? After a week here, you actually believe *you* decide anything? The duke decides everything.'

The icy, knowing smile she favoured Kael with chilled Zara. 'You have turned my daughter's head with half-truths and lies, Mr Gage, and who knows what other damage you've done. Are you proud of yourself? She is a vulnerable young girl, coming out of a tragedy. She is easily led astray. A known seducer of women, like yourself, should have exercised honour and restraint.' She gave him a look of disdain, a look Zara had seen freeze Austrian diplomats before. 'What possible pride could you take in such an easy mark—?'

'Mother! I'm not a child,' Zara interrupted, flushed and embarrassed. Her mother portrayed her as a halfwit incapable of thinking for herself.

But Kael put a hand to her shoulder, his touch counselling caution. 'What lies and half-truths would those be, Lady Aberforth?' How could he be so calm when her mother had slandered him?

'She thinks you have made this decision on your own, the two of you. And yet, she knows this party is about Brockmore helping arrange matches. The two ideas are irreconcilable, Mr Gage. So you tell me, how is that you're the only one the duke hasn't helped along? What has he offered you to convince you to reach above yourself to my daughter?'

Zara's stomach dropped. Her mother was so sure of her argument it was frightening. 'My daughter doesn't know about your arrangement with the duke, does she?' Her mother inclined her head. If it was a bluff, it was a brilliant one. 'Perhaps you'd like to tell her what the duke has promised you if you marry her.'

This was the nightmare he feared. Zara's panicked gaze flicked to his in horror and disbelief, urging him to deny it. He should have told her and they would have laughed about it. Now, there would be no laughing. This was serious. 'There is no deal, Kael. Tell her,' Zara insisted, but Kael hesitated a moment too long. He watched every last ounce of hope that flared in her green eyes fade, become extinguished. The seconds that followed might have been the worst of his life.

She let go of his hand and edged away from him as if he were now a leper, her eyes reflecting her betrayal as consequences began to roll over her. 'Kael?'

He wanted to strangle her mother—hardly an appropriate feeling to have towards one's mother-in-law. Her mother was a master. The viscountess knew Zara would never take her word for it so she'd forced him to incriminate himself. He could always lie, but the duke was sitting right there to countermand him. No one would believe him over a duke and a viscountess any way. Not even Zara.

He couldn't think about that. He could only think that she was leaving him, taking his happy-ever-after with her. He missed her already. He had only to say the words that would compromise them both and he could make her stay. But instead, he gave her one last gift. 'It's true, Zara. The duke offered to help my sister find a husband, to have a real life with a real family of her own, the one thing I can't give her.'

Her mother had her by the shoulders, offering support, but he saw conflicting emotions in

Zara's eyes. Her mother's evidence and his testimony didn't reconcile. 'You would sacrifice yourself in marriage for the sake of your sister?' she said softly. He could see her debate it in her mind: how could such a noble man be so duplicitous?

'It was never a sacrifice, Zara.' He'd give anything to have this conversation in private without the duke and the viscountess looking on. He wanted to take Zara in his arms and assure her with his mouth, his lips, his hands, that the duke's offer had nothing to do with his motivations. 'I would want you without his offer.'

'Of course he would!' Zara's mother snapped. 'You have a dowry he'd love to get his hands on, Zara. He is everything your father and I have warned you about, everything we've protected you from. He is here because he was caught *in flagrante delicto* with another woman of good birth.' She gave him a viper's glare. 'And now you think to ruin an innocent like my daughter.'

The words stung. Kael would rather have been flogged than to stand there and hear those words and know he could do nothing about them. They were true. She'd always been too good for him and now Zara knew it. He gave the duke a short nod. 'If you'll excuse me, I seem to have spoiled the morning, my apologies. I'll look in on Merlin down at the stables.' And maybe he'd just get on his horse and ride away. Why not? There was nothing left to stay for.

In flagrante delicto! That woman was a maestro of disaster. Kael kicked at the hay. If it wasn't so horribly true, he would have found it quite entertaining to know the oh, so proper Viscountess of Aberforth knew such words *and* what they meant. It just proved everyone had layers.

Except him. He was no better than he ought to be and everyone who saw him knew it. He had no secret layers—a poor gentleman's son who lived on the fringes of society. He should stop reaching above himself, stop trying to change his fate. He should retreat to the country and stay there. He liked the country. He didn't get into trouble there. He only got into trouble in London when he started to dream again.

That decided it. This was done. He couldn't help Zara by staying and he couldn't save her, couldn't save *them*. He found Merlin's saddle in the tack room and his bridle. He would ride out and send for his things later. Jeremy could send them to Sussex. There was nothing he needed immediately except distance. Distance would help him forget how close he'd been to perfection. His fingers worked the tack with lightning speed. He was almost done when Colonel Kennedy ducked in.

'Going somewhere?' Fergus stepped up to Merlin and put a hand on the horse's long face in gentle greeting. 'I thought you'd be deep into the treasure hunt by now.' He stroked the grey's long face, his own face thoughtful.

'I'm leaving.' Kael grunted as he tightened the cinch.

'Hmm. Early and without your luggage? I hope it's not an emergency?' the colonel asked in kindly concern.

'No.' Kael picked up his grooming kit and slid the brushes into the saddlebags.

'Then I can only deduce it's from a broken heart.' Kennedy took a seat on a hay bale.

'Something like that. What are you doing out here? Why aren't you off with Miss Fairholme finding diamonds?' Kael turned the tables on Kennedy with questions of his own.

'I might as well tell you.' Kennedy leaned forward. 'It won't be a secret much longer. Verity and I have decided we don't suit.'

In spite of his anger and frustration, Kael laughed. 'The duke is having a hell of a house party. Zara won't toe the line, his own niece won't toe the line. It makes me wonder how many other little rebellions are brewing beneath the surface.'

'Oh, so it *is* a broken heart? Or isn't it? I'm confused. Aren't you thrilled Miss Titus isn't "toeing the line"?' Kennedy grinned at successfully having drawn him out.

'I think you missed your calling, Kennedy. You should have been an interrogator.' Kael took a seat next to Fergus, Merlin's reins loose in his hand. 'Miss Titus has recently become aware of the duke's offer to me should I wed her.'

'And she is offended?'

'Yes. Although I tried to tell her the deal was irrelevant. I would have married her without it.'

'Certainly, she is wealthy. Aside from Verity, she's the richest girl here.'

'No, dammit!' Kael interrupted vehemently. 'She could be a pauper for all I care.' He wanted to grab the colonel by the lapels and do him violence for the insinuation that he was nothing more than a fortune hunter.

Kennedy grinned again and Kael relented with a grimace, more for himself than the colonel.

Kennedy had tricked him once more, getting him to reveal the intensity of his feelings. 'I see,' the young officer said. 'Miss Titus does not want to be appreciated for her dowry. Does she know how you feel?'

'It doesn't matter. I'm not good enough for her.' Except in bed, but he wasn't going to tell the colonel *that*, no matter how many tricks the man tried. 'I never was. I was merely swept away by her and I foolishly thought I could touch the stars, that I could reach her. She made me feel invincible, alive.'

Kennedy stared down at his hands. 'I know the feeling,' he said quietly. Sincerely. It gave much away.

'Spoken like a man who has walked that path?' Kael asked.

'Who *is* walking it,' Fergus said solemnly.

'But not with Verity?' Kael probed cautiously. This was becoming a deuced odd conversation— two gentlemen talking about their love lives.

'No, not with her.' That was all Kennedy would say. Kael nodded, respecting the other man's privacy.

Kael stood up. 'Well, I guess I should be off.'

The less attention he drew to himself now, the better.

'Are you just going to give up?' Kennedy stood up too, looking disgusted. 'If you leave now, you will prove to everyone you're no better than some say. Look, man, you have to stay and you have to fight for her. Make her believe you. To hell with the rest of them! If you love her, she's the only one that matters.' Kennedy waved a hand in a general gesture to an invisible crowd. 'Who cares what the duke, the mother, what everyone else may or may not be thinking? It's your life, your heart and hers.'

Kael gave Kennedy a strong look. 'Is that what you're doing with your secret miss, whoever she might be? Are you fighting? Is that why you're hiding out in the stable?'

Kennedy wasn't offended. 'I am biding my time, waiting for my moment to come. When it does, I will take it. I am not riding away.' Kennedy paused, his brow furrowed. 'Look, the truth is, I don't know how it will turn out when I seize that moment. I might fall flat on my face. I hope not, but the possibility does exist. Still, I would rather know than always be wondering the rest of my life if things could have been different.'

Kael's hand stilled on Merlin's cinch. Kennedy thought him a coward, had all but called him one. 'I'm not running away. I am leaving to protect her, to make it easier on her.'

'She makes you feel invincible? Then she is worth fighting for, not leaving for. Go back in there and be her warrior. Fight for her where she can see it, where everyone can see it. Go back and slay the doubts others have overwhelmed her with.'

It was somewhat ironic advice considering it was much like the advice he had given Zara about rebellion. Rebellion had to be public to mean much. Fighting did too. He was starting to see Kennedy was right. In his anger, he'd not realised that his act of protection would not be understood as such by others, maybe not even by Zara herself. It would be seen as the careless act of a rogue.

He would do it. He had never run from a fight, he'd not start now when there was so much on the line.

He unfastened Merlin's saddle and winked at Kennedy in encouragement. 'I think I will stay, after all. Who knows, there might be some other surprises tonight that are worth staying for too.'

But it didn't matter if there were other surprises or not. He'd only meant to leave as a favour to her, to spare her the sight of him, the object of her hatred, for surely, she must despise him. But he would do it. Zara was worth it. He hoped he could make her feel the same about him again.

Chapter Twelve

Zara was *furious* and the list of those she was furious with was long and distinguished. She was furious with her mother, with the duke, with the whole ridiculous party, and with her poor maid, Annie, who had only tried to help her dress for a dinner Zara didn't want to attend. The girl had got a bed full of discarded gowns that would all have to be hung up again for her troubles.

That was just the start of her list. There was more. Zara stood impatiently, letting Annie slide the blue gown over her head. She was furious with Kael, although that was complicated. She'd spent the afternoon in her room, pacing and trying to figure out why, replaying the whole terrible scene. He said he'd wanted her without the duke's deal. Surely, that was no cause for her anger. He'd tried to reassure her. But he'd said nothing to her mother's charges of fortune hunting. He'd simply walked away. That was where her anger boiled and her thoughts reached a dead end. Why had he just left? Why hadn't he said that wasn't true? Why hadn't he said he loved her and wanted to marry her where everyone could hear?

That was the part that didn't make sense and it fuelled the anger she held for herself, that *she* had somehow failed *him*. What had she missed? What had she done that caused him to walk away? After an afternoon of searching for answers, it came to her with a shock. If he was a fortune hunter, he'd had the perfect opportunity to expose them and ensure their marriage and he'd not taken it. 'Annie, I need to sit down for a moment,' she murmured, sinking to the little stool set before her vanity.

'Are you all right, miss?' Annie looked concerned and rightly so. The woman who met Zara's stare in the mirror was pale.

'Some cold water, perhaps,' Zara suggested, wanting time alone, a few precious minutes to gather her thoughts. Her mother was wrong. Kael wasn't after her fortune. All he had to do was tell her mother and the duke that he'd compromised her and it would have been done. They would have had to accept him then. Instead, he'd walked away. *To protect her* and at great expense to himself. He'd lost the duke's deal for his blind sister and no one would think kindly of his behaviour. Leaving her would prove he was all the rogue everyone believed him to be, especially coming so soon on the heels of the *débâcle* in London.

What had she done? She had shunned him, questioned him. She'd been horrified at the revelation of the duke's deal. Zara remembered stepping away from him, of seeing the moment of hurt on his face before his mask of insouciance had slid into place while her mother railed at him: a knowing debaucher of innocents, a fortune hunter. Horrible things to call a man.

Annie returned with the water. Zara's hands shook as she took the glass. She had to make amends. She was the villain in all of this, not Kael. She was the one that called up his insecurities with her doubt. She had treated him like the ghost in his past. 'Annie, I've decided against the blue dress after all.' It was too demure, too quiet. Tonight she needed something stunning. 'I think I'll wear the green.' The deep-emerald silk that brought out her eyes and hopefully her heart. Dinner was starting to take on a new importance.

* * *

'Darling, you look splendid,' her mother whispered as they walked across the lawn to dinner. Her mother was benevolent in her victory, believing the issue of Kael Gage had been put behind them. There would be no formal parade into the dining room tonight. The midsummer feast would be held outdoors at the centre of the maze and the guests were all to find their way out to the table by seven. 'I'm proud of you for not skulking in your room this evening. It would be easy to do, given the circumstances. But you are a Titus and you are made of sterner stuff. Keep your head high and show everyone it will take more than the likes of Kael Gage to bring you low.' Her mother shook her head. 'Good riddance, I say.'

'Good riddance?' She almost choked over the words, fearing the worst.

'Gage should not bother you tonight, my dear. He was headed towards the stable, by last report. He'll be long gone by now. His sort always are. He was out of his depth here.'

He certainly was, Zara thought, her hopes sinking, as they turned right and then right again. There was no finer man present. The company, with few exceptions, was far too shallow for him. She could only hope she was not included in that grouping. Had he really left the party altogether? If so, she'd have no chance to make amends. They took the final turn, Zara's heart pounding, and stepped into the centre of the maze. It had been transformed for the Russian-themed evening. Atlas had been moved aside to accommodate the large table and long tables laden with foods lined the perimeter, emanating delicious smells.

Even the footmen were dressed in Russian-styled livery, but Zara spared little time for the details. She was too busy searching for Kael. Kael would want to protect her, but he would not leave her, not if she was right about his motives. The man who had raced for her, who had swam with her, who had touched her, loved her so exquisitely would not leave her. He would find a way to fight for her and she would have to be ready.

Some guests were already there, but not everyone. She took comfort in that. Just because he wasn't here yet didn't mean he was gone. The butler appeared at the entrance, a gaggle of guests at his heel, laughing and in good spirits even though they'd apparently been lost in the maze, something the duke hadn't counted on. Kael would not have got lost. He knew the way.

Then she saw him emerge from behind the parade of lost guests, alone and self-assured, his dark evening attire immaculate, his hair pulled back and sleek. 'He's coming over here,' the viscountess murmured. 'He has balls, I'll give him that.'

'Mother!' Zara said in shocked tones over her mother's language. She'd certainly seen a different side of her mother during this party. Then again, she'd seen a different side of herself as well. It just proved people were not always what they seemed, even the people you loved. Right now, all that love was centred on Kael, striding towards her as if he had every right to be there, to claim her. Which he did. Assuming he still wanted her.

'You have nerve, Mr Gage, to show your face.' Her mother bit out the words, appalled he'd approached them, appalled that others were starting to stare.

Kael ignored the stares and the whispers starting behind fans. He gave her mother a short bow, as if she had received him cordially. '*Enchanté*, Lady Aberforth.' He held out a small roll of paper tied with a ribbon. 'It occurred to me this afternoon that while I don't care a donkey's ass what anyone thinks of me, not you, not the duke, I *do* care what Zara thinks.'

'What a lovely expression, Mr Gage,' her mother said coolly, eyes narrowing as she took the scroll. 'What is this?'

'My written testimony. Read it. I have decried any claims to Zara's dowry.' Zara felt his eyes fall on her. 'You, Zara, can decide what is right for you. But you should do so knowing that I'm not after your money. I want you, just as I told you today in the drawing room.'

Her mother appeared irritated. 'This is starting to sound like a Drury Lane play.'

'Read it,' Kael urged when she made no move to unwrap it. The duke and his wife seemed to materialise at Kael's shoulder, both looking regal dressed in traditional Russian folk attire for the evening.

'Read it, Helene,' the duke prompted. 'I witnessed it, it's a legitimate declaration and I think the man is in earnest. Zara can do no better than a husband who loves her.'

Her mother scowled and unrolled the paper. 'You and Alicia always were romantics at heart.'

'Is there any other way to be?' The duke gave his wife a warm glance and she returned it with a warm smile of her own.

'Kael, I know you aren't after my money,' Zara put in. She had meant to seek him out to apologise, but so far, he'd been the one who had sought her out. They'd both made some missteps in the drawing room that morning. Perhaps he should not have left. Perhaps she should not have recoiled in doubt. He should not be the only one making amends.

Kael nodded, his eyes on her. Waiting for her, she realised. To do something. But what? Her mother finished scanning the short document. 'How could you possibly believe he's not after your money, Zara? Don't be naïve. He can write down anything he wants. It doesn't mean it's true, or that you have to believe it.'

'But I do believe it.' Zara reached out for Kael's hand. She should have never let it go that morning. If she had her way, she would never let it go again. Her eyes held his as she spoke the words. 'When Kael had the chance to expose me this morning and ensure that he would have to marry me, he didn't.'

'What? How could he do that?' The words were

barely out of Lady Aberforth's mouth before she answered her own question. A gloved hand went to her lips, her voice trailing off. 'Oh—oh, my dear.'

The duchess was beside her, a hand at her elbow. Clearly the duchess had anticipated some quiet fireworks. 'It's not the end of the world, Helene. They're in love. They have found their happiness. We should be celebrating. They anticipated their wedding night. Is that so bad? These are modern times, even so, we were not all so chaste in our day either.' She murmured her logic to Lady Aberforth, leading her aside away from any staring eyes.

'I can't believe you told them that.' Kael grinned as the duke slipped away, leaving them alone in the crowd of dinner guests.

'I can.' Zara looked at him warmly. 'I didn't understand why you left today, why you didn't argue with my mother's claims. But then I realised why. It was a way of protecting me.' She rested a hand on his sleeve. 'And it was at a great cost to you. You were willing to sacrifice your reputation for me and in return I gave you so little. I am sorry, Kael. I misjudged at the first opportunity.'

Kael covered her hand with his. 'I did too. When a crisis hit, I let myself believe that I wasn't good enough for you, even when you had all but declared for me in a room full of your peers. You refused to go with Markham. You gave him away to Ariana Falk. You showed me how much I mattered to you and I refused to believe it.'

'We'll do better next time,' Zara assured him. 'We have the rest of our lives to work on it.' It would need work too, nothing was ever perfect, and even when it was, it was hard to accept.

'I like the sound of that.' Kael laughed.

'Which part? The next time or the rest of our lives?'

'All of it.' Kael's stomach suddenly growled, loud and insistent, and they laughed at the intrusion. 'Do you know what else I like?'

'What?'

'The duchess's advice: we should be celebrating. Are you hungry, Mrs soon-to-be-Gage?' His hand was at her back, leading her towards the table where the other guests were nearly all assembled. They found two seats together and the feast began, opening with thin crepes stuffed with imported herring caviar, borscht for soup, followed by Russian salmon and *pelmeni*. There was Russian dancing after dinner while dessert was laid out buffet style and the drinks flowed: vodka and kvass and berry juices for those who were less adventurous.

Kael was a natural at the folk dances and they danced every one of them, she relying on his steady hand as he whirled her through the steps, laughing, eyes sparkling. This was what it felt like to be alive, to be in love, to be with Kael. And this feeling was going to be hers for ever. She could not believe her good fortune.

After desserts of *chak-chak* and *symiki* and countless other delicious and equally strangely named desserts, they walked back to the house, his arm about her. Other couples did too. The folk dancing, the outdoor air, the general tenor of the evening seemed to warrant a lapse in formality. It felt good to walk beside Kael, her head resting on his shoulder, the magic of midsummer heavy in the air. 'I was thinking…'

He chuckled. 'Three very dangerous words, I'm sure.'

'I've been thinking,' she went on, ignoring his tease. 'That we should be married in Sussex, at your home.'

'Not in London or at your family seat?' Kael

asked, surprised. 'I would have thought you'd want a big wedding.'

Zara shook her head. 'Just a big wedding night. I only want you. We'd best send that message from the start.'

They reached the steps and Kael bent to her ear mischievously. 'Send your maid away, Zara. I'll be there in twenty minutes.'

'You are very punctual.' Zara gave a throaty chuckle twenty-one minutes later as Kael slid into her room and shut the door softly behind him.

'And *you* are still very dressed.' Kael raised an eyebrow in mock disdain at her satin robe.

Zara cocked her head to one side, her hand working the sash until it was loose and she could slide the robe off her shoulders. 'I have two things to say to that. First, not any more.'

Kael drank in her nakedness, his body hard and aching. He loved her breasts, the flat of her belly, the dark shadow between her legs…he loved all of it, all of *her*. 'And second?' he asked hoarsely.

'And second…' She stepped towards him, running a finger down his chest. 'You're the only one committing a clothing infraction.'

'Hmmm. So it seems,' Kael murmured, liking where this was going. 'What are you going to do about it?'

She yanked on his cravat, pulling it loose, her eyes dancing as she held up the strip of material. 'I am going to take off your clothes and then I'm going to render you senseless.'

Kael Gage liked the sound of that. But he liked the practice of it even better.

Chapter Thirteen

Saturday June 21st
Brockmore Manor House Party

Programme of Events
Annual Brockmore Midsummer Games
The Midsummer Ball

Zara had come up with a plan to fund their near future. 'We have to win the games,' she informed Kael over breakfast Saturday morning. Kael was enjoying how hard she was trying to appear 'normal'. 'How can you stroll around here as if nothing has happened?' she whispered. 'It seems wicked for us to meet like this, fully clothed, and acting as if you haven't just come from my bed where we've done far more wicked things than fork eggs.'

Kael carried their plates to an empty place at

the table. 'We'll worry about wicked things later. Tell me, why do we have to win the games?'

Zara gave him a shrewd look and whispered *sotto voce*, 'Haven't you been listening to anything? There are *expensive* prizes to be won. I think I could win ladies archery. Are you any good with a knife? A gun? Can you shoot accurately off the back of a horse?' She gave his biceps an appreciative stare. 'Arm wrestling?'

Kael laughed. 'You are an avaricious miss, already turning my finer assets into profit. But you might be disappointed. I can arm wrestle, but I won't beat the village smith. I can ride and shoot, but I won't beat Colonel Kennedy who is a professional.'

'Not to worry. We'll find something you are good at. Besides, Colonel Kennedy isn't competing.' She nudged him with her elbow. 'Knot tying, maybe. You seemed passably accomplished at that last night.'

'Passably? I'd say downright expert from the way you were moaning,' Kael murmured over his coffee. Last night had been a rather erotic version of the Brockmore Midsummer Games. Zara had surprised and pleased him with her willingness to experiment with the more exotic aspects of love making.

'All right, expert, then,' Zara conceded. 'We have to sign up as teams of two today and at the end of the day, the points will be tallied. The winning team gets one hundred pounds. All placements, first through third, earn points.'

Kael grinned. 'So when I come in second, I won't be a total loss?'

Zara looked at him smartly. 'No, so when the village smith comes in second, *he* won't be a total loss.' She tossed her head. 'Perhaps a private wager might inspire you to greatness. If you score more points than I do, I will…' She leaned over and whispered in his ear.

Kael's grin expanded. 'Really? Then I'm sure I could best Thor himself in a hammer throw.'

The games became fiercely competitive. There were individual contests for everyone, men, women and children. Everyone wanted one of the fabulous prizes and the shiny medals that hung on thick blue ribbons. Zara accumulated her share, winning two events and taking two seconds. She won the ladies archery and shooting, but placed second to a villager in a barefoot race and behind Florence Canby in the egg-and-spoon race. She might have won if Kael hadn't winked at her three steps from the finish line. 'Well, I'm really looking forward to tonight.' He wagged his eyebrows when she accused him of sabotage.

There were games for the men: shooting contests, knife throwing, wrestling and riding. Kael won shooting targets off the back of Merlin, but took second in knife throwing to Alexandr, and another second in wrestling the bulky blacksmith. But Zara assured him with a laugh that it was worth it to see him greased up with his shirt off. The ride was last and Kael and Merlin dominated the field, easily romping to victory in a quarter-mile sprint.

Last to come was the couples' three-legged race at the end of the day. A tally board had been posted on the lawn, showing the leaders. 'We're tied for the lead with the blacksmith and his wife,' Zara whispered. Only the top three couples would race, everyone else had bowed out and retreated the field.

Kael grabbed two long strips of cloth from a basket. 'Are you ready for me to tie you up?'

She lifted her skirt so he could reach around her knee. 'We really need this, Kael.'

He laughed. 'Don't you think that's exactly what the blacksmith's wife is saying to him?'

Zara shook her head. 'No, she's saying, thank goodness you beat him in wrestling or we wouldn't even be tied with them.'

'There.' Kael finished the knot and she wrapped an arm about his waist as they experimented with the three-legged arrangement. 'Start slow first. If we fall, we're finished.'

They hobbled to the starting line, finding their rhythm and looking over the competition. The blacksmith and his wife were both burly. Their bulk might slow them down. Florence and Jessamy were struggling to stay upright because Florence was giggling too much.

'I don't want to lose to them,' Zara said.

'Correction. You just don't want to lose.' Kael squeezed her. 'We won't. We're going to do this together.'

The duke raised his hand to start the race. 'Racers must go down to the barrels, circle them and run back. The first team to cross the finish line wins. Runners, on your marks, get set, go!'

They started cautiously, finding their rhythm

again. Their strides grew more confident, their speed increased. By the time they reached the barrel, they were flying, their lead increasing. Oh, this was glorious! Zara's hat came off and she let it go, let her hair fall down as they ran. She was laughing, almost too hard to run, but Kael's arm was hard around her as they sprinted towards the finish line, he would not let her fall. They crossed the finish line, collapsing in laughter on the ground, Kael coming down on top of her and stealing a rather vibrant kiss while the crowd roared, caught up in the excitement.

'We won, we did it!' she breathed as Kael helped her to her feet. Just like the horse race, this race, this silly foot race, had taken on an importance that transcended the race itself.

'I think that means I get to claim my prize,' Kael whispered at her ear.

He did get to claim his prize, much later that night. Zara made him wait. All through a beautiful cold supper on the veranda, all through a breathtaking evening of indoor-outdoor dancing at the spectacular midsummer ball, the ballroom turned out like a fairy wood where guests could not tell if they had wandered in or wandered out.

But the greatest spectacle of all was Zara in her ethereal white gown covered in *brillante*-studded tulle, winking like stars when she moved, a veritable Titania among her subjects as she defied convention and danced not twice with him, but *five* times. It was quite a declaration by London's standards. In town, Zara's snub to etiquette and its significance would be duly noted. Tonight though, Kael wondered if anyone was counting besides him. No one seemed to care. Midsummer magic had them all deep in thrall. Except perhaps Zara's mother, who begrudgingly watched them from the sidelines, but she had begun to come to terms with her daughter's choice and her daughter's right to make that choice. It was the best Zara and he could hope for at present. The rest would come. Zara had chosen her freedom and him over the trappings of tradition and that was all that mattered. She declared it in every dance this evening, letting everyone see how happy she was.

The duke danced by with the duchess, Markham with a blushing Ariana, Jessamy Addington with Florence Canby. It appeared the duke's party had been a success after all despite some rocky spots. That reminded him of Kennedy. Kael looked around to catch sight of the officer. Surely, with so many couples dancing, he would be here with his secret lady-love, not so secret any more. It was a night of declarations. But Kennedy was nowhere to be found. Perhaps that was a declaration too.

Kael whirled Zara through the turn, using the opportunity to bring her up against him. They would leave tomorrow. He to Sussex, she to London to pack and to prepare for the wedding. It would be two weeks until he saw her again. In the meanwhile, he could content himself with having the banns called in his parish church. But it would be hard. He planned to make tonight count.

Kael danced them out of doors to the edge of the floor and into the night. Then he took her hand and they began to run; across the south lawn, down to the lake, to the boat and lantern he had waiting there.

'What are we doing? Where are going?' Zara was breathless, excited, as he helped her into the rowboat.

'To the island—' Kael smiled, wickedly '—where it all started.'

Zara leaned back into the bow of the boat,

watching him work the oars, her gaze speculative, the mischief in her eyes matching his own. 'Hmmm. I'm starting to see why this is called the house party of the Season. I forget why I ever wanted to be any place else.'

Epilogue

January 1818

Brockmore Manor was quiet, blanketed in a fresh coat of snow. The excitement of the holidays was well behind them, the new year ahead of them. It was a time for revisiting the bounty of the past year. Marcus leaned back in his chair, leg over one knee, and looked fondly at Alicia as he lowered his newspaper. 'Addington and the Canby girl have tied the knot.'

Alicia looked up from her needlepoint with a smile. 'That makes eight matches so far that have come to fruition.' The party had been one of the most difficult to date, but the matches had arguably been the most brilliant. She counted them off; 'Colonel Kennedy and Katerina, Markham and Ariana, Catherine and Jeremy, Kael and

Zara, Verity and Desmond, Brigstock and the one Kilmun twin, I forget which one, and now Florence and Jessamy.'

'There were a few surprises in that batch.' Marcus chuckled, recalling some of the rough patches. He patted his coat pocket, feeling the crinkle of paper. 'I almost forgot, Zara and Kael wrote.'

'From Austria?' Alicia looked interested. 'How are they liking Vienna? It's so romantic in winter. I remember when we were there: the opera ball, the tortes. I loved the chocolate.'

'Yes.' Marcus remembered too, as if it had been yesterday instead of thirty years ago. He'd been a young man then, with a new bride on his arm and his first foray into international politics. 'You wore green silk to the opera ball and every man spent the evening staring at you. You were the most beautiful woman I'd ever seen. You still are.'

Alicia gave him a coy smile. 'I don't suppose those memories had anything to do with how the Gages ended up in Vienna for a honeymoon?'

'Gage has a fine eye for horses.' Marcus shrugged noncommittally. 'It made sense to send him. My stables will benefit and so will his. It's mutually beneficial for both of us to have Gage in Austria.' He handed her the letter. 'They may be home early. The honeymoon has borne fruit already. Zara is increasing.'

'An anniversary baby then for their first year,' Alicia said knowingly. They had once hoped for such a thing, more than once actually. 'Perhaps you'll be named godfather. They could do no better. You have a soft spot in your heart for the young man.'

'Maybe I do,' Marcus admitted.

'And Fergus Kennedy too?'

Marcus laughed. 'His circus will be the talk of the New World once it opens. Sometimes even I am surprised by the way things turn out.'

Alicia reached a hand out and rested it on his leg. 'You have a good heart, my husband. You've helped so many young men and women as if they were our own, even if they don't know it at the time.' She gave him a coy glance. 'Do you know what I want to do this afternoon in front of a roaring fire?'

'Plan this year's party?' Marcus grinned at his wife, who still turned his heart after three decades of marriage.

She gave a sultry laugh. 'We can start, but I thought we could do something else.'

'Let me guess.' He grinned broadly.

'Really, Marcus.' The Duchess of Brockmore traced a finger up his thigh. 'After all this time do you need to guess?'

* * * * *

Author Note

Writing any novel is a challenge. Writing one in close collaboration with a fellow writer whom you've never met and who lives many thousands of miles and a seven-hour time difference away certainly ups the ante!

We began our journey with nothing more than an invitation announcing that the Duke and Duchess of Brockmore were hosting a week-long house party, culminating in a lavish mid-summer ball, and a mood board. We had no idea who would be attending the party or how they would be entertained, but we *did* know it would be light-hearted, colourful, romantic and sexy—as the invitation said: a house party like no other.

We started with the concept. We wanted, if possible, to interweave our two stories closely, providing the reader with two quite different romances, both being played out at one sumptuous Regency country house event, sharing the same colourful cast of characters. We wanted to make it a fun party to experience and read about, but we were also determined to have fun writing it. We wanted to let our imaginations run wild when creating the Brockmore Manor world, but we also knew, from working together on the much bigger Castonbury Park series, how vital it was that the world we built looked and felt identical to both of us.

Logistics meant that achieving this was certainly a challenge, but a combination of an active Pinterest board, and a lot of emails flying back and forwards—and we mean a *lot*!—kept us in synch.

Our world-creating began with the Duke and Duchess of Brockmore—a powerful couple with, we decided, a hidden agenda: a Regency Gatsby and his consort, brokering all kinds of matches, political, commercial or dynastic. Naturally that led us both to decide that it would be interesting if our respective heroes and heroines upset the Duke's carefully arranged apple cart. We then populated the party with a guest list chosen as carefully as if we were the Machiavellian Duke himself. With a complement of ten guests apiece, we swapped characters, physical appearances and history, we plotted on the Duke's behalf, and as the stories progressed we meddled in his plans, allowing some to come to fruition, and some to run a very different course.

With a whole week to fill with events, we allocated alternate days as the backdrop for our romances to play out against. And, with a house and grounds to fill, we drew up a garden plan and posted pictures of each of the main rooms where our characters would be acting out their various dramas. Where we both covered the same events—such as the opening drawing room party and the horse race—it meant a lot more time-consuming reading and continuity-checking than either of us had planned for, but it was important to us not only to be consistent, but to give the reader a chance to see those events through the eyes of different characters.

We hope we have achieved what we set out to do—which was to write two fun, sexy romances in one lavish setting. We also hope you enjoy reading our stories as much as we enjoyed writing them.

Bronwyn and Marguerite

MILLS & BOON®

Why shop at millsandboon.co.uk?

Each year, thousands of romance readers find their perfect read at millsandboon.co.uk. That's because we're passionate about bringing you the very best romantic fiction. Here are some of the advantages of shopping at www.millsandboon.co.uk:

* **Get new books first**—you'll be able to buy your favourite books one month before they hit the shops

* **Get exclusive discounts**—you'll also be able to buy our specially created monthly collections, with up to 50% off the RRP

* **Find your favourite authors**—latest news, interviews and new releases for all your favourite authors and series on our website, plus ideas for what to try next

* **Join in**—once you've bought your favourite books, don't forget to register with us to rate, review and join in the discussions

Visit **www.millsandboon.co.uk**
for all this and more today!